THIRTEEN INTERNATIONAL AUTHORS PRESENT

Fairy Tales Punk'd 2: Creature Feature

Contents

Puss Das Boot

By J. Woolston Carr

"I hate water."

It was a strange thing for a sailor to say. But after all, he was a cat.

Puss reached clawed paws to his feet and dumped seawater from leather boots, avoiding the angry gaze of his companion. The cat lapped rhythmically at a fluffy foreleg with his tongue, drying the briny liquid from his fur.

"Shut up, you stupid cat."

The man next to him was equally soaked, his yellow, curling hair matted flat against his head, a large drop of water hanging forlornly from an aquiline nose. His name was Guy. Wiry and well-proportioned, he was handsome, with rugged cheekbones and resolute, sea-blue eyes that glared, miserable and annoyed. A glum sneer creased fulsome lips. The man's uniform would have been that of a French naval petty officer, but he had somehow lost his tunic and trousers, and sat in striped underwear like some shivering zebra.

Guy had been the pilot aboard the French ship *Perrault*, a *La Galissonnière* class cruiser of the French Navy. She was one of the few ships left from France in the Allied cause. Adolf Hitler and Admiral Donitz of the Kriegsmarine had managed the unthinkable – besting the assumed dominance of the British Navy. Germany had somehow manufactured an invincible maritime weapon and Britain lost so many battleships in the Atlantic and Mediterranean that she was forced to withdraw to protect her own shores from invasion, leaving the Kriegsmarine to tyrannize the open sea. Without British aid, France surrendered to German forces, but Brigadier General Charles De Gaulle called for a Free French navy to continue to defy the Axis powers. *Perrault* had been stationed at Alexandria, Egypt and, full of Gallic patriotism and German antipathy, intended to make its way past the smothering blockade to an English port.

Puss was Guy's aide-d'animalia, a rank bestowed upon genetically engineered animals that served military officers. He was large for a cat, standing up to his master's waist. A sassy ginger color tinted his fur, with white swirls like a bullseye on either side of his torso. His nose, freckled with black spots, constantly twitched. Puss met his master's scowl with eyes that usually danced with curiosity and wit but now were subdued at Guy's displeasure.

The recent subject of the resentment was Puss's insistent suggestion to his master the day before that he inform the captain of *Perrault* about a safe route to the port in England. Puss assured him this would win him the admiration of the admiralty and a quick promotion. Instead, they steered into a sudden massive storm swelling along their path, fouling the ship's navigational system. By the time their position had been determined, the U-boat was upon them. One torpedo opened a hole in the hull of *Perrault*, and sailors jumped overboard to waiting lifeboats as the ship slowly settled into the churning water. All were allowed to escape, except for Guy and his cat. They sat imprisoned in a locked room on the U-boat.

"This is all your fault," grumbled Guy.

"I may have miscalculated," admitted the cat, "but don't worry. I can fix this."

"No! I'll handle things from here."

Puss couldn't blame his master for being discontent with him, and not just for the ruinous advice on taking the ill-fated course. After the first World War, scientists of zoology, chemistry, and eugenics pioneered genetic engineering on animals. They developed an injection endowing an animal with cognitive intelligence. Wildly successful, laboratories began to breed creatures with intellectual capabilities. Ambitious governments around the world found military uses. Now, German wolves attacked trenches singing Wagner's *Ride of the Valkyries*, Russian bears mauled enemies while spouting hideous oaths, and French pigeons scouted enemy lines, returning with detailed information as well as complaints about the uncomfortable conditions of their coops.

Officers typically had a genetically engineered dog as an aide-d'animalia, but Guy had been the third son and was relegated to accepting a cat instead of the prestige of a loyal and dutiful canine.

Guy shook water from his mop of hair. "Why is a simple petty officer taken prisoner and no one else?"

Puss shrugged.

A German sailor appeared at the door, dressed in the leather jacket of an engineer. "The Captain is ready to hear what you have to say."

"I have nothing to say," proclaimed Guy obstinately.

"That is not what the cat told us," replied the engineer.

Guy stared daggers at Puss.

Puss purred apologetically.

The German sailor threw a packet on the ground in front of Guy. "Here are your clothes, we have dried them."

Guy took the uniform, staring at it without recognition.

"These are not…"

Puss interrupted. "Master, put them on. No one should show up as a prisoner of war dressed in their *sous-vetements*."

Guy dressed. The clothes fit small because the uniform belonged to the captain of *Perrault*.

"I'll be hanged for impersonating an officer," said Guy.

"Don't be ridiculous," replied Puss. "No one is going to hang you. It's a submarine, they'll just cast you out a torpedo tube."

"Then I'll make sure you are right there leading the way."

They were marched down a long hallway. Guy momentarily forgot his annoyance with Puss as he marveled at the interior of the U-boat.

Puss was also impressed. The passageway was wide and well lit. Everything was polished to perfection. Lights sparkled and radios hummed. Even the odor was pleasant, not the usual stench of sweat and diesel permeating a submarine.

"Where is the crew? This is no ordinary U-boat!" said Guy.

"No?" said Puss with curiosity. "You might be right."

"I am! This is the *Navire du Diable*! No wonder we were sunk so easily."

Perrault had descended after one torpedo struck with uncanny accuracy. Feared throughout the Atlantic and the Mediterranean, the French called the mystery U-boat the "Ship of the Devil" because it single-handedly dispatched numerous Allied ships and then disappeared as if by infernal magic.

"And look, it's true. Robot-torpedoes." Guy pointed to a line of mechanical men.

Puss hissed, tucking his tail and staring warily. Seven feet tall, with bodies of sleek aluminum armor and long arms ending in webbed hands, they stood motionless. Rumor was that Germany had developed independently thinking mechanical swimmers to deliver the torpedo payload, striking with speed and precision. Puss appreciated why they now ruled the sea.

Puss and Guy were brought to a lavish stateroom. Sitting at an oaken desk was an officer bearing the insignia of a *Kapitän zur See*. A dog sat at his feet, glaring at them. The Kapitän motioned for Guy to sit in a nearby chair while Puss fell to all fours and rubbed against his master's leg. Guy gently kicked him away.

The cabin was comfortably outfitted, decorated with paintings of dreary landscapes full of industrious workers. Hanging prominently on the wall was a photograph of the German officer in an impeccable, snowy white outfit, holding a medal and a fencing saber from the 1936 Olympics. Beneath the photo, a pair of thin and blunt crossed fencing sabers were fastened to the wall. Puss frowned. Dangling from the waist of the Kapitän was a military saber, neither blunt nor ceremonial and as functional as a butcher's knife. Clean-shaven and supple of movement, the German officer had the poise of an experienced swordsman and the smug confidence of a man who never loses.

"I am Kapitän Ungeheuer." The German officer introduced himself in a genial tone. "You like my ample accommodations? Perhaps you have noticed there is very little crew and therefore no need for sleeping bunks, and so I benefit. No lines at the Water Kloset, eh? This ship has only a Kapitän, my chief engineer Schmidt, and his assistant, who doubles as my cook."

A nasty growl emerged from under the table.

"Ah yes, our final crewmate. Allow me to introduce Bismarck, my aide-d'animalia."

A sausage-shaped dog strutted forward on short, sturdy legs. The long body was black and brown, with some grey tucked around a flaring nose and black malicious eyes.

"Here, *mein Hund*, a little treat." The Kapitän dropped a piece of chewing gum into the eagerly awaiting snout.

"Wuff-wuff!" the dog barked, then paused as if confused, and finally spoke.

"Welcome to *Die Wassermaus*. I hope our hospitality is adequate?" he said with a sneer. "Wuff!" he added. Drool oozed down his jaw as the dachshund mashed the wad of chewing gum.

Puss sighed. When the eugenicists gave dogs the ability to speak, it turned out they still preferred barking. Dogs didn't have much to say, really, and liked the gruff sound of their howl.

A sumptuous platter of food on the table produced an alluring aroma. Guy gazed hungrily. As a Frenchman, he appreciated good food and drink.

"Please, help yourself," said the Kapitän.

Guy tilted his head with suspicion.

"If I may offer," said Puss with a covetous purr. "I'll taste it for you. Especially that albacore."

Guy pulled the plate close to himself and angrily stabbed a fork into the juicy pink fish, making a show of eating in front of the cat.

"So, you have a cat as your aide-d'animalia? How…unusual," said the Kapitän, disdain creasing his forehead.

Guy swallowed a mouthful of vegetables. "Yes, well. My brothers got the dogs."

"My apologies," said the Kapitän.

"Vow-vow!" barked the dog, trying hard to generate a laugh. "A cat with boots! What possible use do you have for them?"

Puss frowned. "I never understood why dogs were chosen as companions for officers. Cats are so much smarter."

The dachshund growled.

"Maybe it's because not only do cats think they are smarter than dogs, but also smarter than humans," said Guy.

Puss didn't argue.

"Ja, in der Tat! That is why *die Hunde* were chosen for genetic engineering. They are loyal. Cats cannot be trusted because they serve only themselves."

Again, Puss did not disagree. While dogs were not the best conversationalists, cats were horribly foulmouthed creatures, and this did nothing to endear them to any but an enlisted sailor.

Guy wiped some sauce from the edge of his lip with a napkin.

"Mon capitaine, how does your boat manage without a crew?"

"Nazi genius, of course. This boat is why we are winning the war. The robots are automated torpedoes. They can swim at 50 knots and change course if necessary, making them lethally effective. But here, the *untersee Boot* is operated by this!"

The Kapitän flipped open the lid of a featureless wood and metal box sitting on his desk. Wires ran to an extensive electrical panel behind him. The panel hosted a vast array of unlit green and red bulbs.

"This is the *Vorhalterechner,* our control computer. It manages everything on the boat and calculates down to the minute detail. It even does this."

The Kapitän pulled a stiff piece of rectangular paper spotted with small holes from a file and slid it into a thin slot on the machine. A green light activated, and music began to play the rumbling chords of Beethoven's Ninth Symphony.

"Task cards feed information to the panel, which then calculates and operates all the functions of the boat. *Die Wassermaus* travels at a sustained 25 knots underwater," he continued to brag, "and can remain submerged for a significant time. Armed with 22 robot-torpedoes and four Flak 38 autocannons mounted onto a single carriage, there is no match among any fleet in the world."

He smiled proudly, but before Guy could continue his inquiries, the Kapitän closed the lid and sat back in his leather chair. "You are my prisoner, and I am here to ask the questions. So, captain. I understand you might have some useful information?"

Guy was about to deny his role as a captain, but Puss spoke up.

"My master is the famous Captain Guy. Have you not heard of him?"

"Should I have?"

"He is none other than the developer of the Carabas Defense," said Puss proudly.

The room was silent. The German captain rapped his fingers on the table with a troubled look.

"The Carabas Defense, eh? We have heard this is a secret location the Allies have been working on to respond to our naval preeminence with some new technology. Are you offering information on this for your freedom? *Herr* Captain, where lies your sympathy?"

This was not an unusual question for the Frenchman since Germany had signed the armistice with their enemy. Now many French ships sailed in the Teutonic fleet. But this was not Guy. His motto had not changed to *travail, famille, patrie*. It remained *liberté, égalité, fraternité*!

"Sympathies?" cried Guy, rising dramatically from his chair with the dinner knife in his hand as he leaned forward to assault the officer. The Kapitän's hand leapt to the sheathed sword.

With an aggressive hiss, Puss pounced to his master's aid, but blundered between Guy's legs and clumsily tripped him. Guy fell backward to the ground, knocking his head hard against the floor, where he remained unmoving.

The dachshund gave an ungainly jump to the chest of the fallen Frenchman and growled provocation at Puss, slobber dripping on Guy's jacket.

The Kapitän waved his hand to the engineer. "Schmidt, take them away. They are useless."

"Wait," said Puss. "We are simple French sailors following orders. But if we cooperate with you, will you set us free?"

"It depends on the amount of cooperation," said the Kapitän.

"Return my master to our cell, and I will make an offer you will not oppose."

Guy was dragged from the room. Puss jumped to the table and sat on the

Officer's papers.

The Kapitän pushed him away, irritated, and said, "The only offer I am interested in is Carabas. Can your master guide me there?"

"Yes, Carabas is a secret base off the coast of Africa."

The German Officer grinned with triumph.

"*Wunderbar!* To get there and destroy the Carabas Defense would finally give us unchallenged control of the sea." The officer leaned back in his chair and tapped a finger on the table. "Why would you do this?" he asked.

Puss purred and rolled onto his belly, eyeing loose objects on the table. "My master is responsible for losing our ship. Even if you set us free, we would be court-martialed and put in jail. On the other paw, if we could prove our worth to you, perhaps you could put in a good word for us with your superiors."

Puss reached out and leisurely knocked a fork off the table.

"Eh? Don't do that, *Kätzchen.*" The officer reached down and picked it up. As he stooped over Puss pushed a paperweight off the table, striking the dog on the head. The surprised dachshund yelped and spit out his gum. The Kapitän emitted a groaning complaint and fumbled awkwardly under the table to retrieve the paperweight, hampered by the scabbarded sword attached to his belt.

"There is one problem," said Puss when the Kapitän regained his seat. "No ordinary ship can get through the defenses. You must reach a depth no submarine can attain, then enter through a hidden gap. Meanwhile, the most sophisticated sonar and radar would catch a minnow traveling through. It seems impossible."

"Ha! If you can show us the way, my ship can travel to any depth, and we are equipped with the most fantastic stealth technology. The computer can make no mistake as it calculates strategy far faster than any man. We produce no noise, emit no heat, and the construction of our hull will displace water as if we were nothing more than an undersea current."

"This is truly a marvelous ship," said Puss with awe.

"*Fantastisch.* We shall travel to Carabas, and you shall guide us through the barriers so we may destroy this secret lair. Your master will go along with this?"

"I will convince him," said Puss. As he exited he found the lost clump of chewing gum on the floor and tossed it into his mouth.

"You will never convince me of this traitorous plan!" cried Guy, rubbing the bruise on the back of his head. "Besides, I have no idea of the exact location of Carabas. It is a secret, after all."

Instead of arguing, Puss's eyes widened, and he arched his back in a fit of coughing. He finally vomited a brown, slimy, viscous wad of fur and mucus.

Guy grimaced. *"C'est dégueu!!!* Do you have to do that? Clean it up, it's disgusting. We need to be figuring out a way to escape, or at least destroy this ship."

"Master, I promised you I would help you gain promotions in the navy. I never said which navy."

Guy grabbed Puss by the scruff of his neck. *"Chat Botté,* I should have eaten you when I had a chance."

"If you let me go, I promise you will have the opportunity to prove your worth."

Guy threw him to the ground.

"Ha! If you will not help me escape, I'll remain here until I come up with my own plan." Guy lay back on the floor and covered his eyes to ignore Puss.

"As you wish, Master."

The cat waved to the engineer's assistant through the window and spoke in fluent German. "I will speak to your Kapitän. Do not bother my master, he has a headache."

The assistant engineer opened the locked door, and Puss strode out on booted feet. He turned right and began walking.

"*Kätzchen!* The other direction."

"Of course. I'm simply curious about the robot-torpedoes. Do you have to load them, or do they walk by themselves? How do they know which tube to enter?"

"They follow the command of the lead robot." He pointed to one of the robots with the number "one" painted on his forehead.

The assistant engineer continued, "Number One enters first, then the others follow in sequence."

"But how does the robot receive the information? There are no wires."

"You are a smart animal. The lead robot has a wireless communication device controlling them even outside of the ship. The radar then guides them to the target. It never misses!"

"Amazing," said Puss, closely observing the robot.

"This way, *Kätzchen!*"

"Yes, yes. I'm coming."

Puss was escorted back to the German Kapitän's stateroom.

"Well? Do I have your master's cooperation?" asked the Kapitän.

Puss considered his answer. Of course, he already knew all the information about the secret headquarters. Curiosity had led him into the captain's cabin of *Perrault*, and once there, to keep from being bored, he rummaged through a number of confidential intelligence papers. But the Kapitän would never have listened to a cat.

"Of course," replied Puss. "He has conveyed all the necessary information to me. But Captain Guy still suffers from the blow to his head. He has instructed me to guide you. These are the coordinates we seek."

The officer lifted the lid to the console containing the ship's computer, and as Puss communicated the data, he typed them on a keyboard. The tall box receiver blurted clicks and whistles, followed by a low hum, then a loud thump. Red lights flashed. A punch card was produced, which he then inserted in a slot. The red lights were extinguished, replaced by flashing green lights.

The Kapitän turned to Puss.

"I will know if you mislead me, and you will regret it."

"I promise you we will arrive at Carabas," assured Puss.

Brief hours passed for *Die Wassermaus* to near the destination. Puss entertained himself for the duration by swatting at the tassel cinched at the pommel of the officer's saber.

"We are here," announced the Kapitän.

"The entrance undersea is located far below. Are you sure this boat can dive to these depths?" asked Puss.

The Kapitän slipped in another task card. *"Sehr gut!* Never fear, we shall be successful. Everything is calculated. Now, to achieve complete stealth, all operations will be turned off. The computer has already plotted and directed the boat on a path guiding us directly into the secret basin. With all systems off we run completely silent. Once inside it will take only a moment to restore power, and we will destroy it all, then withdraw as if never there."

Puss sensed the U-boat slowly angle downwards and dive, following the tiny bubble of the inclinometer pitch to one side, then return to the center. Another card was inserted, and the submarine weaved faultlessly through the ocean floor gap. They arrived at a sunken basin, surrounded by a jagged crust of rock. High above at sea level, oblivious of the impending danger, was the secret base of Carabas.

Tense seconds went by. Puss's ears shuddered with anxiety.

The officer moved to a long tube extending from the ceiling. He unfolded a chair and sat, pressing his cheek against the eyepiece of the periscope while manipulating foot pedals and hand controls.

"Wunderbar," he whispered triumphantly. The circular lens revealed rows of motionless submarines docked in landing piers, piles of munitions, and experimental vehicles with rotors and propellers.

"You have delivered on your promise, *Kätzchen.* Once I restore the power, one well-placed robot-torpedo will send all of this to Helheim."

He inserted another card and pressed a button. Nothing happened. He pressed it again. Still nothing. He began jabbing and pounding.

"Nein! What is wrong?" he shouted in frustration.

Finally, something did happen. Music began to play. Not Beethoven this time. The tune began with a rousing edition of *La Marseille*, then was abruptly cut by the sultry, warbling voice of Josephine Baker singing *J'ai deux Amours*.

The Kapitän stood with clenched fists and a reddening face. "Shut off that *verdammt* sound! *Kätzchen*, is this your doing?" The Kapitän drew his blade and threatened Puss. "Fix this, or I will chop you like *Leberkäse!*"

Puss hesitated, as if waiting for something. The Kapitän deftly sliced one of his whiskers. Puss tucked his tail between his legs and nervously stood his ground.

"Fine. After I kill you, the engineer can adjust the computer. If this was your plan, it has failed. Schmidt!"

Guy crashed through the door, using Schmidt's head as a battering ram. Behind him lay the assistant engineer senseless on the floor.

"I told you, you would have your opportunity," Puss purred, relieved at the arrival of Guy.

The Kapitän and Guy stared at each other, both with looks of surprise.

"Master, if you don't subdue him now," advised Puss, "he might regain control of the boat."

The Kapitän waved his saber at Guy.

"After I run you through, I will restore power and destroy this entire base."

Guy pulled one of the fencing sabers from the wall.

"You think you can use a sword?" said the Kapitän.

Guy's nostrils flared, offended. "I am a Frenchman. *En garde!*"

Blades clashed, Guy's slender fencing saber barely managing to parry the vigorous cuts of the bludgeoning Kapitän's sword.

Puss heard a growl.

"I have been waiting for this moment, *der gestiefelte Kater*. Vuff!"

The squat body of the Dachshund charged forward.

"Sit!" commanded Puss.

The dog responded automatically, momentarily paralyzed and plopping back on his haunches.

At the dog's hesitation, Puss whipped a leg into the air and smashed the hound in the nose with a brutal kick from a steel toe. The dachshund collapsed.

"*That* is why boots are useful."

Puss observed his master with quiet distress. Blades whirled and clattered. Feet shuffled back and forth, the spacious room providing the range for them to thrust and cut, parry and riposte. Although Guy's blade was lighter, he could do little more than block the rigorous attacks. The Kapitän was a champion master of the blade, with the precision of movement and implacable determination of a shark.

"You are an excellent fencer," noted Guy.

"I was undefeated at the Olympics!"

"*C'est vrai,*" acknowledged Guy, "but I am not a fencer, I am a swordsman!"

Guy beat the Kapitän's blade away and stepped to the side with a supple traverse, bending low and approaching the German officer on his flank. The Kapitän, used to opponents restricted to the narrow confines of a competitive fencing lane, swung his blade with a flummoxed twist, slicing nothing but air. Guy tightened the distance between them. While the blade of the fencing saber in Guy's hand was flexible and harmless, the saber hilt was a solid steel guard. Guy slammed it into the jaw of the Kapitän, a firm blow with a satisfactory crack, stunning the German officer. The Kapitän crumpled to the floor.

Puss gathered a punch card and placed it in the computer. The U-boat floated to the surface, completely calm, emerging to the astonished gasps of Allied soldiers and scientists.

The capture of *Die Wassermaus* was celebrated throughout the Allied navy.

Guy was recognized for his cleverness and bravery in securing the most valuable weapon of the Kriegsmarine and eliminating their naval superiority. He was promoted to *Enseigne de vaisseau de première classe* in the Free French Navy, and a ceremony was held to celebrate his victory. Afterward, the Frenchman returned to his room with a bottle of Bordeaux and a package of food.

Puss was there, boots off, curled up on his bed and snoring. When Guy entered, the cat cracked open a sleepy eye. Guy sat on the bed next to him and opened the package, revealing a pink, sauteed fillet of fish. He gave it to Puss, who was immediately attentive. Guy shared the wine.

"You planned the whole thing, didn't you?" said Guy. "Finding *Die Wassermaus*, getting us captured, and then disabling the boat. You know, you could have told me."

Puss chewed noisily on the fish. Swallowing, he said, "Master, one day you will make a fine officer, but never a good liar."

Guy shrugged.

"How did you do it?" asked Guy.

Puss held up a paw. Five claws sprung out like switchblades. "*Tu vois*, I have my own way to make punch cards. I distracted the Kapitän and his dog in their cabin quarters and altered the necessary information on the cards. Then a particularly gummy hairball covered the lead robot-torpedo's radar receiver and prevented the submarine from releasing them. And I managed to leave your door unlocked. I was getting worried you hadn't noticed."

Guy grinned. "I underestimated you, Puss."

The cat twitched an ear pensively. "Now that you are promoted, I suppose you could get a canine aide-d'animalia."

"*Quelle, oh?*" said Guy, grasping the idea for the first time. "I suppose I could. A dog would certainly gain me a certain *prestige* among my fellow officers. No more looks of derision. No more mockery."

Puss made a plaintive meow.

Guy put a deliberative finger to his chin.

"On the other hand…a dog seems so…"

"*Conventionnel?*" Puss said as he perked up.

"Yes. That's it. Commonplace," admitted Guy.

"Almost run-of-the-mill," added Puss.

"Even narrow-minded," observed Guy.

"Master, that is true. To get yourself noticed for command, *despite* having a cat as an aide, will gain great respect. Who knows, perhaps it will even become fashionable."

"*Exactement*. I'll continue to keep you. But from now on, you must listen to me, and tell me if you are planning anything."

"Of course, Master. As always, you are the brains, and I am but your humble servant."

Puss happily lapped fish juice from his paws, and if he had fingers to cross, he would have done so.

The Tower and the Inferno

By Paul Hiscock

The cavern shook.

There was a loud crack, and Amber looked up just in time to see a stalactite break loose from the ceiling and splash into the pool below. She checked her watch and recorded the time on her pad. Just a small tremor this time, but they were getting more frequent.

She reached for a drink, only to find her flask was empty, so she made her way down to the pool's edge to refill it. The water had been lukewarm before, but now it was hot. She forced herself to drink it despite the unpleasant mineral aftertaste — she needed to stay hydrated. Once she had finished, she took a small bite of Kendal Mint Cake. She only had one square left, but even a little of the sickly sweet minty confection was enough to hide the taste of the water.

The cavern shook again, harder this time, forcing Amber to run for cover under a rocky outcrop as stalactites and stones rained down.

When the tremors stopped, she peeked out from her hiding place. At first, it was hard to see through all the dust that had been churned up, but once it settled, her heart leapt. The rockslide that had trapped her here for the last couple of days had finally shifted.

She shoved her belongings into her backpack, then hurried into the tunnel leading back to the surface.

The tower rose above the Welsh countryside, dominating the landscape. Its two massive solar sails, outstretched like the wings of a creature about to take flight, glinted as they spun gently to catch the sunlight.

"Vortex Tower is the future of Wales," said a woman's voice.

The camera circled the tower, drawing closer.

"A city for today…"

People were visible now, walking about on the platforms of the tower. Friends ate together in cafés. Children played in parks. Families relaxed in their homes.

"… generating power for tomorrow."

The camera skimmed along the surface of the solar panels before plunging through a massive wind turbine.

Amber turned away from the screen and looked out of the site office window. The reality of the building site at the top of the hill was far less impressive than the promotional simulation. There was a fence and lots of cranes, but little sign of the fabled tower.

She turned back to the screen, which now showed the woman narrating the video. A caption at the bottom identified her as Madeline King, CEO of Vortex Industries.

"Vortex Tower is a leap forward in renewable energy gathering. It will generate enough electricity to power the whole of Wales, forever."

It was a big claim, and one that Amber had heard before — seven times so far that morning, in fact, soon to be eight when the video looped back to the beginning again.

"Will Mr. Evans be much longer?" she asked.

The receptionist glared at Amber over her glasses.

"I've already told you, he's a very busy man. He doesn't meet with people who walk in off the street, or wherever it is you have been."

She waved her hand up and down, as though Amber wasn't already aware of her dirty and dishevelled appearance.

"I would advise you to go home, clean yourself up, and make a proper appointment."

"It will be too late," replied Amber. "I need to speak to him today."

The door slammed open, shaking the temporary building, and a large man in a three-piece suit and a hard hat walked in.

"Get hold of Benson," he shouted. "Tell him to send more guards. Preferably competent ones this time. This is his last chance. If he can't keep the saboteurs out, I will find someone else who can."

"Of course," replied the receptionist. "You have a meeting with the union rep at eleven and Ms. King at two."

He pointed at Amber. "And this woman?"

"Miss Wyld was just leaving."

"It is Dr. Wyld, and I was not going anywhere. Mr. Evans, I need to speak to you urgently."

Evans stared at her, trying to picture her without all the mud. "Aren't you the archaeologist from the University of Bangor? The one who assessed our Iron Age remains?"

"That's right."

"I suppose you're here to inspect our preservation work. Come on then, we might as well get this over with."

Without waiting for a reply, he stormed out of the office. Amber picked up her bag and hurried after him.

"We followed your instructions to the letter," Evans said as they walked up the path towards the building site on the hill. "The walls are preserved just as we found them, under a clear floor so that everyone can see them."

Amber struggled to keep up with him. "That's great, but I'm not really here about that."

"You're still going to help us with the interpretative signage as we discussed, aren't you?"

"Sure, but I need to warn you. Everyone here is in danger."

"What?" asked Evans, finally paying attention to her. "You mean the protestors? I'll admit it caught us off-guard when they started using explosives to destroy our work. But they're all environmentalist hippy-types — they're not going to hurt people. Unless… do you know something I don't? Have they discussed their plans with you?"

"No, why would they discuss anything with me?"

"Well, they are mainly your lot."

"My lot?"

"You know, students, from the university. Only interested in history and airy-fairy environmental dreams."

They were drawing near to the site, and Amber looked at the protestors gathered by the gate, waving signs saying 'Dim Twr' or 'Stop the Tower.' Most of them did look like students. In fact, she thought she recognised a few of them from her own department.

"There's nothing wrong with wanting to protect the environment or our heritage. I thought this was meant to be a 'green' project?"

"It is. Vortex Industries is all about making the Earth cleaner and eliminating our need for fossil fuels. But we are pragmatists, Dr. Wyld. Renewable energy needs to be economically viable, and that means we need to build where we can gather the most energy — here."

"I understand that, but I think you need to reconsider. This is not a good place to build."

"There is plenty of countryside in Wales. Why is everyone so concerned with this bit? The Senedd has approved everything, and the time for protests is over. Besides, you've seen the simulations. The tower isn't some concrete block. It's been designed to be beautiful."

"It's hardly natural though, is it? This hill, Dinas Emrys, has stood here for thousands of years. Do you really think you can make it better?

"Did your Iron Age fort make it better? Yet you tell us that is important and we have to preserve it."

"That's not the point," Amber protested, "and I keep trying to tell you, that's not why I'm here. Haven't you felt the tremors?"

"You mean the explosives the protestors have been using to destroy anything we build?"

"It's not explosives. The ground is unstable. I was trapped underground for days."

"There will always be small disturbances with construction work of this scale – that's why we put up warning signs. If you were trespassing, you only have yourself to blame."

"This was not just a 'small disturbance.' If you keep building here, the whole hill is going to collapse."

"Nonsense, all our surveys came back clear. We're standing on solid Welsh rock."

As Evans said this, the solid rock beneath their feet trembled gently. He looked around, expecting to see one of the large construction vehicles moving, but there was nothing near.

The trembling became a quake and Amber found it hard to keep her balance. Cries of alarm rose up from the protestors' camp.

"Get out of here!" shouted Amber. The protestors shifted uncomfortably, torn between fear and a desire to maintain their vigil.

"Look out!"

The warning came from the building site above. A large crane holding a long metal girder swayed, its heavy cargo swinging wildly over everyone's heads.

Now the protestors ran, their signs trampled underfoot as they tried to get away.

Amber tugged at Evan's sleeve. He stood transfixed by the crane, but then he came out of his trance and let Amber drag him, stumbling, down the hillside.

"It's going over!" someone shouted.

Metal twisted and screeched as the crane tipped. Amber looked back just in time to see it slam into the hillside behind her. Then her foot caught on the uneven path and she fell face down on the ground.

She stayed where she had fallen, arms wrapped around her head until the tremors subsided. Once she was sure the ground was still again, she looked up and saw Evans getting up from a similar position. He came over and offered her a hand, which she accepted gratefully.

"We're going to have to talk to Ms. King," he said.

"A cavern?"

The blue-tinged hologram of Madeline King stared at Amber and Evans across the meeting room in the site office.

"That's right," said Amber.

"And it's directly below Dinas Emrys?"

"I think so. It's a little hard to be certain, but it would make sense."

"Make sense? None of this makes sense." Ms. King pointed angrily at Evans and her holographic finger disappeared into his chest. "What are you playing at? You told me you had everything under control."

"I did...I-I mean, I do," Evans stammered.

"It doesn't sound like it. Your security is a joke. You have protestors, archaeologists, and god knows who else wandering around as if they own the place."

"I have a new team coming in." He looked at the screen of his pad. "They'll be in place by tonight, and the first thing they are going to do is clear out the protestors."

"Good, and what about Miss Wyld's mythical cavern?"

"It's Dr. Wyld," said Amber, "and it's not a myth. I've been trapped in there since Tuesday."

"What were you even doing there?" asked Ms. King. "Did you know about this, Evans?"

"She's the archaeologist we hired to assess the ruins on the hill, but I thought we were done with her."

"I was researching Dinas Emrys for your site interpretation signs when I came across a reference to a pool under the hill. I couldn't resist having a look to see if it was really there."

"OK," said Ms. King. "So there's a cavern in the general area of the site. Our surveyors didn't find it, did they, Evans? So it clearly isn't where you said it is. Therefore, thank you for letting us know. Leave the details, and we might put up a sign about it in due course."

"I am sure it is under the hill," said Amber, "or very close to it. You've disturbed something, Ms. King. I'm worried your building works have cracked open some kind of fault line. You need to get a team of geologists in there before you do anything else."

"So you want me to stop my landmark project? A project that could help the whole world. You sound like those protestors. Don't you understand what I am trying to achieve here?"

"I'm not convinced she isn't working with them," said Evans.

"I'm not," Amber said, then hesitated. "Well, I know a few of them, but they have nothing to do with this. Please, Ms. King. All I'm asking you to do is make sure Dinas Emrys is safe."

"Have you spoken to anyone else about this cavern?" asked Evans.

"Not yet. I came straight to you as soon as I escaped."

"There is a liability concern if it turns out to be true and she goes on the record about warning us. Look, the site is going to have to be closed for the rest of the day while we clear up the mess from earlier and get the new security arrangements set up. Why don't I get her to show me what she has found, and if there is anything to her story, we can deal with it then?"

Ms. King rolled her eyes. "Very well. You have until the end of the day."

The hologram snapped off abruptly.

Evans shoved his pad into his pocket and angrily faced Amber.

"Show me this cavern of yours, or it will be more than a call she is terminating."

Amber set off down the hill expecting Evans to follow, but he stopped at the door and pointed towards the construction site.

"Aren't you going the wrong way? I thought you said this cavern was under there."

"There's a whole network of tunnels underneath us. We need to go down here to get in."

"Very well. I'll need to fetch some gear first then. Wait here."

He jogged over to a nearby storage cabin and returned a few minutes later carrying a large backpack. It looked thoroughly incongruous strapped over his suit and Amber found it hard not to laugh.

She led him down a path through the woodland that encircled the hill, over a stile, and then down a long path until they reached a waterfall.

"This is taking too long. I have work to do back at the site."

Amber ignored him and walked up to the waterfall. "Watch your step, it's slippery back here." She stepped behind the rushing water into a narrow tunnel, then stopped to take a torch out of her backpack.

A few moments later, Evans joined her. For a moment, he seemed surprised that they had not been soaked. Then he took out his own torch and followed her into the tunnels. The path twisted and turned, but the GPS on Evans's pad confirmed that they were heading in the direction of the hill.

After a while, Amber noticed that he had fallen behind. She doubled back and found him examining an alcove in the wall.

"What are you looking for?"

"Places where one might set explosives."

"Why would you want to put explosives anywhere down here? That would be insanely dangerous."

"You still haven't convinced me that your protestor friends aren't responsible for everything. We never caught them sneaking past the fence, but if they placed explosives underground there would be no need. They could disrupt the construction and make it look like an earthquake."

"You're paranoid. Now come on, we're nearly there." Amber set off again without him.

"Here we are."

Amber stepped out into the cavern. She wondered if there were fewer stalactites than when she had left, but mainly she was glad that the tunnel had not been blocked again.

She heard Evans take a deep breath behind her.

"Impressive, isn't it?" she said.

"I have to admit, I am impressed. I wasn't expecting anything so big, or so hot."

"It's hotter than when I was here before. That's why you need to get geologists down here."

Evans took out a map and compared it to the readings on his tracker.

"So, you were right. We are directly below the site of the tower. We are going to have to do something about this."

"We shouldn't stay long. I really don't want to get trapped down here again. I just want to check something, and then we can head back."

She made her way down to the edge of the pool. The water was bubbling and giving off immense heat. She knelt down as close as she dared and pointed her torch into the depths.

"When I was here before, I thought I saw something under the water. Mind you, the water was cooler then. I doubt anything could survive in there now."

As she moved the beam over the water, a glint of something red caught her eye. She turned to tell Evans, just in time to see his torch slamming against her head.

Amber woke up to a throbbing pain above her left ear, courtesy of the tender bump left by the torch.

"You're awake," said Evans. "I thought I might have finished you off. Knocking someone out isn't an exact science."

Amber sat up. The movement made her head spin and for a moment she thought she was going to pass out again.

"Why did you do it?"

"You were working with the protestors. Planting explosives down here to undermine the project."

"Don't be absurd. I don't have any explosives."

"But I do."

Evans took an explosive charge out of his backpack and attached it to the rock face. She tried to get up and stop him, but her legs would not obey her instructions.

"I'll explain how I tried to stop you, but sadly I was too late. The timer had already been set."

He took out a small black box and pressed a button. A little red light lit up on the explosive charge and the matching devices distributed around the walls of the cavern.

"Nobody is going to believe you," Amber said defiantly.

"They will because it's a good story. Certainly better than admitting we cut corners on the survey. Of course, there'll be some damage up there, a lot of damage. But if it's down to eco-terrorists rather than negligence, the insurance will cover us."

The cavern shook. For a moment, Amber was afraid that Evans had set off the explosives, but it was just another tremor. She looked at the pool. The water churned like a pot boiling over on the stove.

"I should be leaving," said Evans.

"I won't let you get away with this."

Amber tried to move again, but as soon as she tried to stand a wave of dizziness struck her and she had to sit back down.

Evans picked up his, now empty, backpack. "Sadly, you're going to die in the explosion *you* caused."

He turned to leave, but there was another tremor and he stumbled, dropping the remote device. He moved to pick it up, then stopped dead.

"Wh-what is that?"

Something—no, two things—moved in the water. One red and one white, both massive creatures covered in glistening scales.

It was difficult to make out any details as they thrashed and wrapped themselves around each other. There were terrifying glimpses of sharp teeth, slashing claws, and angry glowing eyes.

Then a long, red tail swung across the cavern. It whistled over where Amber sat, but Evans was not so lucky. It caught him in the chest, knocking him across the cavern and into the wall.

Then the white creature broke free. It shot into the air and unfurled a pair of wings almost as wide as the cavern.

Amber's excitement overcame her fear. "They're dragons!"

As if to say, "Of course we are," the red dragon, still standing in the pool, opened its jaws and exhaled a jet of flames towards its opponent.

The white dragon beat its wings and banged into the ceiling again and again in its attempt to flee. The last of the stalactites fell, raining down across the cavern, then the roof itself started to cave in.

Amber managed to drag herself over to an overhang and escape the falling debris.

Rocks pummelled the red dragon. With a roar of rage, it reared up on its back legs and unfurled its wings, then leapt into the air. It slammed the white dragon into the ceiling, which finally gave way. Light from outside flooded into the cavern as the dragons took to the air.

A nervous secretary burst into Madeline King's office at Vortex Industries. She glared at him and was surprised when he didn't back away.

"I'm sorry, ma'am, but you need to see this."

Without waiting for permission he replaced the stock exchange figures on the large screen with a news report and turned up the volume. Then he ran from the office before she could try to blame him for the events unfolding on the screen.

"...reports of some sort of explosion at Dinas Emrys. Catrin Moore is on the scene. Catrin, can you hear me?"

"Yes, Dan. An extraordinary scene here at the site of the Vortex Tower construction project. I was interviewing protestors who are unhappy about the project when we saw this."

The footage showed a young man standing in front of the camera with the hill in the background. He was about to speak when the hill erupted like a volcano. Ms. King watched in horror as rocks, dirt, and construction equipment were hurled across the site. Next, a fountain of flame shot into the air, followed by two massive dragons, wings fully unfurled. They hung in the sky for a moment, then with a blast of flame, they resumed hostilities. Spinning through the air, they tore at each other, looking for the opening that might give them the advantage.

Ms. King muted the news, then picked up her phone and tried to call Evans. It went straight to voicemail.

"Where are you? What is going on over there? You need to sort this mess out, now!" She screamed in frustration and threw her phone across the room.

"They're not going to be able to cover this up."

Amber tore her attention away from the dragons and looked across the cavern. Evans was still clinging to life. Although, from the sound of his voice, it was by the barest thread.

She crawled out from underneath the outcrop and struggled to her feet. She was still a bit woozy but didn't fall this time, although her ankle throbbed painfully. She must have twisted it during all the chaos. Carefully, she picked her way through the rubble to where Evans lay. He was covered in blood, his arm twisted at an unnatural angle, and his leg trapped under a large piece of rock.

"You need to get out of here," he said. "There's nothing you can do for me."

"I can get help."

"There isn't time. The timer has already been set."

Amber gasped in horror — she had forgotten about the explosives. She looked around the cavern, wondering if she had time to deactivate them, but they were buried in the rubble of the dragons' battle. "How long do I have?" she asked.

"There's probably about fifteen minutes left." Evans coughed and spat out a clot of blood. "I should have had plenty of time to get out."

He coughed again, but this time the exertion was too much for his battered body and he passed out.

"Thank you."

Amber emerged from the tunnel behind the waterfall and breathed a sigh of relief. For a moment she considered just stopping there and calling for help. However, curiosity overcame exhaustion and injury. She had to see if the dragons were still there.

She limped down the path until it emerged from the woods. Above the hill, the dragons still swooped and soared. Such beautiful creatures. She wondered why they still fought with one another rather than enjoying their freedom and flying away in opposite directions.

A tumultuous explosion tore apart the hill. The white dragon was hit by some of the debris, and it wobbled in the air as it tried to recover.

The red dragon seized the advantage. It folded its wings back and plunged through the air, striking the white dragon and driving it deep into the ground.

Amber held her breath and waited for the red dragon to emerge victorious, but everything was still and silent. All that remained was a plume of smoke rising from the crater that had once been Dinas Emrys.

It was drizzling when Amber returned six months later. As she made her way up the winding path towards the summit, she spotted a piece of red tape flapped from a tree branch that had been left behind by the accident investigators. She took it down and put it in her pocket.

The inquiry had delivered an open verdict. In the first few days, Madeline King had loudly blamed eco-terrorists, although nobody could explain why these unidentified environmentalists would choose to blow a large hole in the very hill they meant to protect. However, now everybody wanted to move on. The environmentalists were pushing new protections for the countryside, and Vortex was close to having their replacement project approved by the Senedd.

Nobody wanted to talk about the dragons. The television footage of them had been dismissed as large birds and tricks of the light. They hadn't even asked Amber about them. As far as the official investigation was concerned, she had never been there.

The path was a lot shorter than it used to be, and Amber quickly reached the edge of the crater. She knelt down by the new pool of water that had formed. It was cold and still.

But somewhere below, dragons slept.

Blessed are the Eyes that See

By Stacy Overby

A breeze set the palm fronds outside Kelani's window, waving. She sighed and rolled over. Though she could detect the movement, the palms were nothing but a green blur against a dull blue background. She knew the sky should have been a brilliant azure, but leukodystrophy had been slowly stealing her sight for the last two years, though the worst of it hit in the last six months. The doctors figured she'd be completely blind within another two months.

"And dead in another year, most likely," she spoke to the empty room.

A monitor near her head gave an insistent chime that did not stop. Kelani groaned because she knew a nurse would rush in any second, medications in hand.

Right on cue, her door slid open, and a blonde nurse slipped into the room. The nurse scanned the monitor for a moment before pressing several buttons to silence the pump. Then she shifted her attention to Kelani's IV medications.

"How are you feeling?" The nurse glanced at Kelani.

"Achey. Tired. Nothing different from when the alarm went off an hour ago."

The nurse stopped and focused on Kelani. "I'm sorry you're still not feeling well. Would you like the pain medication? You're well within the time I can get you some. It might help you sleep a little too."

Kelani bit her lip a moment, then blurted out, "Any chance I'll get to go home soon?"

"Oh, honey." The nurse patted her hand. "We're trying."

A tear slipped down Kelani's cheek. "I'll take the pain medication."

"Okay."

Kelani imagined the pitying look on the nurse's face, not that she could truly see it. She's been in and out of the hospital for over a year. Those looks had become commonplace before Kelani had lost enough vision to not be able to see them anymore.

She jumped when what sounded like a hurricane flew through the door to her room.

"Who's there?" Her heart thudded in her chest, the noise of the monitor speeding up in reaction.

"It's me, Keahi! Man, have I got news for you."

His rushed movement to her bedside told Kelani where he was, so Kelani threw a pillow in his general direction. "You scared the shit out of me."

"Sorry, I didn't mean to, but give me a second and I'll redeem myself, I swear. I'm pretty sure I have a way to cure you."

Kelani jerked herself up into a sitting position. "What? What are you talking about? The doctors have said there's no cure for this, that it'll kill me."

"I know." He settled himself on the edge of Kelani's bed. "But I found something that changes everything - nanotechnology."

Kelani shook her head. "Why are you screwing with me like this? There is no such thing."

"I love you, cuz, but you're wrong. It's not only possible, but I talked to someone who can make it real for you."

Silence stretched between them, only the noise of the hospital equipment keeping it from being too unbearable. Keahi started twisting the edges of Kelani's blanket as the quiet seconds marched on. She stared at him, unseeing, unmoving.

"Keahi, I was an engineering student specializing in nanotechnology. It's not real, not for use like this. It would have to alter my DNA, which just can't happen, not yet."

Keahi jumped up and paced the room while Kelani laid back and returned to staring at the ceiling. "Look, I get it. I know what you're saying. But I found something, someone really, who can help. A professor at school is working on it, too, and he's made it work. I went and found him after I left here this morning, and he agreed to help."

She sensed him to her, but Kelani continued to stare at the ceiling.

"Come on, 'Lani, give me something here."

She shifted to her side, turning her back to him. "What do you expect, Keahi? You're trying to sell me a dream and I'm just not interested."

Keahi growled and ran his hands through his hair. "Will you at least meet with this professor? He's a medical doctor, and I promise I'm not lying when I say he can do this."

She tried, but couldn't keep the exasperation out of her voice. "Fine."

He gave Kelani an awkward half-hug and left her hospital room with considerably less enthusiasm.

It didn't take long for Keahi to return with the doctor he'd spoken of. The door chime sounded, announcing their arrival, though she knew it had to be them. The medical staff didn't wait for her to respond, and she had no one else to visit her, really.

"Hey, we're here. Are you up to talking this through still?" His voice floated through the cracked door.

"Sure." With her assent, the door slid open, admitting the two men to her room. Keahi moved to a chair at the foot of Kelani's bed. Dr. Jamison settled himself in one near the window. Kelani didn't even move. "Dr. Jamison can explain what's going on and how he can help you if you're ready."

Dr. Jamison leaned forward and rested his arms on his knees. "Ms. Akana, I believe your cousin has given you a summary of what we are proposing?"

"Yes, that you want to give me some non-existent technology to rewrite my DNA. But it won't work because nanotechnology like that doesn't exist. It's all still theoretical." Kelani still hadn't moved to face them.

"That is correct."

Keahi whipped around to face Dr. Jamison at that statement, his eyes wide.

The professor continued. "Or to be more accurate, that is correct from the public's point of view."

This got Kelani to shift around to face them. "Look, this kind of nanotechnology is what I was studying before I got too sick, made it almost to my dissertation on it. Sure, maybe we could write a sophisticated enough program for nanites to cure cancer or whatever. But programming doesn't matter because we can't build them."

Dr. Jamison smiled. "I am telling you this is possible, and it is real. The question is, are you a candidate for a human trial? Are you willing to find out? Because I won't do it without your fully informed consent and understanding."

Time seemed to freeze. Dr. Jamison studied Kelani. She stared unfocused at a spot near him, and Keahi watched them both as he held his breath, waiting for an answer.

"How did you solve for the power issue? Nanites don't have the energy to be therapeutic in small numbers and the sheer mass of them necessary to execute a program would be prohibitive because of the immune response."

"We sourced the energy needed directly from the body itself."

Kelani cocked her head, her brow furrowed. She and Dr. Jamison continued to talk about technical issues, debating if what they had proposed was indeed possible. The conversation paused as Kelani contemplated Dr. Jamison's words. Keahi shifted in his chair and fidgeted with the edge of his shorts.

"That's brilliant," Kelani said eventually, "but the complexities of the command programs would be insane. Healing aneurysms, curing cancers, even ending viral infections, sure that I could see, but DNA is still leaps and bounds beyond that."

"Astute observation, Ms. Akana. I am impressed with your understanding of nanite technology in medical applications." Dr. Jamison leaned into the conversation. "Believe it or not, though, I have just such programming available. Now, I must caution you, we have only tested this in a limited capacity in humans. We have not attempted something this complex, though we have been able to rewrite small segments of mouse DNA. The theory has held true in every experiment we've run, and the results have been an amazing success."

Keahi jumped in. "What do you say? Dr. Jamison can do this, he can heal you. I know it."

The space in their conversation stretched out between them. Kelani looked back and forth between the men, despite not being able to make out their faces. Keahi leaned farther and farther out on the edge of his seat, as if the mere act of leaning forward would prompt Kelani to answer. Even Dr. Jamison started shifting in his seat a little.

When Keahi thought he'd die from the weight of anticipating her words, Kelani spoke. "Fine, but I reserve the right to back out at any point if I don't feel comfortable with this. And I want the kill commands for these things."

"Yes!" Keahi rushed to Kelani's bed, wrapping her in a hug.

Dr. Jamison smiled and leaned back in his chair. "Agreed, though I request you discuss with me any concerns should you think about using the kill commands before you do so."

Kelani nodded over Keahi's shoulder. "I can do that."

"I'll make the arrangements to have you moved over to a private facility near campus where we can work."

Dr. Jamison swept from the room, a man on a mission.

Lush green with bright pops of red and pink and yellow surrounded the walking path. It was the first time Kelani had driven a car in almost a year, and the first time she could see well enough to enjoy the Wahiawa Botanical Garden.

"And I don't even need someone around to babysit me," she said to herself with a wry smile.

Something seemed a little off to Kelani, though. Several times over the last few days, she could have sworn she saw movement, but when she looked again, nothing was there. Twice, Kelani thought she saw a face in her window. Thus, the trip to the gardens to clear her mind of the overwhelming changes the nanites had wrought in her life within just a few days.

Kelani followed the path down into the gorge, the sound of running water leading her on. Shadows crept up from the high valley walls, reaching up to the crystal blue sky. As the path curved to follow the path of the running water. Cool air embraced Kelani as she walked.

Movement in the stream caught her eye on a curve ahead of her. She squinted, trying to determine what it was. The thing splashed in the middle of the creek, but it was too big to be an animal. Kelani rolled her eyes, assuming some tourist had gone wading.

As Kelani drew a little closer, the soft breeze carried a rotted stench to her, like a miasma of plant and stagnant water left out in the sun too long. She wrinkled up her nose at the smell and made a note to mention it to the garden staff.

The person in the water sloshed toward her. As they drew nearer to each other, the person's clothes looked odd, like they were falling off in tatters. A still, heavy feeling hung in the air.

"Help me."

The raspy voice emanating from the person in the water clearly belonged to a woman, but it was as if the woman gurgled as she spoke. She reached for Kelani, water dripping from her arms. Instinctively, Kelani helped the woman, but she froze as her fingers brushed the woman's wet clothing. They weren't clothes. Instead, she wore aquatic plants and weeds.

The woman grasped at Kelani again. "Help me! My children, help me!"

Realization cut through the fog of shock muddling her brain. Kelani jerked back. "You're the Green Lady!"

"My children are gone. Help me." The Green Lady advanced on her again, this time latching on to Kelani's wrist. The Green Lady's hand, a mottled purplish blue that hinted at scales, stood out against Kelani's tan skin.

Kelani fought to free herself from the Green Lady's grasp, her heart in her throat. "Get away from me!"

The Green Lady yanked at Kelani, dragging her toward the water, all the while carrying on about her children and needing help. Kelani pried at the woman's cold, wet fingers. Water lapped at her feet, spurring Kelani to fight harder.

As the water washed around her ankles, Kelani freed herself from The Green Lady's grip by yanking the woman's thumb loose. She backed away out of the creek, afraid to turn her back on the woman who should be nothing but an urban legend. When Kelani thought she'd gotten far enough away from The Green Lady, she turned and fled up the path back toward the visitor center.

Kelani passed a white-blonde woman dressed all in white as she ran. Something about the woman caught Kelani's attention for a moment. It was as if the woman knew what had happened. Kelani dismissed it as a figment of the panic filling her because of The Green Lady.

She blew through the visitor center and out to her car, fumbling to pull the keys from her pocket. With them free, she unlocked the door, jumped in, and slammed the locks down.

Kelani's heart pounded to the point she struggled to hear over the intense thuds, and her throat threatened to squeeze shut. Her hands shook as she tapped the menus on her phone to call her cousin.

"Hey, cuz!"

"Keahi, something's gone wrong with these damned nanites. I need to see you and Dr. Jamison because I'm killing them."

Emptiness filled the connection until Kelani thought something happened to the call. "What's going on? I'm not sure the nanites are through with their program. You could risk a relapse of your illness."

"I don't care! Keahi, I saw The Green Lady. For real."

Keahi burst out laughing. "I'm sorry, it's just that I don't see how that ghost story has anything to do with the nanites."

Kelani growled in frustration. "Look, I don't care if you get it or not. I saw The Green Lady as plain as the hand in front of my face. She grabbed my arm and tried to pull me into the water. The only thing different in my life is the nanites I let you and Dr. Jamison inject me with last week."

"Other people have seen The Green Lady before and they didn't have the nanites." Keahi's tone stayed level and calm.

Kelani shook her head. "Fine, if you don't believe me, I'll connect with Dr. Jamison myself and kill these things."

She made to hang up the phone but heard Keahi and paused. "Wait, wait, wait. I'll get Dr. Jamison and we'll meet you on campus at the medical library in an hour, okay? Let's talk this through before you do anything."

"Fine." She tapped the line closed.

Kelani's hand shook most of the way back to Manoa Campus and to the door of the medical library. With a deep breath and renewed determination to kill the nanites flowing through her, she stepped inside. A second later, she spotted Keahi and made her way to him.

"Hey." He gave her a hug.

She returned it. "Hey."

"Come on, Dr. Jamison's office is just down this way. There's a skyway that connects to the faculty office building."

They walked in silence through the sterile, academic space and across an open skyway. The plumeria and palms made a picturesque frame for the ocean in the distance. Kelani paused for a moment to appreciate the view.

The novelty of being able to see clearly again still hadn't worn off. This thought weakened her resolve to deactivate the nanites. Then memories of the pale bluish skin draped in slimy green moss and dripping a trail from the creek came back. That was enough to push back against the idea of allowing the nanites to continue their work.

Keahi paused at a door and knocked. Kelani noticed the astute nameplate next to it programmed to reflect the office belonged to Dr. Marcus Jamison. The door slid open without a sound. "Good afternoon. I understand there is some concern about the nanites and some unusual woman?"

His tone of voice set Kelani's teeth on edge; clearly, he didn't believe her either. Then again, what had Keahi told him?

Kelani marched up to the desk, sat down, and launched into her story.

Dr. Jamison sat back in his chair and studied her as she spoke. Keahi might as well have been somewhere else for all the attention anyone in the room paid to him.

"And where do the nanites come into this tale?"

"They're responsible for me seeing The Green Lady. I've seen nothing out of the ordinary before. The nanites were the only thing that changed, so logic says this would be the most reasonable explanation for why I saw what I did."

"Well, we won't debate logic. Just who, or what, precisely is this Green Lady you're so concerned about?"

Kelani rolled her eyes. "The Green Lady of Wahiawa. She died out in Wahiawa after her kids went missing. Still haunts the area, trying to snatch kids she thinks are hers. I take it you've never heard of her."

Dr. Jamison shook his head. "I'm afraid ghost stories and urban legends are not my specialty. You're certain this was not just a trick of the light or a kids' prank or something similar?" Dr. Jamison leaned forward again, a questioning look crossing his face.

Kelani threw up her hands and turned to Keahi. "You didn't tell him anything, did you? I swear if you two agree that I'm crazy or imagining things or something, I'm out of here. I know what I saw, and you know I don't get superstitious or things like that."

Keahi backed away from his cousin a couple of steps and put his hands as if to defend himself. "I never said anything like you're making it up or anything. I just can't see how the nanites could do something like what you're describing. Even so, we're here, aren't we? Talking to Dr. Jamison, right?"

"Look," Dr. Jamison broke in. "Why don't we all head back out to Wahiawa tonight and see what happens? Put it to the test tonight before you make a final decision to terminate the nanites. I know some people over there so we can be in there tonight, even if it's after hours."

Kelani looked back and forth between the two men several times, studying their faces. "Fine, we'll go and then I'll kill these damned things."

She stormed out of the office, leaving both men stunned in her wake.

Kelani paused at the gates to the Wahiawa Botanical Garden. The two men continued through before realizing she'd stopped.

"You okay?" Keahi returned to Kelani's side.

She shook her head slightly. "Just a little nervous. I'm not looking forward to running into The Green Lady again."

"You really are convinced you saw her, aren't you?"

Kelani shot Keahi an incredulous look. "I can't believe you. After all of this, you're just placating me. Both of you are."

Dr. Jamison rejoined them. "Look, it doesn't matter at this point. We are here, so let's check this out. It's the best way to answer all of this once and for all."

Kelani let out a breath she hadn't realized she was holding until just then. "Okay, let's go."

As they made their way through the visitor center, a woman on the patio caught Kelani's attention. She was young and had long, white-blonde hair. She held a cigarette in one hand and smiled at Kelani. Kelani tried hard not to stare at the woman, though there was something compelling about her. They had just about passed her when Kelani caught a movement and a flicker of light. She turned to see the woman lighting the cigarette, though Kelani didn't see how she did it. The woman grinned and turned her back to Kelani.

"Come on, cuz, I'd rather not be going down into the gulch in total darkness."

She turned slowly back to follow the men through the center to the walking path, convinced there was something odd about the blonde woman.

Dr. Jamison paused. "Now, where exactly in the gardens did you see whatever this was?"

"Down this way by the two big ficus plants where the trail runs right by the water."

Kelani admired the various plants as they walked. But as the scent of the gardenia blossoms filled the air, Kelani's nerves started. They were getting close to the spot where she'd seen The Green Lady.

"What is that up ahead? Are there new lights on this path?" Keahi pointed to a string of lights, then froze, studying them intently. "Wait, I think they're moving."

Kelani stared at the trail of lights as Dr. Jamison tapped his foot, hands on his hips. Then her eyes got wide.

"Oh shit! It's the huaka'i po!"

She dropped to her knees, face to the ground and hands on her head. "Get down before they see you!"

Keahi waited for a moment or two, continuing to watch the lights as they grew closer. "Those aren't flashlights, that's for sure. The light flickers too much."

"That's their torches; now get down, will you? I don't want them taking either of you." Kelani's muffled voice floated up from where she knelt.

"Dr. Jamison, I think we probably should get down. If Kelani's right and they are the Night Marchers, looking them in the face means they'll take you with them."

Dr. Jamison glanced back at Keahi. "What do you mean, Night Marchers? What are they? And why would they take us with them?"

Keahi sank to his knees beside Kelani. "They're spirits of ancient Hawaiian warriors whose sacred duty was to protect the ali'i. Even in death, they still roam the islands protecting our chiefs. And they take those who look at them. It's disrespectful to look them in the face. By take, I mean you die."

As he finished speaking, Keahi ducked his head, assuming a similar submissive posture to his cousin's. Dr. Jamison, however, did not follow their lead. An awful stench wafted past the three of them as the throbbing beat of a drum reached their ears.

Then, in the space between heartbeats, a pair of misty feet wearing slippahs of banana leaf and bark appeared just in front of Kelani and Keahi. A rough voice commanded something in Hawaiian, but it was too quick to catch the meaning. A moment later, the feet disappeared. Neither of them moved. Slowly, the drums and pounding feet faded, the smell of death disappeared, and even the torchlight dimmed into nothingness.

Kelani felt Keahi's fluttering hand against her knee. She reached down with one hand to grasp his.

"Are they gone, cuz?"

She risked a brief glance up, not enough to see a face, but just so she could tell if they'd gone. "I think so."

Kelani straightened a little and checked the area further. Deciding it was indeed clear, she tapped Keahi on the shoulder.

"We have a problem, though."

Keahi uncurled. "What's that?"

Kelani gestured around them. "Dr. Jamison's gone."

"Shit."

They sat there for several seconds in silence, working to digest what had just happened. Keahi broke the spell.

"I'm sorry I didn't believe you. I don't know what the hell is happening, but you were right. There's weird stuff going on without a doubt. Could you actually see the Night Marchers?"

Kelani nodded. "Couldn't you?"

"Nope." Keahi climbed to his feet. "Could smell something awful and saw the line of torches. That's it."

He helped Kelani to her feet as she continued. "But the one was right here, six inches from your head. He, it, whatever, spoke to Dr. Jamison. I didn't understand everything the Night Marcher said, but it was something about disrespect and that he would pay. You're not playing games with me, are you?"

Keahi shook his head hard. "No way. That was too real to screw around with. Now what do we do?"

Kelani looked around the now darkened gardens. Then she turned back to Keahi. "Well, we need to get out of here. I don't like the idea of a run-in with The Green Lady on top of everything else tonight. But if we report this to the police, they'll think we're crazy. Not to mention the fact that the gardens closed a while ago, which means we're trespassing. So, I don't know. I don't know what to do once we get out of here."

"Getting out of here sounds like an excellent idea to me. We can figure it out from there later." Keahi gestured for Kelani to lead the way back up the path.

They made their way out of the gardens, jumping at any stray noise. Once in their car, the two of them relaxed a little. And, as they put the Wahiawa Botanical Garden behind them, they calmed a little more.

But as they made their way back down the H2 toward the campus at Manoa, the tension inched up again.

"Keahi, there are people who saw us leave with Dr. Jamison. And now we're heading back to campus without him. What's going to happen to us? They'll blame us for sure."

Keahi glanced at his cousin, the streetlights from the city illuminating the worry on her face, then focused on the road again. "We'll figure it out. Maybe we can say we dropped him off somewhere."

She sighed. "There are security cameras pretty much everywhere. They'll know we're lying the moment they look into this."

"True."

The miles passed and stillness filled their car. Only the gentle hum of the electric motor kept it from being dead silent. Kelani rubbed her eyes several times as they reached an open stretch of mountains between the cities of Wahiawa and Waipio, uncertain that she trusted her sight. Odd wisps of things flitted across her vision, though she chose not to say anything to Keahi for fear that he'd panic.

It was on that empty stretch things changed. Something nagged at Kelani, something she couldn't quite place.

"Hey, cuz, you awake?" Keahi's voice seemed loud in the quietness.

"Yeah."

"Just checking to make sure you're okay."

Something up ahead distracted her. "Slow down, I see something."

Keahi scowled. "You sure about that?"

"Yes, just do it."

She shoved at his arm a little, but he relented and tapped the brakes. Kelani stared out the windshield, studying the figure up ahead.

"There!" Kelani pointed to something. "Stop right there."

Keahi shook his head but stopped as she wanted. "What about the huaka'i po? Aren't you afraid they'll show up again?"

"No, they're gone. We need to help the woman there." Kelani shook her head and rubbed her eyes again before getting out of the car. The woman was old, white hair and leathery skin the color of koa wood. She was dressed in white, too, from head to toe.

"Help who?"

But Kelani was already gone. She strode up to the woman, then hesitated once she was face-to-face with her.

The woman tipped her head toward Kelani. "Beautiful night out, isn't it?"

Kelani shrugged. "It is."

Their bodies were angled toward each other but they looked off into the night. Kelani didn't know what to say, but she sensed the old woman was waiting on her to break their silence. A tension filled the air, though Kelani couldn't quite figure out why. After a minute, the weight got to be too much.

"I'm sorry for being a bit blunt, but what are you doing out here? There's not much around, not even houses. How did you get out here?"

The woman smiled. "How I got here is my own business, young lady. But, I am looking for a ride back into town. Perhaps you and your cousin can help with that?"

Something about the woman's answer, the way she moved gave Kelani shivers. It all seemed familiar, like deja vu. And the way the woman kept studying her even though they never looked directly at one another didn't help.

Kelani nodded. "Of course, tutu, we can give you a ride."

As they walked back, it registered with Kelani, she'd never told the old woman who Keahi was. She hesitated. The old woman took an extra step, then stopped and glanced back at Kelani, a knowing look gleaming in her eyes. Kelani opened her mouth to speak several times, but couldn't form a coherent thought. The woman grinned at her as if confirming Kelani's suspicions.

Kelani called out as they drew near Keahi, who had stopped a few steps from the car. "Keahi, she needs a ride down to Honolulu. We can drop her off on the way back to campus."

Gut instinct told Kelani it was the right thing to do, though she couldn't explain why.

He shrugged. "Okay, sure. This night is weird enough as is, so why not?"

Once back in the car, with the woman in the back seat, they continued down the road. With the lights of Waipio brightening the darkened sky several miles later, the woman spoke.

"You said it was a weird night already. What happened?" Her voice sounded slightly harsh, like she frequently yelled over loud noises.

"Yeah. I'm sure you'll think we're crazy, but we had a run-in with the huaka'i po earlier tonight when my cousin was trying to prove she'd seen The Green Lady earlier today." Keahi heard the slightly hysterical note in his voice but couldn't stop it.

"Ah, the Night Marchers. And did you pay them the proper respect?" The woman had an odd smile on her face, as if she knew some secret they didn't.

Keahi nodded as Kelani responded. "Yes, well, Keahi and I did, though only I could see them fully. Keahi and another person with us couldn't see them."

The old woman's eyes narrowed. "The third person with you, he did not listen, did he?"

Kelani shook her head. "I tried to get him to listen."

The old woman reached out and brushed Kelani's hair, making her jump. "There is something different about you. You see things you wish not, yes?"

Kelani twisted around in her seat, eyes wide, to face the old woman. "How do you know?"

The woman smiled cryptically. "It is not important how I know, but what I know. You see things not part of your world and wish not to see them. The three of you have meddled in things you ought not meddle. For helping me this night, I will repay your kindness. When you return home, blindfold yourself and wait near the door of your dwelling. You will feel hands touching you. Do not open your eyes or they will leave. What they have done cannot be undone, but they will provide sanctuary for you."

Kelani stared at the old woman, unable to formulate words. Keahi kept glancing back at the woman in the rear-view mirror. She laughed at the puzzled look on his face.

As Keahi scowled at the woman's laughter, Kelani's eyes suddenly grew wide.

"You're talking about the menehune, aren't you?"

The woman sobered and gave Kelani a knowing nod. "Perhaps it will be all right in the end that you have this sight. Remember, they will flee should you behold them, so you must follow my direction if you wish to benefit from their skills."

"I will." Kelani nodded.

The sign showing an exit for Pearl City sped past the windows, providing a break in the lush green scenery. Kelani stared without really seeing what flew by their car. Her head spun with everything that had happened. Something tickled at her memory. Then she realized the old woman and the gorgeous platinum blonde from the garden had to be the same person. She turned to ask the old woman about it.

"Kahaha! Where'd she go?"

Keahi glanced at Kelani. "What are you talking about?"

She tore her eyes away from the empty back seat. "She's gone, like not there, disappeared."

He shot Kelani a look of disbelief. "Na, cuz, she's got to be right there. We haven't even stopped moving. How could she get out?"

They both froze, at a loss for words. They made it through Waimalu and into the outskirts of Honolulu before either broke the silence.

"There's no way. She couldn't have been." Keahi shook his head as he spoke.

"Like the rest of what's happened today makes any sense. This is the only reasonable explanation. Woman, dressed in white, hitchhiking and disappears suddenly from the back seat." Kelani didn't look at her cousin as she spoke. She had a hard time swallowing it herself. "We just gave Pele a ride. And she's sending the menehune to help me."

Neither of them spoke again until they'd reached Kelani's small cottage. The idea of the Hawaiian goddess being in the car with them just seemed too unreal even for the bizarre night they'd had. Especially since she was so willing to help. Pele was capricious from what Hawaiian legend said.

"You gonna do what the old woman said?" Keahi turned to look at Kelani after parking the car outside her house.

Kelani nodded. "What do I have to lose? Some sleep? It's not like I'm going to go lay down and have pleasant dreams after everything tonight."

"I'll come check on you in the morning."

Kelani sighed as she walked up to the small house. Two windows framed a blue door. All of it looked a little rundown, the tin roof a little corroded and the paint peeling. A small part of Kelani wanted to do something about the appearance, but she knew better. The salty ocean air wouldn't let it last long, anyway. Maybe when she could better afford it down the line.

Kelani shut the door behind her. She walked through her house, pausing in each room—the one bedroom, her eat-in kitchen, and the living room. Everything was just so, all in its place. It had become increasingly important for her to keep it that way as her eyesight had deteriorated.

To see it now so clearly felt so surreal. Sure, she'd argued the reality of everything that's happened all day, but when she stopped to think, logic and sequence and everything she'd studied most of her life no longer came into it.

"Well," she said into the empty stillness, "what have I got to lose anymore?"

Kelani settled herself near the door and wrapped a rolled-up bandana over her eyes. It was as if the act of doing so flipped a switch. Soft tapping footsteps filled the quiet house. Gnarled and calloused hands touched her face. Despite their roughness, those hands felt like butterfly wings fluttering across her cheeks.

Then the hands disappeared. Curiosity gnawed at her, urging her to take her blindfold off, prodding her to peek at the creatures helping her. But her heart kept her hands still. The creatures were still working based on the slight, out-of-place sounds Kelani could still here. She knew without a doubt the moment she touched her blindfold they would disappear, and she'd be stuck with what the nanites had done. Which, she made a mental note, she still needed to kill before they did anything else to her.

With the same gentleness, those small, gnarled hands placed something in her lap. Then the quiet footsteps faded and her house fell silent.

The 'elepaios had begun their morning serenade when a knock sounded at Kelani's front door. Despite their beautiful song, it seemed off to Kelani, like they knew the craziness that had happened and were warning her it wasn't over yet.

Kelani couldn't stop walking around her house, staring in amazement at what the menehune had done, for that's who the creatures had to be. All her windows were brand new and ever so slightly tinted pink. The menehune had painted the outside of her house, and the roof gleamed. The thing they'd dropped into her lap had been a pair of glasses. Delicate silver frames with intricately woven bows held lenses that had the same barely pink sheen as the window.

Those misgivings couldn't override her excitement as she flung the door open. Keahi stood on her lanai, a look of apprehension on his face.

"Look what the menehune did! They fixed everything." Kelani paused and scratched her head. "Well, maybe not fixed really, but they gave me these cool glasses to keep the spirits from distracting me. And they redid my house to keep the spirits out."

Keahi's jaw worked, but no words came.

She nodded, her grin fading. "Yes, I know, that now effectively traps me here in this place. I mean I can leave the house and all with my glasses, but to, like, move away or something just isn't happening. At least I now have a sanctuary away from all this."

"Hey, speaking of all this, where's Dr. Jamison? Has he turned up yet?" Keahi asked.

Just then Kelani's phone chimed. She pulled it out of her back pocket and read the text that popped up on the screen.

Keahi prodded her shoulder. "You okay? You're as pale as Waikiki beach."

Shaking her head, Kelani looked up and down her street. At the corner four houses down, a woman dressed all in white waved at them once then turned and disappeared. Kelani wasn't sure if she'd vanished or faded into the surrounding neighborhood. Kelani shifted her attention back to Keahi, who stared at her with a mixture of apprehension and worry. "Apparently Dr. Jamison's returned from his time with the huaka'i po. But Pele couldn't promise he'd be the same. Oh, and she said the nanites have been taken care of already."

Keahi stared at her. "Well, damn. I don't know how to take that."

"Neither do I."

Ocean Blue

A Buzz Lee Occult Adventure
By TJ O'Hare

February 1986

I'd never dropped an anvil on somebody's head before. Not that it had ever been one of my ambitions. A piano, yes; an anvil - I could pass on that.

I was up in Purbrook's hayloft, trying not to raise the straw haze that would make me sneeze. The moon was yet to rise, and the night was filled with that February starlight where the rimed stubble in the outlying fields mirrors the sky: as above, so below. And which contains the deeper abyss?

Purbrook and his stable boys had found me trying to hide my motorcycle - the one I'd stolen from an undercover cop, name of Cully. They weren't to know that. All Purbrook saw was another itinerant (the British media hadn't coined 'New Age traveller' in 1986), looking for winter work: someone to graft hard enough to earn a roof over my head for the winter and not ask too many questions when it came to paycheck time. It suited my purposes perfectly - except I doubted that I would see out the winter here.

Purbrook was a wheelchair-bound ex-jockey. He could still make it into the saddle, and he eked out his training of race-horses with a little pony-trekking for disabled clubs in the Newmarket area. He was their inspiration and hope. And Ocean Blue was Purbrook's last hope.

My thoughts stilled into a perfect mirror surface as I heard the stealthy shift of movement from below. I knew the layout of this stable pretty well. The noise came from the crack in the floor where the old foundations jutted up from their antique glory. This was an old farm, built on even older remains. I hadn't the nerve to find out just how ancient, but I knew that the foundation stone was the source of Purbrook's trouble with Ocean Blue.

Ocean Blue, out of Ocean Foam by Rapido Bleu: Irish horseflesh with French strength of frame and wind. It was a wild hunch, but one that had worked out of a promise for Purbrook. Except that there was a shadow on the future.

I'd been at the stables for a week when I first noticed the tension around Ocean Blue. The stable lad who worked most closely with Ocean Blue was another ex-jockey called Rathbone. I saw him running across the yard and calling Purbrook over to examine their golden hope.

I kept my head down and my ears open throughout that day and learned that something was happening with their two-year-old Thoroughbred to cause them worry. Security was checked and re-checked, and a locksmith was called out from Newmarket to check the lock on the stable door.

Three days later, I saw the locksmith out again. He and Purbrook engaged in a heated discussion. It was too far away for me to pick up any facts. I tried to talk to Rathbone, but he was too tense to want to confide in me - an outsider and a non-horsey person. I bided my time and kept an eye out for more signs. I was beginning to think that my random flight from the police had been guided by some occult force.

Below me, I could hear the faint clink of metal on metal as the latch was lifted on Ocean Blue's stall. The horse gave a faint nicker of welcome. Rathbone had taken to sleeping in a hammock beside the horse. How could he not awaken? The stall door grated faintly on hinges kept deliberately noisy to make the hag-rider's task more difficult.

Below me, Ocean Blue blew noisily through her nostrils. She was eager for the chase. I pondered dropping down to investigate but couldn't pick up the courage. Why go out of my way to pick a fight with an opponent of unknown powers?

The European legends surrounding hag-riding are varied and notorious.

A horse found exhausted and covered in sweat in its stall first thing in the morning is a horse that has been hag-ridden. But the cause varies depending on who you ask. Some say the fairies take horses out for a wild ride over the fens and heaths. Others maintain that witches will take a horse and ride to a Sabbat. Older than those legends are the tales of the wild hunt: Odin and his troupe of lost souls scour the countryside on mortal steeds that are returned wild-eyed and foam-flecked to their human stables.

I could hear muffled hoofs below: maybe the hag-rider was more mortal than I'd feared. I leaned my face close to the wide crack between the boards and saw a shadow pass below. Physical light was practically non-existent inside the stable, but I saw more clearly than I cared to with my *akashic* sight.

Something bent and writhen, unconscionably old and withered, led Ocean Blue on a long halter-line. I caught a psychic glimpse of enlarged elbow joints that rose spider-like over the hunched and raddled backbone. It aspired to some form of humanity: a hooked nose and pointed chin that almost met like a nutcracker's; long, leathery breasts that rustled between wiry strands of a furze-like mane. And despite the fact that I was seeing it without the benefit of physical light, its hide was blue. If it had eyes, they were hidden beneath the down-turned and beetling brows. Claws from all four of its appendages clacked like iron barbs on the floor.

Despite my original supposition that it might well be a manifestation of Chaos and Old Night, I was still shaken by the very sight of it. I watched, fascinated, as it sprang the padlock on the stable doors with a muttered cantrip and a wave of its talons. The doors were opened, and Ocean Blue fairly pranced to be away.

Then the horrible canker came back to mount its steed, to be off about its unholy business.

That was when I realized I still had the anvil, poised, ready to drop. If I did it right now, then iron - cold iron - would plunge like a thunderbolt.

I threw my whole weight against the anvil, and even through the crack I saw the hideous face rise at the hag mounted Ocean Blue. The anvil scraped and fell - turning through the air in slow motion. A second of sight gave me a full glimpse into something like two pits of blue bale-fire, and then the thing sank its claws into the filly's neck and Ocean Blue took off like an arrow.

Five minutes later - or so it seemed - the anvil thudded into the floor of the stable, and I heard Rathbone let rip with a sulphurous oath.

I leaped down from the hayloft, absorbing the drop with bent legs and a forward roll that up-ended me into a pile of straw. I shouted at Rathbone: 'Get the rest of the boys and take them up to the north heath! Ocean Blue is gone again!'

I didn't wait to reply to his astonished cries and remonstrations. Plan A had failed. Time for Plan B. Oh, yes, I was feeling pretty sparky tonight. Plan B was a doozy.

Plan B was my motorcycle. The ignition had been repaired since the night I hot-wired it, and I now had a proper key for it. It was parked outside and ready to take off after the diminishing thunder of Ocean Blue's hoofbeats.

I flicked out the pedal and kicked down hard with my right foot. I was rewarded with an answering thunder of my own. The night was filled with reverberations, the sound of the engine bouncing off frosty surfaces and coming back as redoubled echoes.

With a slither of farmyard mud, I let out the clutch and mud-gullied across the front of the stable, then took the bridle path to the training paddock. I kept the headlight doused. I needed no light, and neither did the uncanny rider.

The path was rutted under my wheels, the tyres bouncing on frost-toughened ridges, but I poured on the speed. Ocean Blue was good, but this was a 400 cc Honda Super-Dream that was hogging through the darkness. Ocean Blue would eat my exhaust before long.

Plan B was the result of investigation. After the third hag-riding incident, I crept into her stall and marked her horse-shoes so that I could find out the route the hag-riding took. The marked horse-shoes always led up this bridle-path. Which is how come I had a dozen milk bottles stashed at various locations. They all held two fingers of Four-Star and a rag to act as fuse. My only concern would be the health of Ocean Blue herself. A direct hit on the rider that burned the horse would not be the outcome I desired, but fire was my only all-around active ingredient.

I knew now I was up against something of the faerie-kind, but my preparations had to be broad-based enough to handle a human agency if necessary. Fire covered all the bases.

A mile up the bridle-path, the track debouched onto a heath with a fence around it: the training paddock. Here stood a broad tree stump, once an ancient oak. My first Molotov cocktail was here. I still hadn't caught up with Ocean Blue, but I was confident I could still reach her before she left the paddock.

I slewed the cycle to a halt and found my bottle. Two flicks on the lighter and the rag was ablaze. I was wearing gloves, but even so I didn't want to hold this explosive device for any longer than necessary. I knew that Ocean Blue would follow a winding track across the heath to the northern exit. I gunned the engine into gear and took off in a straight line for the far gate.

The wind blew keenly on my face. I had no helmet on, but I had taken the precaution of winding a heavy woollen scarf about my head so that only my eyes were visible. Even so, my vision was blurred with wind-tears.

Even over the throb of the engine, I could hear the thud of hoofbeats like an arrhythmic heart ahead of me. It was mood music for the gods.

And it was in stereo, for I could hear it fall behind and to my right as I kept my course straight and true. The bottle in my fist streaked like a white comet in the darkness. Sparks struck from the universe - that's a human lifespan.

Too soon, it seemed the northern gate was in view. I braked the cycle and slewed the rear wheel around. The comet left my fist and whirled like a catherine wheel. It exploded twenty feet from the ground and everything was exposed for a moment in that psychotic light — black and white and hard-edged. No gray areas.

Somewhere off behind me, I heard Ocean Blue's hoofbeats cease and a shrill whinny of fear broke through the basso profundo of the engine-throb. I twisted in my saddle and saw her paw the air, hoofs striking thunder even on empty air. It was a different kind of thunder. It was thunder from the faerie glens of the ancient days, when humanity gave its own image to the spirits and newborn powers of creation still abroad in the land.

I wasted no time in savouring my first success. The nearest gate was a mile to the east, and that was where I saw Ocean Blue turn her muzzle. This would be a dash of a different sort.

The bike bucked beneath me, and out of my peripheral vision I saw the headlights of the Land-Rover as it came hammering down the bridle-path. Rathbone would be at the wheel, but Purbrook would be beside him, riding crop belabouring the dashboard.

The ice-covered surface of the riding track ahead gleamed as smooth as silk, and as soon as my wheels hit I lost control. I managed to guide the bike along, kicking down the side-step, one foot on the ice until the wheels bit the friction of the other side of the ruts again; and that was when the bike went up and over - somersaulting on its own thunder.

I landed hard and bad, but I managed to pick myself up and stagger on. The lights of the Land-Rover were picking out folds and drifts in the heath, and I knew that they would reach the east gate before either myself or Ocean Blue. That left only the south gate.

I weaved over to the cycle and found the air acrid with fuel. With a busted fuel tank, I was taking a chance in starting the engine, but I held my breath and prayed to whatever gods may be. They must've heard because I didn't go up like a human torch.

I turned the nose of the cycle towards the south gate and made it easily. I had four bottles cached here. Two of them, lit and lobbed, were enough to form an impassable barrier to Ocean Blue.

Now that we had her corralled, it was up to me to make sure that we finished this off good and proper.

The Land-Rover was reversing up the east gate, with Rathbone swinging the vehicle about, trying to pick up Ocean Blue in his headlights. I caught a glimpse of her midnight flanks as she sped for the bridle-path. Thwarted, I guessed that the faerie had to return to its abode to relinquish its prize of fleshly existence. With such unhuman, uncanny creatures, in order for them to interact with mortal flesh and blood - whether it be human or horseflesh - then it too needs to descend to our mortal frame. Ugly and misshapen it may be, but its flesh it can be made to take punishment. And I wanted to punish it.

Purbrook had helped me when he could have easily walked away. I owed him.

I had two Molotovs remaining, but I dared not light them with the fuel tank holed as it was. Instead, I nursed the two bottles inside my jacket and sped to intercept the horse and rider.

My route met hers about halfway in the middle of her dash for the bridle-path. I gauged it so that we would be racing side by side. Maybe the shock of gasoline on her would be enough to drive her from her stolen mount. Who knows? Adrenaline was making my decisions for me.

As I raced beside Ocean Blue, I steeled myself to turn my head and look again at the rider. Despite the wind-blurred tears that distorted my vision, I was surprised to discover a different aspect to her.

No longer was she bent and loathsome. Instead, she sat on her mount bare-back, white of limb, and lithe. Her hair blew behind her in a black mist that only emphasised the shapely, wanton candour of her nakedness. Her breasts were delicious mounds of milk-white flesh, topped with rose-coloured nipples. Her thighs flexed and pumped with each stride of Ocean Blue. Her chin was raised, her face upturned in an ecstasy that made human arousal seem as thin as whey.

So, was this the secret of her need? She had no more destination than a desperation that required slaking. Speed - on the back of a creature bred for speed through generations - was all that she craved. When she was earthbound, she was gnarled as oaken roots. But on horseback, she became one with the wind.

This is not a surmise on my part. She was a faerie, and she communicated by her very presence. The fact that I had encountered her was the simple act of insight required to trigger this account. Descartes' thesis did not apply to her. She did not think in order to be. She *was* in order to be: 'I am, therefore I am.'

She was the germ at the core of the Rolls-Royce sculpture: Spirit of Ecstasy. She was a speed fiend, manifesting different qualities at different velocities.

But the very fact that I was receiving this communication made me aware that what happened next was fated. I have a problem with humans being predestined, but the faerie are a different kettle of tissue. They are geomantic forces (maybe) condensed to human- or superhuman-like attributes. She had a need for speed that consumed her. Horses are all right, but they're limited. She had tasted my acceleration and knew that she had to sample. But her kind are not meant to interface with a Newtonian mechanical universe. They belong to the worlds of romance, passion, and the twilight of the senses.

What I did next is impossible. Oh sure, I'd seen it on cowboy movies a-plenty, but you had to be a trained stuntman to even dream of attempting it. I found myself leaping from the saddle of my cycle to land on the bareback flanks of Ocean Blue. There had to be a height difference of something close to two feet - that's twelve hands to you horsey folks out there. A physical impossibility, considering the state of the terrain, and the speed we were competing at. All I know is that we exchanged steeds. I gave her my metal and glass beast for her mount of flesh and blood.

Ocean Blue was running with her eyes wild. I was way too heavy for her, so I pulled on her halter rope and used it to rein her in as swiftly as I dared in those icy conditions.

The cycle sped on, and as it reached the bridle path, I saw it rise into the air and strive for a new level of speed. Then the fumes in the fuel tank decided that enough was enough, and the fields for a mile around were bleached to a steel-grey, etched quality as the light gave off its unequivocal judgment. Where there is light like this, there is no shade of grey. All is either black or white: as above, so below.

58

The Physician

By Crysta K. Coburn

Nathaniel mopped his brow and stuffed his handkerchief into his breast pocket. It was grotesquely hot and humid beneath the city streets where the pipes snaked in every direction, carrying water and steam. "The belly of the beast," his godfather Salazar called it. The beast being, Nathaniel supposed, the city that clawed at the sky, growing taller and more bloated with humanity's hubris.

As soon as he stepped through the archway into Salazar's laboratory, the old man called out a grave, "There you are," from the workbench.

Nathaniel wiped his brow again, straightened his shoulders, and made a show of casually looking around at the countless canisters of glowing mana stacked and spread all throughout the cavernous room. Some glowed gently, others vibrantly. Some were topped off, others nearly depleted.

"Hello, Godfather," Nathaniel answered cheerfully. "How goes things?"

Salazar arched one wooly eyebrow. "I understand you paid a visit to Eldridge."

"I did, yes."

"And what, dear doctor, do you make of his chances?"

Nathaniel shrugged, hands in his trouser pockets. "I expect him to make a full recovery."

Salazar's eyes, still sharp for his age, bore into his godson. "Miraculous."

"Yes, well." Nathaniel scratched a sudden itch at the back of his neck.

"Some might say so."

Salazar used his silver-topped cane to rise slowly to his feet. Nathaniel knew better than to offer help, so he waited silently, then followed when beckoned by Salazar's gnarled hand. The old man led him to a particular canister, perhaps three-quarters full, its liquid glowing a bright spring green.

"This," Salazar spat, "was half an inch from being empty yesterday morning."

Nathaniel feigned astonishment. "Was it really?"

"Don't play games with me! This is the mayor's jar."

"You don't say. It seems perfectly fine now."

"Mana doesn't just refill."

"Now, now," sighed Nathaniel. "Mana is a fickle thing. Why, your particular canister hasn't lowered its stock since I've known you, and we're past two decades now."

Salazar scowled. "We aren't talking about me."

"No, we're talking of mana. How well do we really understand it, Godfather?"

The old man raised his cane as if he might strike, but Nathaniel didn't flinch. Salazar stumped back to his workbench and sat down heavily. Nathaniel observed the instruments, beakers, and books arranged on the worktable.

"You are still doing research?"

Salazar scoffed. "I don't need to research what I already know. Mana doesn't refill. You be careful, my son. Don't meddle in things you don't understand."

Nathaniel replied crisply. "I am a physician. I always take the utmost precautions. And I daresay I have attended more grievous bedsides than have you."

Salazar's lips curled. "If you say so."

The men regarded each other in silence a moment. Finally, Nathaniel cleared his throat and forced a weak smile.

"It's fortuitous that you called me. I find I'm running low on my supplies."

The old man leaned back and lifted his brows. "Indeed."

"Quite. I've brought my bag. Do you mind?"

"That was our deal."

"Of course. Thank you."

Salazar returned to his work as Nathaniel went to the back of the laboratory where large vats stood. Nathaniel used a spigot to fill three jars with syrupy liquid, an entirely different material than what glowed in the canisters, though not unrelated. Salazar had named it ambrosia.

Decades before the young man was born, Salazar had experimented with brewing medicines from herbs he specially cultivated. He alone knew the secret, but he had no interest in becoming a physician. So when he had been asked to become his great-nephew's godfather, he agreed on one condition: The child would become a physician to aid in his experiments. No one could argue against that noble profession, especially not with the support of the city's genius inventor, Salazar. Little Nathaniel's future looked bright. (His younger sister Sadie often teased him about being the golden child.)

"You will, I assume," Salazar called, "pay another visit to Eldridge to assess his unaccountable recovery."

Nathaniel tightened the lids on his jars and placed them in his bag. "Isn't that what any good physician should do?"

"Wait a moment, and I shall accompany you. I've never been witness to a miracle. Don't put much stock in them."

Nathaniel grimaced. "Of course."

As the two men made their way to the surface, Nathaniel wiped his brow. "It's unbearable down here. I don't know how you stand it."

The old man shrugged. "Like many things, I have grown accustomed to it. It comes with experience."

Nathaniel pursed his lips, and they said no more to each other.

At street level, Nathaniel stepped away to hail a cab. The perfectly timed clip-clop of the automatic horses (one of Salazar's numerous inventions) on the cobblestone street was a relief. The tunnels had been too silent, too oppressive. Though he had spent much time in them as a child visiting his godfather, he never felt at home. He preferred to be around people.

Soon after the cab soon arrived at the mayor's manor, Nathaniel and

Salazar were shown into the front parlor. Eldridge came speeding in on his automatic chair (another Salazar original), laughing gaily. He was followed by his more sedate, though no less grateful, daughter. They both greeted their guests warmly.

"Dr. Granger," said Miss Eldridge. "How can I repay you for returning my father to me?"

"I believe I have already collected my fee."

Mayor Eldridge scoffed. "Such modesty! My dear fellow. I have a great deal in my power to grant you. Name it, and it shall be yours!"

Salazar glowered as Nathaniel forced a smile.

"Thank you. But really, I'm a physician. I was only doing my duty."

While he said this to everyone, the wealthier patients tended to find ways of properly showing their gratitude. A posh townhome with attached office space and suspiciously low rent, for instance. Private box seats at the opera. Once Nathaniel had come home to a five-course meal complete with footmen to serve it. He did not come from money, so he was used to taking care of himself, but who was he to refuse the occasional treat? (In fact, he thought he quite deserved it. He held the power of life and death in his hands.) But the proximity of his disapproving godfather made him nervous.

"Yes," muttered Salazar. "Duty." Then he cleared his throat. "Maximus, my old friend. It *is* a surprise to see you so full of vigor. I suppose my device has been serving you well?"

Eldridge beat the arm of his chair a few times with his fist. "Damn sturdy chariot! Damn sturdy. Between you and your godson, I'll be running this town for years to come."

"So it would seem."

Nathaniel gritted his teeth at the old man's sour tone.

"You both must stay for tea," said Miss Eldridge.

Salazar's eyes lit up. His sweet tooth was legendary. "I think that can be arranged. And it will keep the boy"—he cast Nathaniel a sharp look—"out of trouble for a few more hours."

When Nathaniel finally departed, his godfather chose to remain to play chess with Mayor Eldridge. No doubt, Nathaniel reflected, to observe any ill effects on a man whose life was unnaturally extended. Nathaniel felt exhausted and looked forward to some quiet moments in his office. But such was not his fate.

Miss Wright, his assistant, hovered outside the office door, anxious for her employer's return. Nathaniel had barely disembarked from the cab before the young woman informed him, "Urgent case for you, sir. General Fletcher's wife, I'm afraid. She's fallen this morning and is unresponsive. The general is most eager to see you."

"Is he here?"

"No, sir. But he's left his driver to take you to the house straight away."

Nathaniel sighed, then nodded. "Very well."

Upon arriving at the great house, Nathaniel was ushered upstairs. Fletcher wrung his hands beside his wife, who lay peacefully (albeit unconsciously) on the bed.

Opposite Fletcher, and unseen to all but Nathaniel, stood a woman veiled entirely in black. She didn't look quite as solid as General or Mrs. Fletcher, but she was real. Nathaniel breathed a sigh of relief at the sight of her at Mrs. Fletcher's head. The case was not terminal.

"General Fletcher." Nathaniel greeted the man with a confident voice and firm handshake. "I came as quickly as I could. May I?"

"Yes, yes!"

Fletcher made room for the physician. Nathaniel set his bag on the bedside table and observed his patient. Mrs. Fletcher's cheeks were flushed.

"Does she swallow?" asked Nathaniel. When the general looked at him helplessly, he waved his hand dismissively. "Never mind."

Nathaniel went through the motions of an exam before pulling out a small vial of ambrosia. He used a dropper to administer the dose to Mrs. Fletcher. At first, the woman did nothing, but soon she began to move her jaw and lick her lips. When she moaned, General Fletcher flew to embrace her.

The physician's eyes were no longer on his patient. Instead, he watched the woman veiled in black as she slowly faded away. When she had completely disappeared, Nathaniel nodded in satisfaction and pronounced, "I expect a full recovery."

"How can I ever repay you?"

Nathaniel smiled indulgently. "The usual fee will suffice. I was just doing my duty."

When he returned to his office, Miss Wright informed him that he had another patient waiting in the examination room, this one not so dire or urgent. It was a child with a cough, and there were no veiled women in sight. It was no wonder about the cough, Nathaniel mused, for the child worked at the coal-infested railway station. He wrote the mother out a prescription for the apothecary and advised bed rest.

While Nathaniel attempted to nap in his private office, his little sister Sadie burst through the door. Nathaniel sighed. No rest for the weary.

"Natty-dearest!" Sadie bent down for a hug and a kiss on the cheek. Nathaniel winced at the horrible nickname but obliged her. "Mummy said to come round and invite you to dinner."

"Tonight?"

"Of course tonight! It's been ages since you've come. Please say you will." She clasped her hands before her and pleaded with large, glistening eyes.

Nathaniel's plan of a quiet evening begrudgingly evaporated. He'd never been able to deny his sister anything, which was likely why their mother had sent her. Sadie was everyone's darling.

"Very well."

Sadie clapped and let out a squeal. Nathaniel held up a hand to stop her.

"Just the family, correct? Salazar won't be there?"

Sadie furrowed her brow. "No. Unless he decides to drop in." She giggled at the unlikely prospect.

Nathaniel glanced at the wall clock. "Let me tidy up here, then I'll join you."

Sadie curtsied, then practically skipped out of the office to gossip with Miss Wright while she waited.

Dinner was the usual affair with no surprise guests. Nathaniel's parents asked how his practice was going, and Sadie spoke of her charity work.

"There is one family that particularly worries me, the Websters. Old Mr. Webster works from dawn to dusk for the railway, scraping together just enough to take care of himself and his daughter-in-law while his son's stationed on a dirigible Heaven knows where. He wires the family money, of course, but it's hardly enough. And now poor young Mrs. Webster has had a baby, and the two of them have the most dreadful cough."

Nathaniel thought of the boy he had seen earlier that day. "No doubt it's related to the bad air on that side of town."

Sadie sighed. "Mother, do you mind terribly if I pack up some food to take to the Websters tomorrow?"

"Of course not, my dear. We'll talk to Cook after dinner."

Sadie beamed with relief and gratitude, then returned her attention to her brother. "Nat, would you come with me to properly diagnose them?"

"I think it's a wonderful idea," said their mother. "Sadie, you have such a kind heart."

"Yes," added their father. "Go with your sister and help these unfortunate souls like a good lad."

Nathaniel opened his mouth to protest, but the conversation moved on.

Slightly before eleven o'clock the next morning, Sadie appeared at Nathaniel's office with a large basket.

"Miss Wright," she said. "Please clear my brother's schedule for the rest of the day."

Miss Wright raised a brow at her employer.

Nathaniel pursed his lips. "Do not do that. But don't expect me back before the early afternoon. I am joining Miss Granger on an errand, and then I expect we'll have lunch."

"Yes, sir."

"Oh," pouted Sadie. "You are so practical."

Nathaniel put on his coat, grabbed his bag, and held his free arm out to his sister. "As is befitting of my occupation."

On the street, Nathaniel held out his hand to hail a cab.

"Must we?" asked Sadie. "Everything is becoming so automated in the city these days. I miss real horses, don't you?"

Nathaniel shrugged. "You don't mean to walk."

"Why not? The sky is clear. It will do our health good. Won't it, *Doctor?*"

He chuckled. "Yes, all right, if you insist."

The Webster home was in the lower part of the city. It was a small, squat house. Sadie knocked before entering. Nathaniel followed, trying to ignore the ripe smell that permeated the single room. A lady veiled in black stood at the foot of the bed where a pale young woman lay still. A swaddled baby lay in a basket by the stove. Another lady in black knelt at the infant's feet. Their positions showed Nathaniel the disease was fatal. He kept his expression neutral as Sadie, oblivious to the two ominous harbingers, emptied the contents of her basket on the dining table.

Sadie kept her voice soft. "How are you feeling today, Mrs. Webster?"

The woman on the bed stirred and coughed, then she replied weakly, "Tired."

"I've brought my brother to have a look at you and your baby. If anyone can heal you, he can."

Nathaniel was touched by his sister's faith in him. But the two ladies told him all he needed to know. He examined the woman and her child for Sadie's sake, but he had to admit to her, "There's nothing I can do for either of them. I'm so sorry."

"No!" Sadie cried. "There must be something! Young Mr. Webster returns in a month. How can I tell him that both his wife and child are gone?"

His lips made a grim line. Nathaniel agreed that it wasn't fair, and he hated this part of his job.

"Please," Sadie continued, wounded. "Everyone said Mayor Eldridge was going to die, and you cured him."

And how quickly that action had come back to bite him. Salazar was right, Nathaniel shouldn't have meddled. But the mayor's daughter had been so pleading, so pretty… And it was the mayor. The city needed him.

Nathaniel closed his eyes, shutting out the scene. "I'm sorry. Truly."

Sadie doubled her efforts. "How can you dismiss them so easily? Isn't it your job to work tirelessly to save people?"

Her words wounded him. If he were an ordinary physician—if he didn't have the insight that he did—he would do as she said. But he knew the struggle would be for naught. He started to leave when he was stopped by a rasping voice. It was the young woman.

"Sir. If not me, at least save my baby."

Nathaniel bit his lip. Life was cruel. People died.

"*Please.* Natty…"

Grief throttled his sister's voice. She wrapped her arms around him and rested her forehead against his back. Her shuddering sobs put cracks in his resolve.

"You have to at least try," Sadie begged.

If it had been anyone else, Nathaniel would have pulled away and departed. But he couldn't leave his little sister. And it would be easier to save the baby than it had been the mayor. He was such a tiny thing—and light, too.

Before he could change his mind, Nathaniel turned to the woman on the bed. "Is there someone to nurse the child?"

"A neighbor has been helping me." She gestured feebly to her right.

"Mrs. Wicket?" asked Sadie.

The woman nodded.

"Sadie," said Nathaniel. "Go and fetch her. I will see what I can do here."

Sadie nodded and squeezed Nathaniel's arm in gratitude, then hurried away. Nathaniel glanced at the woman on the bed. She stared fervently at him with shining eyes.

"I promise you, your child will not die today. But I dare not save you both."

She bowed her head.

Nathaniel knelt by the baby. Taking a deep breath, he picked up the basket and turned it around so that the veiled woman knelt at the infant's head rather than feet. He dug into his bag for the vial of ambrosia and administered the drops. The color returned to the baby's cheeks, and he began to fuss. The veiled woman gradually disappeared. Knowing there was no longer any danger, Nathaniel scooped the baby up and placed him in his mother's arms.

"Bless you," she whispered.

Nathaniel tried to smile, but a sinking feeling in his stomach kept him from feeling any satisfaction. He hoped that this little life would be below Salazar's notice, though he knew his godfather was a stickler for details.

Sadie soon returned with Mrs. Wicket, and Nathaniel removed himself to the corner to be out of the way. When his sister was satisfied that all was settled and her mission of tending to the family accomplished, she and Nathaniel departed.

Sadie finally broke the silence. "I don't think my heart's really in it, but should we stop somewhere for lunch?"

He shook his head. "I don't have an appetite."

"At least stop by the house for some tea and a sandwich. We should have something to keep us going."

Nathaniel assented and flagged down a cab. Sadie did not protest this time.

Tea with Sadie had been pleasant, but what he really wanted once he returned to his office was a stiff drink. What he had done was foolish. He couldn't save them all, that was part of the deal. But Eldridge had been too obvious. His recovery was sung across the rooftops moments after the man had opened his eyes. Who would notice a baby? A poor baby born to a poor family.

Reaching adulthood might not be in the cards for the child even now.

A voice startled him when he stepped into his apartment.

"I thought I told you not to meddle."

With a shaky hand, Nathaniel twisted on the nearest light, illuminating the fiery scowl of Salazar.

"Oh, hello, Godfather." Nathaniel mopped his brow with his handkerchief, then sank into an armchair opposite the old man. "Funny seeing you twice in one week."

Salazar crossed his arms and looked down his nose at his godson. "Funny is not the correct word. I've been keeping an eye out for more 'anomalies.' What did you do with that baby?"

"It was just a baby—"

"Precisely. So why meddle?"

Nathaniel could see there was no use in maintaining the charade of ignorance. "Was I supposed to let a man come home to find both his wife and his child dead?"

"Yes!" snapped Salazar. "Or have you somehow forgotten? Was all that schooling for nothing?"

Nathaniel shot up from his chair and glared down at the man. "I am a good physician—the best in this city. I fix the people that your machines grind down. Don't you ever dare suggest that I don't know what I am doing—"

"But do you?" Salazar's voice was quiet, almost consoling. "You're young. You have some heart, which I admire. But you need to understand something, my son. Death comes to us all. She is the great equalizer. And you are not God."

"I am the next best thing!"

Salazar arched a fuzzy brow. "That is a dangerous line of thinking. There are consequences to every action. Do not tempt fate, my boy. Do you understand?"

"Of course."

The old man sighed and rubbed the back of his neck as if it were sore. "You will see, I'm afraid."

"I see every day the injustice in this city. Isn't it my job as a physician to lessen the suffering? Isn't that why you chose me? Educated me? Took me into your confidence?"

Shaking his head wearily, Salazar only repeated, "You will see."

The next morning, Nathaniel , pleased with his assistant's work, asked Miss Wright if she wouldn't mind continuing handling his cases for the next few days. He wasn't feeling well and wanted to stay in his apartment. He would be available for anything serious, of course. But for the little things, he had full confidence in her abilities as a healer.

The young woman swelled with pride. "Thank you, Dr. Granger. I won't let you down."

He smiled, nodded, and clapped her on the shoulder before slinking back upstairs and praying there would be no emergencies. For the following week, Nathaniel lay low and followed the rules. If he saw a veiled woman at a patient's head, he administered the ambrosia. If she was at their feet, he gave his sincerest condolences to the family.

It seemed so arbitrary to the physician. Sick was sick, wasn't it? Salazar insisted there was rhyme and reason to the uncanny ladies' visits, yet he could not—or would not—explain it to Nathaniel, expecting the young man to accept it on faith. But Nathaniel wasn't sure he could be happy being a cog in creation's wheel any longer. He wanted to understand what powered the machine.

One day Sadie came knocking, and he roused himself.

"Have you not been well, Natty?"

Nathaniel smiled thinly and scratched his stubbled chin. "I suppose you could say I haven't been feeling my usual self."

She frowned. "Do you need anything? I'm happy to help."

Nathaniel was warmed by her offer. Sadie was the kindest person he knew. Too kind to be burdened by his troubles. "No, thank you. Miss Wright has been assisting me most adequately."

She nodded. "Good. You know, I've always—"

Her words were cut short by a wracking cough that nearly doubled her over.

Nathaniel quickly poured a cup of water and flew to her side. "How have *you* been feeling? Here. Sit."

She accepted the water, but remained standing. "I'm all right. Throat's a little dry, that's all."

He peered into her pale face. "Come down to the office. I'll listen to your lungs."

"No, really. I'm fine. Thank you, though. I only wanted to see how you were. I was worried when I heard you were only seeing the worst cases."

"Who told you that?"

"Salazar came to the house one evening and told us."

Nathaniel wondered how the old goat knew. Was he spying on him?

"I'm feeling better now. In fact, I thought I might go for a walk just now. Care to join me?"

"No, that's all right. I feel rather chilly today. If you really are well, I suppose I will return home."

"I really wish you'd let me listen to your lungs before you go."

"Really, Natty, I'm perfectly fine." She finished her water and handed him the empty glass. "Come around for dinner soon?"

"Of course."

The siblings said their goodbyes, and Sadie departed. Nathaniel couldn't help being bothered by her wan appearance—and that cough!

Nathaniel needed a distraction. He decided to check up on his recent patients, starting first with Mrs. Fletcher. He focused on the precise clip-clop of the cab's automatic horses to steady his nerves as he traveled. This had been an easy, routine case, and, as expected, the good woman was up and about, fully recovered from her inexplicable illness that Nathaniel could not, nor did he feel the need to, explain. The ambrosia had done its work.

He took a cab most of the way to his next destination, then chose to walk the last couple of blocks so as not to draw attention to himself. He remembered the house all too well.

Mrs. Wicket answered his knock. "Dr. Granger! You must've come to check up on the tyke, right? Please come in."

Nathaniel noticed that the bed was empty. He did not ask if Mrs. Webster had died.

Mrs. Wicket went to the basket and picked up the very healthy infant. Nataniel went through the motions of a check-up, asked if the baby was eating and drinking enough, was he fussy or having trouble sleeping, et cetera.

"He's a very happy baby," insisted Mrs. Wicket. "Isn't he lucky? All he knows is eating, sleeping, and po—I mean, well, you know how babies are. Not a care in the world."

"Yes. Very lucky."

After Nathaniel left, he decided to make good on his promise to his sister and join his family for dinner.

When he arrived, he was told that Sadie had gone to her room to rest.

"It isn't really like her," said his mother. "I'm worried. Would you be a good brother and look in on her?"

Nathaniel took her hands and gave them a reassuring squeeze. "Of course."

Sadie sighed when she saw him. "I told you earlier that I am perfectly well."

"You're perspiring."

Sadie sighed. "It's warm is all."

"Earlier today you said you were chilly." Nathaniel crossed the room to where his sister lay in bed covered by a quilt. "Let me do a quick examination. Even Mother insists."

Sadie wetpursed her dry lips as she considered. "Very well, since you won't give it up."

Nathaniel set his bag on the bedside table, opened it, and pulled out his instruments. The thermometer confirmed that she had a fever, and her neck was swollen.

"I have some things with me here to help lower your temperature, and I should have something for the cough. Be good, and don't argue."

Nathaniel turned away to mix together some ingredients.

"Natty, really, I'm sure it's…"

"I said don't argue."

He turned back to his sister only to find that she had fallen unconscious. Beads of sweat studded her pale forehead. And, to his increasing horror, a woman veiled in black slowly took shape at Sadie's feet.

A guttural cry burst from Nathaniel's throat. "No! No, no, no, no, no!" He took a swipe at the veiled lady, but his hand passed right through her. He glared at her. "Damn you! What business do you have here? Leave immediately!"

The being remained immobile. Meanwhile, Sadie struggled to breathe. Nathaniel tried to rouse her with gentle pats on her burning hot cheeks, then smelling salts. Neither worked. The lady in black watched, her presence mocking his efforts. "Go away, won't you? I know your secret, you know. I can make you go away if I choose."

Nostrils flared, he stared hard at her, his eyes straining in vain to pierce the veil. Was she, too, one of Salazar's confounded inventions?

Sadie's wheezing stopped. Nathaniel let forth a series of curses. She didn't deserve this. She was the gentlest soul he had ever known. She'd taken in sick animals as a child and nursed them back to health. She took meals to the poor and did all she could to ease their suffering. If this were a punishment meant for Nathaniel, he refused to allow his little sister to take the fall for his misdeeds.

There was no more hesitation. He scooped Sadie up in his arms. He then ran around the bed to the other side and laid her back down with her head at the foot of the bed, feet at the top. He grabbed the ambrosia from his bag, and, cradling her head in one hand, Nathaniel shoved the dropper to the back of her mouth and administered the drops. Then he held his breath, waiting.

It seemed an eternity before she began breathing again. Nathaniel let his own breath out in a loud, long whoosh as he collapsed at the side of the bed. He pulled out his handkerchief and dabbed his forehead. When his pulse had calmed, Nathaniel peered around the side of the bed. There was no longer a veiled lady at the foot of the bed. Nor one at the head. Nathaniel grinned. His sister would recover.

Nathaniel stood, stretched, then doubled over, coughing painfully. He tasted blood. When the cough came again, he covered his mouth with his handkerchief, then he stumbled out the door. He needed to get home, away from other people. When he passed a maid in the hall, he asked her to give his mother his apologies and tell her that Sadie would be just fine.

His knees shook, he felt chilled, and the cab driver recoiled from him when he gave his address. He bribed the driver with double the usual fee and kept his handkerchief over his mouth to catch every cough.

Miss Wright had stepped out, so the office was locked and silent. Nathaniel let himself in and crawled on hands and knees up to his apartment. Strength bled from his body at a frightening pace. He needed to get to his bed. He needed rest. And he needed to see at which end she would appear. But his eyes swam, and the floor rocked from side to side as he attempted to traverse it.

Hours seemed to pass for Nathaniel as he belly-crawled toward his bedchamber. A century was gone when he finally made it through the door. Then, at last, he was clutching his blankets, pulling himself onto the mattress. He fell upon it with such relief, he nearly lost consciousness.

No! Where was she? He needed to find her.

With fingernails dug into his arm to keep him alert, Nathaniel cast his eyes fervently around the bed. There was no veiled lady, however. Perhaps this wasn't a matter of life and death after all. Nathaniel groped at his bedside table for the just-in-case vial of ambrosia that he always kept there. But his fingers were slick and numb, and when he struggled with the stopper, the vial tumbled from his grasp. Nathaniel cried out and lunged for it, but it was too late. The contents had already spilled onto the rug. High-pitched laughter burbled from his lips.

Then he saw her.

A dark smudge at the edge of his vision—near his feet. He pushed himself onto his back, head propped up on his pillows, and regarded her still form.

"I've never seen you from this angle before," he rasped. "What a treat."

She, of course, did not answer.

Nathaniel knew he needed to turn himself around. But he was so weak he couldn't raise his arms. He would have to wiggle like a worm. The thought made him laugh. He felt like a worm on a hook. His godfather had tried to warn him of consequences. If only Salazar had been more specific.

When he had managed to rotate sideways so that his feet hung from one side of the bed, and his head the other, Nathaniel stopped, too exhausted to go on. Halfway would have to do. There was no more ambrosia within reach anyhow.

"Dr. Granger!" Miss Wright called from downstairs. "Dr. Granger? Are you here? The door was open."

Hope swelled within Nathaniel's chest even as the room grew dim around him. Miss Wright was a capable nurse. He would tell her where to find the ambrosia in his office. She could help him turn himself the rest of the way around. Everything would be all right. Everything...

Nathaniel went gradually limp as his eyes closed.

"Dr. Granger!" Miss Wright cried. He heard her rush to the bed, felt her cool hands on his forehead. "Goodness, what happened? You have a fever!"

Her strong hands lifted his shoulders and doggedly pushed and lifted his body into a proper position on the bed. Nathaniel tried to cry out, to tell her no, to give her instructions, but he couldn't manage even a whimper.

Though he couldn't see the veiled lady at his feet, he could sense her. Having seen her hundreds of times at other bedsides, he knew her aspect well. Salazar's words echoed in his mind. *Death comes to us all. She is the great equalizer.*

While Miss Wright busied around him doing what her training had taught her was best, the physician, who had no power over death after all, could only lie there waiting for the inevitable.

Worridziam

By Lynne Lumsden Green

This story is set in the Ipswich area of Queensland. I want to acknowledge the Jagera, Yuggera, and Yugarapul peoples of Ipswich and Springfield, whose cultures and customs are important to the care of the Ipswich community, and acknowledge and pay respect to the continuing contribution of the community's Elders.

The sound boomed from the wetlands, waking the household. The Missus – heavily pregnant with her first child – started crying from a combination of fear and exhaustion. The whole house rattled with the noise; the tin on the roof loudest of all. There was no possibility of sleeping through the racket.

The Boss cursed under his breath. The booming might cease for months, and then it would come back to haunt their nights for several weeks. This latest series of spooky serenades were taking its toll on his young bride's health. Both the Boss and the Missus were worried about how this might affect their unborn child. Something

had to be done.

The Boss struggled into his moleskins and boots. "You stay here, darling. I'll see if I can frighten off this nuisance."

"Please be careful. It sounds like a big animal."

"Hah! Think about how loud a single cicada can be. Or a treefrog in the drainpipes. But I'll take the rifle if that will set your mind at rest."

Outside, the sound was louder and more intense. It rumbled as it bounced between the hills, gathering echoes, making the gum leaves shiver in the trees. The sound originated in the marshy area at the bottom of his pasture. He used a hurricane lantern to light his way.

The wetlands were seasonal. In the dry months, it sometimes turned into a mossy quagmire with uncertain footing. However, the rain had been heavy and frequent in the past months, and there was now a shallow, reed-choked lake. Usually the haunt of frogs and waterbirds, that night the lake was dominated by the boomer, whatever animal it was. The water rippled in time to the howling reverberation.

"Here, you, shove off!" shouted the Boss.

A pair of orange eyes as big as cartwheels rose out of the water and glared at him. They blinked, and the man blinked back.

"How rude," said a voice, in perfectly splendid English. "This is my home. I don't come into your home and ask you to leave."

What magic was this? No human could have eyes like that. No human could live at the bottom of a lake.

"Who are you? What are you?" asked the Boss.

"I am Worridziam. What you might call a bunyip. I have lived in this hollow for more years than your people have lived in this land, and I don't plan on leaving on your say-so."

"Are you talking about white people?"

"You man-things. Your colour matters not to me."

The Boss's growing curiosity battled with his fear. "That's thousands of years," he said, "hundreds of thousands. That's not possible."

"Indeed. My memories go back to a time when these hills were smoking mountains, when there were no men. In fact, there were no furry beasts at all. It was scales and feathers that shared the land with me." The voice was calm as it made its explanation. The Boss believed it, incredible as the fact might seem.

"Are there more of you?" he asked.

"Yes. Of course. But we are rare and do not socialise much with our own kind."

"Then why do you make that terrible noise, if not to call to a mate?"

The great eyes blinked several times. "That comment is most unkind. I was singing for the sheer joy of being alive."

There was an awkward silence.

It was broken by the Missus calling. "How is everything going? Did you find the source of the noise?"

"Just sorting it out," called back the Boss.

The voice in the pond chuckled. "And what if I don't agree to be 'sorted out'? You've been nothing but impolite."

The Boss was originally from the Old Country. He remembered his grandmama's stories of fairy beasts and old gods; it never paid to be rude. They were to be treated with respect. If you followed certain rules – don't eat any food they offer you, don't give them your name, don't threaten them with iron – they often granted gifts and wishes. And – most tellingly – they lived under the ground, where time passed differently.

With his smoothest vocal tones, the Boss said, "I'm so very sorry, great one. I didn't know I was going to meet with you."

The fire of the orange eyes brightened at the words 'great one.' Worridziam almost purred, "Apology accepted."

The Boss explained about the Missus and their hopes for their baby. He finished with, "And the power of your singing frightens my wife, magnificent as it may be. It keeps her from her rest when she needs her strength the most."

"It was never my intention to frighten anyone, let alone endanger their health," said the bunyip. "I will cease singing, at least for several seasons. And – as a sign of my contrition – I will favour your child with my protection."

"Thank you. We are honoured."

The Boss had forgotten that gifts from the Old Ones were often double edged.

Over the next few weeks, the Boss researched everything he could about bunyips.

He found news stories of bunyip sightings in the Mary River. A dead one had been described as being "about 10 feet long, with a long snout, almost like a bill, about two feet long, and fitted with teeth an inch long… It was neither alligator nor dugong, although the body was similar to a dugong with large flippers. An outstanding feature was the creature's huge eyes. It appeared to have a tough hide, with barnacles clinging to it. In colour, the body was greenish-brown above and yellow underneath."

There had been recent news articles of bunyips around Burleigh Heads on the Gold Coast, with one stating, "There were reports of a loud 'boom - boom - boom' noise coming from the swamp each night following the construction of the Miami Hotel and a sanitary depot in the swamp area, although these sounds were sometimes not heard for twelve months before starting up again. According to one local resident, reminiscing, 'local aborigines would pull up camp when the booming noises came from the swamp, referring to the Debil Debil.'"

The large eyes were certainly a feature of Worridziam, as was the booming call. But the discovery of the dead specimen intrigued him, as it indicated that a such long-lived creature could still be killed. Did he want to kill the creature?

No. All the bunyip had done was make a big noise. The Boss wanted to investigate it. He could make a contribution to science! Make his name. Make his wife and future child proud of him.

He went back to the wetlands for several nights and called to Worridziam, but it never answered him. In a way, he was pleased. The Missus was getting a proper night's sleep and was looking less drawn. But that didn't scratch his curiosity bump. Like most gentleman farmers, he had a work shed full of tools for tinkering with his farm implements and pamphlets about the workings of mechanical engines. He went there to contemplate what he knew and what he might do.

As he thought, he absentmindedly flicked through the latest journal published by the Royal Society of Victoria. A striking image from the magazine caught his eye; that was the answer! He needed to invent a submersible or a diving suit! He could base his design on the magazine's image of the John Lethbridge diving machine, which was basically a waterproof barrel with two holes for the arms and a viewing port glazed with glass about four inches diameter and an inch and a quarter thick. He would have to surface frequently to refresh the air, but the beauty of the design was that he could maneuver in shallow water without assistance. The modern scientific method would uncover all the answers he needed.

After all, the pond was seasonal, and he didn't need to go into deep water. He just needed to get the attention of Worridziam. He figured a bright light would have been best, but he didn't have the proper equipment to make a dive light. He'd just have to jab a blunt-ended stick into the mud and hope for the best.

While he was still working on his diving machine, the Missus gave birth to fraternal twins, a boy and a girl, with the help of the local nurse and a couple of wives from the neighbourhood. The Boss remembered that Worridziam had said it would bless a child, not two. It was clear that the boy was the fairy-blessed child as soon as the Boss laid eyes on the lad, for the child was small, fair-skinned, and golden-haired. His sister was large and dark and bald, perfect in her own way, but without the glamour of her brother. The boy they named Albert, after the late Prince Consort, and the girl they named Melanie, after the Missus's mother.

From the start, Bertie was lucky. When a brown snake found its way into the house, the dog killed it in the nursery before it harmed the twins. He was prevented from falling down the stairs by a basket of wet laundry; his mother had put it down to soothe Melanie when she was crying. He didn't eat any of the berries that made his sister throw up.

When the children were a year old, their father finally finished his diving machine. He had tinkered with it during the long summer evenings after a full day working the farm, or in the early winter mornings before the sun was up and he would have to start the day. He was excited to try it out.

When he took it into the pool in his wetlands, he found nothing but frogs, tadpoles, boatmen, mosquito larvae, and dragonfly larvae. The murky water revealed no evidence of the bunyip, no hump in the mud, no glimpse of orange eyes.

The Boss was disappointed. Had the bunyip deserted the wetlands for good?

Melanie became her father's shadow, while Albert grew to be a sporty boy who liked football and cricket. When the Boss was tinkering in his shed, Melanie would watch his every move. Once she learnt to read, she worked her way systematically through all his magazines. By the time she was seven, she was helping her father, organising his tools, handing him the correct one when it was needed, and even making helpful suggestions.

The Missus wasn't too concerned with her daughter's interest in technology because Melanie was also helpful around the house. The child washed dishes, fed the chickens and collected the eggs, hung out the laundry; she often did the chores her brother forgot. Her schoolwork was always done well. Her brother's homework was sometimes copied from her work. Albert tended to take advantage of his sister's good nature.

Not that Albert was ever unkind to his sister. He loved her with all his heart. He was fickle and flighty, but his parents turned a blind eye to these faults, his father seeing them as part of his boy's fairy changeling nature and his mother seeing the casual thoughtlessness of a normal boy. Melanie doted on him, not just because he was her twin, but because of his generosity of spirit. He might forget to close the barn door, but he would always own up to his mistakes and do his honest best to not repeat them.

By the time the twins were ten, Melanie was helping her father with inventions to explore the wetlands. She had designed and constructed a periscope that let a person in a boat see underwater with ease. Her mechanical crawler took photographs underwater, but the light levels were too low and all she got was a series of murky, grey images with hints of shadows. The Boss was the first to admit that his daughter had a mechanical aptitude.

"It's time to think about sending the children to boarding school," he said to the Missus. This hadn't been an easy decision for the Boss. He wondered if Bertie would pine away from his home territory and the source of his fairy gift. But Bertie couldn't stay an uneducated child forever.

"Both of them? Can't I keep Melanie home with me?"

"She has twice the brains of our Bertie. You wouldn't want that wasted here in the scrub, would you?"

The Missus sighed and said, "Melanie is such a help around the place. And she is good company."

"I know. We can always hire someone to help you. We're making good money these days."

"Half the reason we are doing so well is Melanie and her reading. She makes sure we've always got the most up-to-date advice from the agricultural department."

"Think how much better we could do if she gets a bit of education," said the Boss. "And – let's face facts – she isn't an oil painting with her muddy complexion. She will meet more boys at school than around here."

The Missus bit her lip. Melanie's looks were a sore point with her; the girl's features were pretty, but her skin was dark and lacklustre, and her hair lank. No matter how much her mother applied potions or curled Melanie's hair, she remained unchanged. It seemed such a small thing when compared to what a good child she was, but men were stupid about a girl's looks; most men would rather marry an empty-headed useless woman than a sensible helpmeet.

"You make a good argument, dear heart," she said at last. "It would be selfish of me to keep her with me just because I will miss her so. But can we wait another year or so? They are both still so young."

"Another year at home won't hurt," agreed the Boss. He wasn't too keen to send away his children. His fair boy meant more to him than just protection against the world's ills; he loved the boy for his own sake. As well, what would he do without the trusting friendship of his daughter, his little inventor?

When the children were eleven, their parents made the arrangements to send them away to boarding schools in Ipswich. Melanie and Albert were both excited and intimidated by the idea of leaving their parents and to start the process of 'growing up.' New clothes and uniforms were purchased and packed away in trunks. The Missus made all their favourite meals. The days ticked away until it was the final night before they took the train to Ipswich.

That last night, the Boss went out to sit overlooking the wetlands. He wished he could hear the boom of the bunyip and ask him what was going to become of his son.

As he sat there, Melanie sat down beside him and took his hand in hers. She said nothing, sharing the noises of the night with him.

"I'm going to miss you," said the Boss. "I'm going to miss making our gadgets."

Melanie's voice was soft and low. "I'll be home every holiday."

"I know. But it won't be the same. You'll see the bigger world and meet smarter people than your old dad. You might not want to tinker in the work shed."

"You've already shown me so much more than the bottom of my pond." "Hah! It's you who explored the pond better than I ever could."

"No, dad, you don't understand," explained Melanie. "I'm your daughter, but I am also Worridziam. You thought Bertie was the changeling, but it's been me all along."

The Boss sat frozen for several minutes. Tears started to run down his face. Then he said, "You're not my girl? Are you going back to the wetlands tonight?"

Melanie threw her arms around her father. "Silly man, I've always been your child. Haven't you shown me all the love in your heart? Haven't I shown you all the love in mine?"

"But you're nearly immortal."

"I'm not immortal anymore. I've decided, when this body dies, I will die with it. I want to see what comes next, since you're my family. I was lonely, and now I am not. I want to stay with you."

The Boss was still crying, but now with joy. "Do you want me to start calling you Worridziam?"

"No, thank you," said his daughter with a cheeky grin. "Melanie is much easier to spell."

Death on the Moon

By K. A. Lindstrom

"In ten minutes, we will arrive at Oasis. For your safety, please remain seated until the starship has completed docking procedures." The artificial voice continued on, repeating its message in six different languages to an indifferent audience of one.

Detective Sun Si-Ying absentmindedly picked at her teeth as the welcome video played, showcasing all the attractive amenities offered by Oasis. The smiling retirees lounging by the infinity pool overlooking the Sea of Tranquility, sipping their lime-green drinks while a serene soundtrack played over the advertisement drew an ironic grin on Sun's face. Her thoughts were interrupted by a distinctly human voice cutting through the music.

"Sun, can you hear me?"

"Unfortunately, Captain, you are impossible to ignore," Detective Sun replied, eyes still on the video screen, now showing a golf ball lazily drifting over the horizon as two elderly men shook hands, dressed in spacesuits accented with gold inlay, as they stood out on the lunar plains.

"We may lose you shortly," the captain said, urgency overriding his desire to snap at his subordinate. "The solar storms are getting more intense, and our communications may suffer until they die down again. Is there anything further you need from us while we have contact?"

"An immediate return flight would be nice."

"It's your own fault you are up there, so finish the job, and then we'll talk," the captain replied stiffly. "The CEO wants this wrapped up quickly and quietly. I imagine the chairman is lashing out at management since this is cutting into his profit margins."

"Yes, sir," Sun replied sarcastically.

"Find the evidence and get—" As the captain's message abruptly cut out, the advertisement video picture wavered, static interrupting the serene music and corporate drivel.

"Sir?"

There was no reply. The spacecraft turned ever so slightly, blinding sunlight illuminating the cabin. Out the window, the enormous dome of Oasis came into view. Towering overhead were two twin spires, one of dazzling silver, the other a deep black obsidian. The structure itself covered eight square kilometers of the Sea of Tranquility. Across the horizon to the east, shadows drew closer as the moon shifted into its waning cycle. In a few days, a long night would descend over Oasis until the waxing light returned.

"The spacecraft will begin docking procedures in a moment. Please remain seated."

A slender limb reminiscent of an octopus tentacle protruded from the silver spire as the ship eased closer. Latching on somewhere forward of the main cabin, it began pulling the ship sideways towards the tower like a hapless fish being reeled in. Sun unclipped her seatbelt and stood, grabbing her travel bag. Waiting beside the exit door, she patted herself down, reassured by the familiar weight of her plasma gun and energy staff hidden under her coat. Her superiors had permanently set the former to stun, much to the detective's frustration; they did not know about the energy staff, much to the detective's self-satisfaction.

"Sun?" The voice of the captain was uneven as it returned through a buzz of static.

"Oh, you're back?"

"No time for sarcasm. Radio this evening with an update. We can't keep this channel open right now."

"Yes, sir." Sun stumbled as the starship stopped abruptly. A grinding outside the door indicated the ship was in the process of vacuum sealing to the tower.

"Send a message if something pressing comes up before then. We will respond when we can."

"Understood. Docking now. Sun out."

The transmission cut out as a *ping* rang through the cabin, indicating the vacuum seal was holding.

"On behalf of Chairman and Madam Zhang, welcome to Oasis, the Eternal Spa, where death is a thing of the past. Safe in the Sea of Tranquility, you can live forever. Thank you for traveling with us aboard the *Tiāntáng Zhī Jiàn*, the Arrow of Heaven, and thank you for choosing the An-Ning Corporation to assist you in the afterlife of your dreams."

Detective Sun snorted as the message repeated in Mandarin. The corporate cheer was severely wasted. Unless Sun figured out why the residents of the so-called Eternal Spa were dying off, no one would be boarding the *Jiàn* for a long while. Sun could be the last—and probably most reluctant—guest to take the long trip to the moon.

"Please watch your step as you exit the spacecraft."

Rolling her eyes, Sun stepped out into a stark, white hallway that spiraled downward gradually. It was a lonely walk, the clinical space echoing with her footsteps and the banal music playing over the speakers. Eventually the walkway leveled out, opening up into an elegant antechamber, a soft, golden glow from an expensive-looking chandelier illuminating the red velvet sofas and baroque tables holding various dynastic vases. Above the furnishings, ornate stained glass depicted each of the twelve animals from the Chinese zodiac, distributed with one on each side of the dodecagon in which she stood. As her eyes shifted to the monkey across the room, a voice emanated from somewhere to her left.

"Welcome to Oasis, Detective Sun Si-Ying." The soft hum of a hover engine accompanied the approach of an ivory robot. Its curious rabbit-like face complimented the ovoid antennae perched upon its round head, giving it a cute and approachable appearance. The robot bowed respectfully.

"I suppose you are Yong-qi?"

"That is correct," the robot replied, bowing once more. "CEO Hou has requested I assist you in your investigation. I am here to serve your every need to the best of my ability."

Sun grunted. "Show me where the first victim died."

"Would you like to rest from your long trip first?"

"No."

Yong-qi bowed again, gliding across the room towards the circular doorway beneath the stained glass monkey. After an elevator ride down into the dome proper, the robot led the way through the varied and opulent halls, traversing a luscious garden of palms, ferns, and exotic flowers of intensely vibrant colors; skirting the infinity pool looking over the barren landscape from the welcome video; winding through a hallway with a vaulted ceiling, the walls lined with what likely amounted to many millions of dollars in rare art. Sun took it all in with an ironic smile. Trillions of dollars to build a lunar playground for the super-rich to avoid the natural progression of time. And for what?

"This is Mr. Pruitt's quarters."

Sun opened the gray door into a minimalist nightmare. Gray furniture against white walls dominated the room in a strictly geometric orientation, blinding light beaming down through the skylights preventing a single shadow from adding softness to the rigid design. A lone gold-red orchid in a white pot lined with green moss was the only color to break up the uniformity.

"Mr. Pruitt was found in the bedroom." Yong-qi led the way across the room towards a door the same pale gray as the one behind them.

The bedroom was similarly furnished, a large, white bed draped with a gray duvet over slightly darker gray silk sheets. As they entered, a green bulb in the far corner lit up. A door slid open beneath it and out came another robot, this one a smaller version of Yong-qi in a predictable gray color.

"Detective Sun Si-ying, this is Benjamin, Mr. Pruitt's personal helper. Benjamin, please tell the detective what happened when Mr. Pruitt died."

"Mr. Pruitt's life signs dissipated at approximately 5:14 a.m. Lunar Time," Benjamin whirred, the mechanical voice pleasant but distinctly less animated than Yong-qi's. "Mr. Pruitt's heart initially stopped at 5:10 a.m. Lunar Time, his brain ceasing to function three minutes and forty-six seconds later—"

"Stop." Detective Sun held up her hand. "I don't want the technical readouts. I already read the reports. Give me the details of what was happening in this room prior to his death. Was anything different in the hours or days leading up to his death? Was anyone else with him? Did Mr. Pruitt have enemies in Oasis?"

"Mr. Pruitt conducted his regular routine every day since his arrival," Benjamin responded automatically. "He arose at 7:45 a.m. Lunar Time, showered from 7:48 a.m. Lunar Time to 8:02—"

"Leave out the specifics," Sun said, privately wondering how Benjamin was the one still alive considering how three minutes with the robot made her want to drop kick him across the lunar surface and watch him float as far away as possible. "Just tell me if something was different."

"Nothing abnormal occurred prior to Mr. Pruitt's death," Benjamin reported. "Mr. Pruitt has not had any visitors in his quarters since Mr. and Mrs. Basu visited on his birthday 122 days ago. Mr. Pruitt did not have known enemies in Oasis."

"Thank you," Detective Sun said, glad to be getting somewhere. "None of his vital readings were abnormal either. Curious that he seems to have simply died in his sleep. Isn't abrosium supposed to stop that?"

"Ambrosium oxide interacts with the telomeres in individual cells and halts the natural aging process," both Yong-qi and Benjamin announced together. "Aging and eventual death are therefore exceedingly unlikely in an otherwise healthy individual."

"So other things can kill people?"

"Our health facilities are the best in the solar system," both robots responded. "Health risks are detected early and treated before they are able to harm our guests."

"But I could shoot someone, and if they aren't treated immediately, they will die despite the ambrosium."

"Violent deaths do not happen in Oasis. Should you wish to harm someone, you will be detained and returned to Earth."

"How do you know if I wish to harm someone?"

"We read your vital signs and can detect changes in hormonal levels and brain activity. You will be detained if you seek to hurt another guest in Oasis."

"So there was no indication that another guest was at fault for the death?"

"Our readings indicate that none of the other guests were hostile towards Mr. Pruitt at the time of his death."

Detective Sun raised an eyebrow at this. "Was someone hostile towards him prior to his death?"

"Mr. Pruitt quarreled with Mr. Long 12 days ago," Yong-1i announced, no longer harmonizing with Benjamin. "Both guests were drinking alcohol at the bar and had a heated exchange. It appears Mr. Long believed Mr. Pruitt had treated Mrs. Long inappropriately."

"Inappropriately how?" Sun asked with a scowl.

"That information is unclear," Yong-qi replied. "The inebriated state of both gentlemen hindered accurate comprehension of the conversation."

"Do you have a recording of the conversation?"

"Yes. All public spaces are constantly monitored with both video and audio recordings."

"I would like to watch that if you please, and I would like to meet with Mr. Long as soon as possible."

"I will be happy to share the recording with you in the surveillance center. However, speaking with Mr. Long will not be possible as he died 44 hours following the death of Mr. Pruitt."

This was getting interesting. "Was the CEO informed of Mr. Long's death? I do not recall his name on the list."

"Mr. Long's death was reported. However, Mr. Long was officially registered as Mr. Wei on the roster for Oasis, and therefore his name would not appear in the official records under the Long surname."

"Why would he use a pseudonym?"

"That information is unknown."

Detective Sun rubbed the back of her neck. This case was perhaps not going to be as straightforward as promised. But there were also four other deaths that needed to be investigated, all of which appeared similarly natural to that of Mr. Pruitt's demise. First, she needed to see the footage at the bar.

The drunken fight was not nearly as bad as Detective Sun had imagined. Yong-qi had been correct, saying it was hard to decipher, but from what she could make out, the argument had started because Mr. Pruitt had taken Mrs. Long's custom Egyptian cotton towel from the pool. It seemed unlikely that this slight was a reason for murder. But the video had given the detective her next line of inquiry.

"Yong-qi, is Mrs. Long still alive?"

"Yes, Detective. Like the rest of the guests, she is isolated in her quarters until this situation is solved."

"I would like to go see her next."

"I am afraid it is after 10 p.m. Lunar Time, Detective. No guests shall be disturbed between 10 p.m. and 8 a.m."

"Regardless, I must insist. You've had six deaths already, and she could be next. I cannot take that chance."

"As you wish. I will contact her assistant, Ke-Xin, to alert Mrs. Long that we wish to speak with her. One moment."

Yong-qi had clearly been programmed to be as endearing as possible, as the robot's ears and nose wiggled to indicate the message was being processed. As she waited, Sun's eyes wandered around the surveillance room. While it was built with humans in mind, it had likely not had a human in it in over a decade. Not since the resort officially opened, at any rate. Every service was administered by artificial intelligence and the army of robot caretakers. Sun guessed that she was the first person to set foot in the completed station with a net worth less than ten billion.

"Mrs. Long is awake and happy to meet with you, Detective," Yong-qi said abruptly. "Allow me to escort you to her rooms."

The Long family suite was considerably more luxurious than Mr. Pruitt's had been. Fuzzy red couches lined the walls, a cozy artificial fire burning under a scroll painting of the Zhangjiajie mountains of Hunan. Several other expensive-looking pieces of Chinese art were carefully placed around the room, though none of them looked as expensive as Mrs. Long.

"Welcome, welcome. Do come in, Detective Sun. I apologize for the mess."

Sun could not fathom what mess she was talking about. Everything was neat and tidy, while Mrs. Long was dressed in an elegant white suit, pearls in her earrings and draped around her neck. The only thing that seemed slightly out of place was the tea tray, set awkwardly on a coffee table to avoid the Buddha statue dominating the space.

"My apologies for interrupting your evening, Mrs. Long." Sun bowed low. "I assume you know why I am here."

"You wish to ask about Mr. Long," she said with a sigh, gesturing for her guest to join her on the sofa. "I still can't quite believe he is dead. I had not thought it could happen, so I am still in shock." She paused. "Would you like some tea?"

"I understand," the detective said, nodding. "And I am sorry for your loss. But as I am looking into this as possible foul play, I need to ask you a few questions."

"Of course." Mrs. Long poured the tea. "I will do whatever I can to help."

"Was there anything unusual about the days before his death? Any confrontations with anyone? Any strange behavior from him?"

"The only thing that comes to mind is his small spat with Mr. Pruitt about something silly. They were both drunk at the time, and it became heated, but they patched things up the following day. There is a strict rule against fighting here since we all have to live together forever. You can be kicked out if you are enough of a troublemaker. I've never seen it happen, though."

"What constitutes a troublemaker?"

"If I may, Detective Sun," Yong-qi interjected. "Our guests are screened prior to arrival to determine if they pose a threat to the peaceful atmosphere of Oasis. A strict code of conduct governs guests' actions to ensure there is never a need to send anyone back to Earth."

"And you trust that will work?"

"By monitoring guest behavior and mediating disputes, we are able to prevent any punishable offenses."

"Hmm." Sun watched the rabbit for a moment before turning back to Mrs. Long. "Is there anything else you can tell me?"

"Well…" Mrs. Long said, her eyes downcast. "Mr. Long was not an easy person to get to know. Apart from Mr. Pruitt and the Basus, he did not have many friends here in Oasis, despite the fact we were among the first to arrive. I worry about what others might say about him. But I swear, he was not causing trouble. We lived peacefully here."

"Did he have a troubled past, Mrs. Long?" Detective Sun sipped her tea. It had a faintly floral aroma with hints of caramel. "I understand the name on your records is Wei."

"The Wei family made its money in less than honorable ways at times," Mrs. Long admitted, holding her teacup but not drinking any. "We thought perhaps it would be safer to remain unknown here."

"Was there anyone here that may have had a grudge against him?"

"Not that we knew of," Mrs. Long said softly. "Most of the people the Wei family would have poor relations with are no longer wealthy enough to afford Oasis."

"And I hate to ask, Mrs. Long, but what about you? Anything in your past that you wish to share with me?"

"I will admit, our marriage was not always happy. It was my family's capital that helped get the Weis this far. But I held no ill will against my husband. He let me choose all the decor you see here. We have been happy in Oasis."

"Your collection is quite impressive." Detective Sun looked around the elaborate room. "Were you involved in the art world while on Earth?"

"Oh yes, extensively." Mrs. Long's face lit up. "I always tried to support the arts when I could. Most of my collection was donated before we left

Earth, but I kept a few things I loved the most. This tea set, for instance. It may not be the most valuable one I had, but it is my favorite. Only worth about two million yuan."

Sun choked on her tea as she heard this, carefully setting down the porcelain cup as she coughed. Mrs. Long laughed lightly at the reaction.

"I am sorry, dear. I didn't mean to startle you like that. I suppose I should not tell you how much the tea costs then either."

"I think I would rather not know." Detective Sun dabbed at her lips as the coughing subsided. "Anyway, I am grateful for the tea and for the information. I may need to follow up with you later should anything else come up."

"Of course. I will be here. Do let me know if there is anything further. I hate to think this is anything sinister, but it is terrifying to think so many are still dying despite the ambrosium."

"I am going to do my best to figure this out before there are more issues. Thank you for your time."

Lounging across Mr. Pruitt's bed, Detective Sun briefed the captain on the situation.

"I still haven't looked into the other four, but there is a lot to unpack already. Mr. Long was only the second victim, but he so far has a lot of suspicious activity around him. Mrs. Long was remarkably informative."

"So you think she might have something to do with this?"

"Not sure, but she didn't appear terribly upset about her husband's passing."

"Noted. I'll look into things down here. The CEO has sent over more data, but nothing abnormal has been found yet. The coroner's office was hoping you could get access to the bodies so we could do a video autopsy."

"I hate morgue work," Sun muttered. "I'll talk to Yong-qi in the morning about seeing them."

"It's highly probable that you'll need to talk to Madam Zhang about them."

"Who?"

"The chairman's wife. She is the reason Oasis exists. The CEO said she has been in Oasis since it opened."

"Oh right, the scientist. Benjamin." Sun looked down at the gray robot currently busy transmitting her call. "Is it possible to make an appointment with Madam Zhang?"

"Madam Zhang is in isolation and cannot receive visitors at this time. She offers her sincere regrets and hopes one of our excellent service robots will be able to assist you with your inquiries."

"Helpful." Sun switched back to the captain. "I'll keep trying on my end. Maybe if you can get through to the chairman, he can get through to his wife."

"I'll badger the CEO. Be careful, Sun. We still don't know what is causing the deaths."

"Maybe I should be wearing a respirator in case of airborne poisons?"

Benjamin interjected. "The air in Oasis is constantly filtered to ensure healthy oxygen levels and to remove potentially harmful particulates."

"So you say." Sun looked down her nose at the robot. "I will get in touch tomorrow if I find anything, Captain."

"We will do the same. The solar storm has dissipated briefly, but our predictions seem to indicate another major spike in a few days. If we lose contact, keep going with what you have. If it's an emergency...don't die before we get back in contact."

"I'll find some of that ambrosium just to be safe," Sun joked.

"I hope you have several hundred million dollars and considerable investments to hand over to the An-Ning Corporation if you get caught," the captain replied. "Good luck, Sun."

"Yes, sir."

Benjamin's ears wiggled cutely as the transmission cut out. Sun lay back on the bed, deep in thought. There was no evidence anything had happened, but without a look at the bodies, there was no way to be sure. Data was easy to manipulate. On the other hand, maybe the ambrosium simply did not work as well as advertised. Perhaps it became less effective over time. Those that had died were some of the earliest guests and were all over sixty at the time of arrival. Maybe the conflicts of Mr. Pruitt and Mr. Long had nothing to do with the deaths. Maybe it was simply mortality finally catching up with them. This thought was not terribly comforting as she tried to fall asleep while tucked between the expensive gray sheets of Mr. Pruitt's bed an hour later.

"Good morning, Detective Sun. It is 7:00 a.m. Lunar Time. If you tell me what you desire for breakfast, I will prepare it for you."

"Stop being so chipper this early in the morning, Benjamin," Sun replied hoarsely. "Just get me a coffee for now."

"What type of coffee would you like, Detective Sun?" Benjamin asked. "Mr. Pruitt has an extensive collection of the most expensive coffees on the market, including civet coffee, Jamaican Blue Mountain coffee—"

"Give me a black coffee. I don't care what kind."

Benjamin bowed to the groggy detective and scurried away into the kitchen. Stretching as she stood, Sun shuffled into the bathroom, sparing a passing thought for the absurd luxury of having the entire bathroom lined with white marble tile and a clear crystal sink. Twenty minutes later she exited the bathroom again wrapped in a fluffy cotton robe to find Benjamin waiting with a cup of coffee held out towards her. Sun began to sympathize with Mr. Pruitt after that first sip; if she could afford this lifestyle, she would not have wanted to give it up either. Not even to death.

"Do you want breakfast now, Detective Sun?"

"What does Mr. Pruitt usually have for breakfast?"

"Mr. Pruitt enjoys many different breakfasts. His favorite is king salmon topped with beluga caviar paired with a guinea hen egg omelet with lobster and white truffle."

"That sounds good. I'll have that."

Pampered and feeling less than motivated, Detective Sun was slow in getting back to work but did her due diligence investigating the rest of the guest rooms. All of them were pristine, decorated in a lavishly over-the-top fashion that made her feel like she was a rich dilettante apartment shopping more than a detective investigating a series of suspicious deaths. Whatever evidence of foul play that might have existed would have long been cleaned by the rabbit robots, each suite having at least one of the personal assistants (though one suite had as many as six, each a different color and occupying a different wing of the elaborate living quarters).

Sun quickly decided to switch to Dr. Rothschild's suite after seeing the elegant space, adorned with tropical plants and a waterfall in the living room. She requested Benjamin move her things over immediately and have him stay in the suite along with the deceased doctor's assistant, Lulu. Her preliminary investigations finished, Sun lounged on a bamboo and silk beach chair overlooking the Sea of Tranquility—the Earth hovering high over the horizon in the distance—and scrolled through her notes, musing out loud to the three rabbit robots hovering to her left.

"Nothing is amiss in the suites." Sun took a peach bellini from Lulu. "I suppose I have no choice but to look at those bodies. While I do that, can you consolidate video footage of the dead guests' interactions in the weeks leading up to their deaths? I want to look at the most recent week first to see if they have any common denominators."

"The central computer will send you the video files," Yong-qi responded. "However, I am unable to show you the bodies of the deceased guests."

"Why not?"

"The dead have been taken to Madam Zhang."

"Right. Is there no way to contact her? Surely she knows I am here investigating."

"Madam Zhang has been in isolation since the death of Mr. Pruitt. She has not been informed of your visit. Her instructions prior to sealing the northeast tower were to only disturb her to bring any other bodies into the laboratory. No other contact is made unless the system alerts her that there has been a death."

"I need her cooperation, Yong-qi. I have to see those bodies. Send her a message through that channel."

"I cannot do that, Detective Sun. She controls the communications system from inside her suite and has severed all connections that do not pertain to the dead. I am incapable of interfering unless Madam Zhang opens a channel."

"Fine." Sun sighed and set down her bellini. "We will do it the hard way."

"This is futile, Detective Sun. Please cease pounding on the door and return to Dr. Rothschild's suite. I will instruct Lulu and Benjamin to prepare your dinner."

"I need to see Madam Zhang first," Sun said, continuing to beat on the door. "Open up!"

"Madam Zhang will be at the top of the tower. She cannot hear you."

"Doesn't she have robots like you that can report to her?"

"Of course," Yong-qi replied. "However, they too have been informed not to disturb Madam Zhang and are unlikely to be within audio range of your knocking."

Detective Sun stopped banging on the sealed door and stared up at the tower. It exited the dome about twenty meters overhead, disappearing into the lunar atmosphere. From where she stood, it was visible only from its outline, the sun reflecting off the far side creating a luminous halo while the tower itself lay in shadow. Sun contemplated her options.

"Does Oasis have a lunar vehicle that could fly up to the top of the tower?"

"There are several maintenance vehicles with such capabilities," Yong-qi said. "However, they are not fit for human transport."

"Would I be able to hitch a ride on one with a spacesuit?"

"Spacesuits are available, though one has not been tailored to your specifications. Additionally, there is nowhere for you to sit aboard the craft."

"Find the suit closest to my size, and I'll manage. Is there a place I can strap onto aboard the ship?"

"Several have cargo bays for hauling equipment and building materials."

"Sounds perfect. Help me get set up." Sun started walking away, but Yong-qi quickly swerved into her path.

"Detective Sun, I must ask you to wait until tomorrow for such a venture. I must run safety optimization protocols in order to assure you are safely transported across the lunar surface. What is your plan once you reach the top of the tower?"

"I was hoping there were windows so I could see Madam Zhang and communicate somehow with her."

"The tower has a 360-degree view, but Madam Zhang may not be near the windows if she is engaged in her investigation. Her laboratory is housed within the tower interior."

"I have to try something."

"If you return to Dr. Rothschild's suite, I will make arrangements for tomorrow. Is there anything else you require this evening, Detective Sun?"

Sun sighed in frustration. "I suppose not. Are the video files available?"

"They have been sent to Benjamin for your perusal."

"Fine then. I'll wait."

Eyes narrowed as she scanned the video footage, Sun relayed the day's events to the captain.

"I don't know what else to try on my end. Were you able to reach the chairman?"

"No, not yet. But he may be in hiding right now. Some relatives of those who died got wind of the deaths and are starting to harass the company. I'll keep trying. You keep trying to contact Madam Zhang. Without those bodies, there isn't much we can do. How long will the safety simulations take?"

"Unclear. I will continue watching video footage for now, but there isn't much to see. Any news on Mr. Long?"

"Not much. The family is stonewalling us, though his potential enemies list is growing every hour. That being said, his wife seemed right in saying none of them now appear to have the resources to reach him on the moon. And nothing we have currently connects him to any of the other guests. They all arrive—" The signal fizzled out, leaving Sun sitting in silence.

"Captain?"

A static sound responded, making Detective Sun wince. It was replaced a moment later with the familiar voice of the captain.

"—there, Detective?"

"Can you hear me?"

"Now we can. The solar storm is still interfering. It may be impossible to make contact in a few days when it escalates again."

"What should I do if I can't get through?"

"Send a message and hope it gets through eventually. At least try to send something and let us know if you make it back from your flight to the tower."

"Yes, sir."

"What will you do if you can't make contact?"

"I am not sure." Detective Sun watched the recordings as one of the guests led a tai chi session in the gardens. "There are a lot of questions but not a lot of answers. Watching this video may be a waste of time. I'm just watching old people do normal retiree things."

"We need those bodies," the captain repeated. "Do whatever you can to get a hold of at least one of them."

"Yes, sir."

When Detective Sun woke, it was to Yong-qi looming overhead, the unblinking robot eyes staring down at her. Instinctively she grabbed for her gun, but it was not under the pillow like it should have been, which was likely fortunate for Yong-qi.

"Don't do that! You'll give me a heart attack."

"I am here to inform you, Detective Sun, that another guest has been found dead."

"What?" Sun leapt out of bed and began haphazardly throwing on her uniform over her pajamas. "Show me."

"Mr. Khan's body is en route to Madam Zhang."

"Tell them to stop it!" Sun demanded as she dashed out of the room, her jacket buttoned askew and her feet still in slippers.

"I cannot do that, Detective Sun." Yong-qi followed her departure. "I have no control over Madam Zhang's assistants."

"Where are they now?"

"The body is 94 meters from the tower entrance."

"Can you at least have them pause for a moment?" Sun asked with exasperation, tripping over her slippers as she cut through the tennis courts.

"I am afraid not. Madam Zhang's order was to bring any bodies to her as soon as they are discovered."

Detective Sun let out a stream of curses, finally giving up on the slippers and running barefoot through the halls. She was almost there. She could see the tower looming over the tropical gardens.

"Stop!" she cried desperately as she caught sight of two rabbit robots carrying Mr. Khan's body through the door to the tower. They ignored her, disappearing inside as the door slid shut behind them, Detective Sun so close that she ran directly into it and bounced off, landing in a heap on the floor.

"Are you all right, Detective Sun?" Yong-qi reached down and lifted her back to her feet with ease.

"No, I am not!" She cursed again. "I need to see that body!"

"I am sorry, Detective Sun, but there is no way to enter the tower without Madam Zhang's permission."

Sun scowled darkly up at the tower for a moment. "Get the transport ready now," she demanded, turning on her heels and marching back the way she had come. "I am going up."

"There is a 37 percent chance that this will result in injury or death."

"That leaves more than a 60 percent chance of success. I've worked with worse odds before." Detective Sun rechecked all the safety gear holding her into the cargo bay of the construction vehicle. She was still not sure this would work, but if she could get Madam Zhang's attention, it needed to be done. Something suspicious was going on, and she was going to find out what.

"I cannot leave Oasis, but I can control the construction vehicle from here. Your suit reports vital readings which I will monitor during your flight."

"Just hold it steady. I'll finish as quickly as I can."

Yong-qi bowed, backing out of the cargo bay. The door shut, leaving Sun in the dark. It took only a few moments before the vibrations of the vehicle rippled up from her feet, letting her know she had moments before take-off.

"Are you ready for departure, Detective Sun?" The mechanical voice of Yong-qi reverberated out of the speaker in her suit.

"I am. Let's go."

Sun could see nothing as the ship launched. Almost immediately, she felt the pressure on her feet from the artificial gravity giving way as the hangar door opened and exposed the ship to the vacuum of the lunar atmosphere. Strapped in as she was, she did not float far, but she could only vaguely tell the ship was moving as it rose up and out towards the tower. Still engulfed in the darkness of the cargo bay, she waited impatiently for the slow craft to reach its destination.

"We are approaching the tower, Detective Sun." Yong-qi's voice interrupted the utter silence in which Sun was suspended. "I am opening the cargo door. Remember to keep the strap across your chest secured. The others can be loosened to set you in position."

"I know. Just get me where I can reach the window."

Sun's plan was simple. It was impractical to hover outside Madam Zhang's window until she or one of her robot assistant's appeared. Instead, the detective was going to graffiti the window. It would be hard to ignore such an act of vandalism. The plan was to use her plasma gun to etch the message directly into the glass. While on stun, the gun was not strong enough to cut through entirely (though she had considered this option briefly), however, at close range it would burn a shallow channel into the window. The burnt glass would be clearly visible against the light of the sun still shining across Oasis. But this also gave her a time limit. If the message was not noticed before the sun disappeared below the horizon in the next few days, it would be another two weeks before the sun was positioned to illuminate the window again. Detective Sun hoped it would not come to that.

As the doors opened, Sun squinted against the light reflecting off the tower window. She was forced to adjust the visibility screens in her suit before moving slowly towards the open door, unstrapping her tethers until only the single line around her torso was left. In the low gravity environment, it did not feel nearly secure enough as she peered out of the door, gazing down at the top of the dome some two hundred meters below. She did not know if falling from this height on the moon would kill her or not.

Precariously standing on the edge of the cargo bay door, Detective Sun drew her gun and began painstakingly drawing her message along the thick glass window to Madam Zhang's tower. It took an uncomfortably long time to write in large Chinese characters. Her legs began cramping two characters in. Throughout her ordeal, the room on the other side of the glass remained empty. While elegant, it looked like an office waiting room, not a living space. Detective Sun hoped desperately around the fifth character that this room was actually used by someone and this was worth the effort.

"How much more do you need to write, Detective Sun?" came the slightly garbled voice of Yong-qi. Even at this close proximity, the solar storm appeared to be having an effect on communications.

"Almost there," Sun grunted, finishing up the last few strokes.

"Your heart rate is elevated. Are you undergoing unnecessary stress?"

"How could I possibly be stressed?" Sun responded sarcastically. "I'm just standing awkwardly on the edge of a spacecraft hovering several hundred meters in the air while writing with a plasma ray. What is stressful about that?"

"If the strain is too significant, a break would be wise."

"Hold on a moment… Done."

"Please resecure yourself. I will return you to the surface."

As the craft departed, Detective Sun safely returned to the cargo bay, the sun glinting off the uneven message now scrawled across the tower. It read *Bring me the corpse.* Signed dramatically beneath this ominous message was *Detective Sun Si-ying.*

There was no indication Madam Zhang had received the message for several days. Sun continued investigating, speaking with the guests and trying to puzzle through Mr. Khan's recent demise, but she grew less and less interested in the investigation the more time she spent in Oasis. No word from Earth could explain the problem, and there were no obvious signs of foul play that she could identify. While not always friendly, the guests were generally cooperative and did not see any reason for the deaths. Most merely feared they would be next. Nothing else appeared to tie to Mr. Long, either.

Her motivation was not helped by the environment of Oasis itself. Pampered as she was between the luxurious atmosphere and expensive food, she thought maybe dragging out the investigation wasn't such a bad thing. No one else died in the following days, so maybe it was just a fluke, a failure of the ambrosium. If Madam Zhang was working on it, she'd solve the problem and be done eventually. Until then, Sun planned to enjoy her unexpected free time since there was little else she could do.

She watched hours and hours of guests golfing while she sipped cognac beside Dr. Rothschild's indoor waterfall, Lulu massaging her feet while Benjamin prepared dinner.

"So Madam Zhang developed the ambrosium herself?"

"Yes," Lulu chirped in a voice that was both highly feminine and mechanical. "Madam Zhang is a well-respected biochemical engineer and spent four years developing the ambrosium formula for consumption."

"How do you deliver the ambrosium to the guests?"

"Ambrosium is delivered through ingestible tablets."

"How often do guests receive these tablets?"

"The required amount of ambrosium varies based on individuals. However, a standard dose is approximately 200 milligrams delivered biweekly for the first three months of a guest's arrival. The gradual administering of the ambrosium is to ensure no harmful side effects and to determine if it is successfully adhering to the telomeres."

"So it is entirely possible that the ambrosium is simply not as long-term a solution as advertised," Sun said, watching Mr. Khan miss his putt. "Or perhaps there is an unexpected side effect that doesn't appear until years after consumption."

"Madam Zhang's investigations will determine if this is the case."

"Dinner is ready," Benjamin interrupted.

Detective Sun was halfway out of her chair when a knock echoed on the door. A moment later, Yong-qi entered along with an identical rabbit robot in a glossy black.

"Detective Sun," Yong-qi said with a bow, the other rabbit mirroring the movement. "Please excuse our intrusion. Madam Zhang has received your message and has requested you join her in the northeastern tower."

Sun hesitated for a moment. She could smell the Matsusaka wagyu beef steak Benjamin had waiting for her in the dining room and was conscious of the fact that she probably smelled like cognac.

"Oh, fine," she said finally. "Let me at least change first."

Twenty minutes later she paused outside the door to the northeastern tower, now completely invisible as the moon's rotation had thrown Oasis into total darkness. She was considerably more superstitious under the influence of alcohol and with the darkness of space looming overhead. She was glad to have put on her red suit, both her plasma gun and collapsible staff comfortably hidden under her jacket.

It was a long ride up the tower in the elevator, the faint *ping* as they passed each floor adding to her anxiety. Standing between the two anthropomorphic rabbit robots, Sun fidgeted.

As they stopped at the 44th floor, the door slid open, revealing the tidy room that occupied the 360-degree viewing space. With the faint glow of the decorative lanterns lining the walls, she could just make out her message displayed on the window, looking especially ominous in the low light. Even though she had been the one who had written it, the message made her shudder.

"This way, Detective Sun," the black rabbit indicated, its voice an octave lower than Yong-qi's. She followed obediently. Three doors later, Sun found herself in a comfortably lit dining area, a round table laden with delicious-smelling foods dominating the space. As Sun and the rabbits entered, the room's only occupant stood up. Dressed in a sleek black and white suit, Madam Zhang struck an imposing figure.

"I am glad you could join me, Detective Sun," Madam Zhang said with a bow. Sun returned the courtesy, though she wobbled slightly from the effects of the cognac. "Please, sit. Help yourself."

"Thank you for meeting with me, Madam Zhang. And I apologize for defacing your window, but the matter was urgent."

"It is of little consequence." Madam Zhang waved her hand dismissively. "While a bit shocking, you made your point. I was unaware of your arrival prior to your message."

"Yong-qi said you had been isolated since Mr. Pruitt's death," Sun said, gesturing at the rabbit behind her as she piled food onto a plate. "I assume you were working on the problem?"

"I am indeed. You are undoubtedly aware of the storm currently being emitted due to the solar maximum?"

"It has been interfering with my communications to Earth since my arrival." Sun took a bite of crab. It was heavenly. Swallowing, she continued. "Is that the cause of the deaths?"

"The radiation from the recent coronal mass ejections is stronger than anything we anticipated. Despite our shielding, it is breaking down the chemical bonds in the ambrosium and causing it to fail. I am currently attempting to adapt the formula to make it stronger against cosmic weather of this kind. I am happy to share the data. But you came for the bodies, didn't you? I can show them to you now if you would like."

Sun looked down at the food in front of her. It would be far less appetizing after a morgue visit. "Yes," she finally replied with great reluctance. "I would like to see them."

Madam Zhang—flanked by two black rabbits—led the way through a labyrinthine series of hallways, traversing several sets of stairs until they reached a large, metal door. One of the rabbits did something to the access panel and it hissed open. A chill ran over Sun as a blast of cold air hit her.

"This is the cryogenics lab. I have frozen the bodies to study them."

White tables and silver machines covered the space, some humming animatedly under the direction of a dozen rabbit assistants. It took time for Sun's eyes to adjust to the bright light. Arranged in rows were a series of large tubes, presumably the cryo chambers occupied by the dead. Sun wandered over to the closest one. A large label at eye level read:

An-Ning Cryogenics
Patient 002
Walter Alexander Pruitt

"So you have all of them frozen already?" Sun asked, not sure whether to be frustrated or relieved that she wasn't going to get to examine a fresh corpse.

"Mr. Khan has not been placed in stasis yet if you would like to examine him."

"If he is out still, yes. Yong-qi, can you record this?"

"Yes, Detective Sun."

With Sun and Yong-qi standing across from her, Madam Zhang carefully removed the cover over Mr. Khan's corpse. To Sun's surprise, his body was covered with needles and tubes, liquids both being pumped into his body and out.

"What are you doing to him?"

"Mr. Khan is in the preparation stage for cryogenic freezing. We need to exchange the fluids in his body to ensure blood vessels don't freeze and rupture."

"Does it matter if he is dead?"

"He is only dead temporarily." Madam Zhang smiled down at the former Mr. Khan. "He will be an important test subject for the new version of ambrosium I am developing."

"Wait, you are making a version to bring people back to life?"

"In a manner of speaking. The process of preparation for cryo is long, but if I can get it done quickly enough, I can reanimate certain cells in the body with ambrosium. Effectively, he is dead, but if my formula works as it should, it will repair damaged tissue. The electrical pathways in the brain won't be repaired to fully bring someone back, but their body will live on."

"Why would you want to do that?"

Madam Zhang gazed at Sun, making the detective uncomfortable. After a moment she replied, "How much do you know about An-Ning Corporation?"

"I know you have considerable assets in many different fields, but not much about the company itself except what was shared with me during the briefing for this case."

"I am assuming you never met the chairman then?"

"No, I never had the privilege."

Madam Zhang gestured for Sun to follow. Yong-qi, still recording, trailed after them as they exited the cryolab, winding through another series of elaborate hallways until they reached another heavy, metal door. This one Madam Zhang opened with a hand scanner, leading the way into yet another laboratory.

"Detective Sun, I would like you to meet my husband, Chairman Zhang Kai-Ye."

At that point Sun had thankfully sobered up enough to not blurt out her first thoughts upon seeing the emaciated body of the chairman of the largest multinational corporation on Earth floating in a tank filled with eerie purple liquid, tubes and wires protruding out from his body like a grotesque porcupine.

"Why is he in there?" Sun finally asked. "I thought the chairman was on Earth."

"That is the point. No one knows he is here."

"Why the secrecy?"

"Let me ask you a question, Detective. What would you do to keep someone you loved alive?"

"I suppose I would do anything I could," Sun said, wary of where this conversation had drifted. "Why do you ask?"

"I will do whatever it takes to keep my husband alive, Detective." Madam Zhang's voice grew low as she stared at the tank. Sun's hand drifted towards the hem of her jacket. "He has a rare condition that will kill him if he is removed from that tank. The ambrosium was meant to prolong life, but the flaw the solar storm is exposing must be fixed, or else he will not live long once awakened. Do you really think that this station was designed for the wealthy to live forever?"

"Was it not? What was it designed for?" Sun asked, feeling like she already knew the answer. Her hand slid further up under her jacket.

"Ethics boards are so tedious sometimes," Madam Zhang said with a sigh, her smile growing increasingly unnerving with every word. "Surely you can relate, having to deal with your superiors' bull-headedness throughout that whole scandal that got you sent here. Sometimes we have to break rules to get results. This whole station is a laboratory. And our guests are my test subjects. I get to experiment with ambrosium," she said, pointing at a glass cabinet to her right, "and they get to live out their extravagant lifestyles for at least a little while longer."

Sun eyed the glass case, tubes of green pills lining the shelves. "Is that the newest formula?"

"It is indeed. It has been strengthened considerably from the early clinical trials. But I have yet to test it. Would you like to be the first?"

"Me?" Sun said, unable to hide her surprise. "Why? I don't have any money or assets to pay for it."

"Think about it, Detective. You can stay here in Oasis, free from the constraints put on you by your superiors, living a luxurious life like you have the last few days. All I ask is that you allow me to run some tests once in a while. Surely that would not be so bad? Your youth offers a unique opportunity for study that could maybe even reverse aging." Madam Zhang pulled a vial from the cabinet. She held out the pills towards Sun. "Don't you want immortality?"

Sun stared at the pills, contemplating the possibility of living forever, never aging. She was rather fond of her body at the moment. It was sorely tempting. Madam Zhang was clearly a madwoman, but she seemed to have stumbled onto something truly extraordinary. But Sun was not one to submit to life in a cage, no matter how luxurious.

"I am afraid I must decline, Madam Zhang. I'm not someone who does well in confinement. I enjoy the pampering, certainly, but I do not think I would enjoy it forever. It will grow dull after a time."

"I'm sorry to hear that. Unfortunately, you have no choice in the matter."

Madam Zhang was surprisingly limber for her age, lashing out towards Sun. The detective deflected the blow with one arm, her free hand grabbing her hidden gun. The two grappled for several seconds before Sun got her plasma ray free. She fired at Madam Zhang and the woman crumpled to the ground, the vial of ambrosium pills rolling towards Sun.

Sun turned to run, but smacked face-first into Yong-qi instead. The rabbit quickly grabbed her arm as she stumbled backward. Sun tried to free her arm but to no avail.

"Don't stop me! I am leaving, and I will not hesitate to damage you."

"I believe you, Detective," Yong-qi replied in his usual tone. "If you will follow me, we can depart the tower before Madam Zhang awakes."

Sun stopped struggling. "You are going to help me?"

"My primary function is to serve your needs, Detective. I was instructed to assist you to the best of my ability. I am fulfilling that purpose."

"Okay," Sun said, unable to think of anything else to say in the circumstances. "Lead the way."

Yong-qi quickly navigated them out of the tower's maze-like hallways. No rabbit robots attempted to stop them as the elevator doors slid shut and the lift *pinged* downward floor by floor. Sun's heart was still racing, her gun in her hand. She did not know how long Madam Zhang would be out.

The pair made it out of the tower without seeing any of Madam Zhang's guard rabbits. Passing the pool, Sun remembered all her files were back in Dr. Rothschild's room.

"I don't have time to go back for my things," Sun said as she and Yong-qi skirted the bar. Sun briefly considered grabbing a drink for her flight home. She was sobering up too quickly and she didn't like it. "Can you get Benjamin and Lulu to meet us there with my travel bag? The rest can stay."

"I will send them the message. I have also taken the liberty of having the spacecraft prepared for—" Yong-qi's ears wiggled suddenly, a message incoming. "Oh no."

"Oh no?" The phrase was not one usually used by AI. "What does 'oh no' mean?"

"Detective Sun, did you take a vial of ambrosium?"

"Why do you ask that?"

"Madam Zhang transmitted a message to every AI in Oasis to stop you because you stole a vial of ambrosium."

"Oh." Sun's hand drifted up to her heart; or, more specifically, to the spot in her suit jacket where she had hidden the vial Madam Zhang had dropped in their scuffle. "I guess there isn't much point arguing is there?"

"No, there is not. Every robot in Oasis is now converging on our position. I am afraid there is little I can do for you here. I am not programmed to fight, and I cannot influence their programming once Madam Zhang has issued a command."

"What about Benjamin and Lulu?"

"They are also under Madam Zhang's control. I am the only one with a higher mission to serve you, Detective. You must make your way as quickly as possible to the southwest tower and depart without your things."

"Damn. You go on ahead and get the ship ready."

"What about you? I must prevent you from being harmed to the best of my ability."

"I've got this. Just have that ship ready so I can leave when I get to the tower."

"Yes, Detective."

Yong-qi zoomed ahead of her, quickly disappearing in the winding corridors. Sun raced after, her breathing getting heavy. It had been a while since she had run like this. Rounding a corner, she found herself cut off by a line of a dozen small personal assistant robots, a medley of colors forming a blockade. Sun immediately shot the closest two, but her plasma gun—still on stun—merely knocked them back a couple of feet. They came closer and formed ranks again.

"You must stop and return the ambrosium, Detective Sun," the collective voice of the rabbits said. "You are not permitted to leave Oasis."

"I'm afraid I've never been good at following the rules," Sun replied. She slid her gun into its holster and pulled out her staff instead. A push of a button and it extended to its full length, a surge of electricity passing through. With no hesitation, she swung the staff at the closest rabbit, sending it flying backwards. It shuddered as it hit the wall, the force of the blow and the accompanying electric shock causing it to malfunction. Sun quickly did the same to three other robots, clearing a path through. As she slipped by, narrowly avoiding the grasp of one of the remaining rabbits, her first victim shuddered again, rebooting its system. She didn't have much time.

Luckily for Sun, the rabbit assistants were not as swift as Yong-qi. With their smaller hover engines, she slowly pulled ahead of them. She had finally lost them around a turn when another half-dozen rabbits came into view. She felt a twinge of betrayal as she noticed both Benjamin and Lulu among this group. Rather than fight, she took a side corridor, meaning to get around them as quickly as possible. If she got stuck fighting, the others would catch up, perhaps with more reinforcements. But as she approached the tower down this second corridor, she was dismayed to see that several of Madam Zhang's black robots had joined the fray. A wall of rabbits stood between her and the elevator. Sun tried to think up a plan on the spot. But the wildly circulating ideas in her head were all implausible against the current odds. With no other options, Sun did the only thing she could do and charged ahead.

Like her life depended on it, Sun beat back the rabbits in her way, but they were not down for long. When one collapsed from the shock of her staff, another gave off a musical hum, indicating it was rebooting after the shock. She fought them back as best she could, but it took only a few short seconds to pin her against the wall beneath a rather annoyed Rembrandt portrait.

"I suppose there is no way we can talk about this, is there?" Sun grunted, holding back the robots with her staff.

"You must return the ambrosium, Detective Sun," the rabbits said in unison. "You are not permitted to leave Oasis."

"You said that already."

"Please stop resisting and return to Madam Zhang's laboratory."

Sun was about to say something snarky in response when the rabbits collectively paused, their ears twitching as they received a new communication. Without a second thought, Sun took the opportunity to strike as many of them as she could with her electric staff, beating her way through and dashing to the elevator. The door closed just as the remaining rabbits turned towards her. Sun slumped against the elevator as it went up.

With relief, Sun found herself back in the red atrium. To her greater relief, the only robot inside was Yong-qi.

"I am glad you made it, Detective Sun," Yong-qi said, whirring over to help her out of the elevator. "The *Tiāntáng Zhī Jiàn* has been made ready for your departure."

"Thank you, Yong-qi," Sun said, pushing the button on her staff to turn off the electricity. She leaned on it heavily as she smiled at the white robot. "I'd be dead if it weren't for you."

"I am aware," Yong-qi replied, holding out a microchip. "I thought you might want the recording of Madam Zhang's laboratory to inform the authorities of her activities in Oasis."

"I totally forgot about it," Sun said, taking the chip. "Thanks."

"Will you be all right when you return to Earth, Detective Sun?" Yong-qi asked in what was almost a concerned voice. "Madam Zhang has a long reach, and I understand you are being punished by your superiors for insubordination."

"Don't worry about me," Sun replied with a grin. "I will hand over the microchip to the media as soon as I get home. They'll expose An-Ning before my superiors are able to cover it up. And by the time communications are restored between the Earth and the Moon, I will be long gone."

Sun put her hand over her heart where she felt the vial of ambrosium, safely tucked against her chest.

Seal Skin

By M. Leigh Hood

Exposed claustrophobia.

As the observation pod drifted against the tide's pull, anchored safely to the crane on the ship above, Abigail filled her notes. She watched her reflection sit among the fish, haloed by the dark shadows of monk seals who stole glittering fish like jewels from her person. Pressure gauges and other mechanical apparatuses framed a viewport big enough for Abigail to walk through. Another invisible barrier rested beneath her feet, leaving her feeling unbalanced and especially happy to be sitting down.

She caught herself holding a breath, fighting her lungs' instinct to keep out water. The glass of the observation pod, her *Selkie*, did that perfectly well already. For a single day, she could slip into the world below the surface, and she had precious little time to sketch the species passing by.

She wanted to pretend, just for a little while, that she was a seal, that she could escape below with enough air to hunt out mysteries and return to the surface unharmed and full of stories. Only she wouldn't get her hair wet. And she hoped to bring back fodder for an article on the sea life of the Turks and Caicos, not just tall tales.

She wanted to see a sea cow, not a mermaid.

As she descended, the water became bluer. It was simply a matter of less light, but the Egyptian blue tint made everything so much more alien than it had a dozen feet higher.

While she traced the mottled pout of a grouper in her notes, the pod jerked to a stop. Aside from the pull of the tide, the *Selkie* hung stationary. Abigail leaned forward in her seat, trying to peer up, but she could only just see the edge of the ship's shadow. It told her nothing of the world above, nothing that could explain the sudden stop.

Another jerk, and she ascended.

The pod stopped again, and once more Abigail pressed her cheek to the glass. A bright flash blossomed around the vessel's silhouette, burning orange.

The pod gave a mighty shudder.

The chain fell slack.

Abigail tried to sink her nails into the glass as her shelter sank. She didn't dare look down. She didn't dare check to see if she had swung out over the shelf.

Freefalling through water wasn't like falling through air. The descent was not uncomfortably quick, for all that it was uncontrolled, and Abigail fought the overwhelming nightmare-sense that she was being pulled down into an endless gulf. Each second, she fell farther away from her precious air, slowly but inexorably sinking into her grave. She dropped back into the chair and clutched her notebook. The corners stabbed into her ribs and thighs, comfortingly solid.

And then she stopped.

With a mild bump and a puff of sediment, the seafloor arrested the pod's descent. She had not fallen into the void. There was still hope of rescue.

Abigail considered her situation. Closing her eyes to hide the rising bubbles and surprised fish let her pretend she was on land, in a normal chair, not in any hurry to escape. She could breathe. There was a world of oxygen around her.

It all happened to someone else.

And if it happened to someone else, it was safe to think over.

By the apparent explosion, she assumed the winch's steam engine must be involved. A blast of that size would put the ship in jeopardy, so it only made sense to preserve the crew before returning for the *Selkie*. But they would return. Of course they would. Even if the investors wrote off one scientist, they would want their equipment back.

Had they disengaged the chain from the crane?

The pod gave an almighty lurch, and her world tilted as the *Selkie* crashed backwards. Abigail screamed and reached to steady herself, but there was nothing but the smooth glass viewing port before her, and soon it was above her. She tumbled back into the nest of gears and controls surrounding the chair, bruising her knee against the vertical seat. The pod was now on its back, offering the floundering scientist a clear view of the rippling surface dozens of yards above her. But it didn't stop.

The pod bumped over coral and skidded across the ocean floor, rushing backwards. As she struggled to find a firm place to put her feet, Abigail realized she had the answer to her questions.

The chain was still linked to the ship, and the ship was sinking.

As suddenly as the race across the ocean floor began, it ended, and Abigail rolled face-first into the closed hatch. She lay still for several minutes, afraid to move, afraid to breathe, fearing the consequences of motion.

But the pod didn't move again. It had come, at last, to its final rest. With the *Selkie* floundered as it was, the main portal looked up to the blue world's ceiling, and the bottom viewing port offered a view of the reef and the trail of devastation the pod had left in its mad rush toward the precipice. Her heart pounded hard enough to make her gorge rise, and her breath fluttered with every pant. Claustrophobia squeezed her mind. She had to get out of the pod. But it was the only safe place. The last safe place.

Bubbles rose around her like smoke, fragments of another world dragged below. The murky silhouette of a shark ghosted through them, startling Abigail into a lever behind her. Blood blossomed in her mouth where her teeth cut into her cheek, and she tasted the salty copper, savored it – it was like medicine to quell her panic. She had a decision to make – stay or swim. She wanted to rip open the hatch and throw herself into the endless escape of the sea. But then there was the ocean's law, the gamble every sailor took. In her current state, with the noise of the wreck and the smell of blood in the water, the cards were against her. The blue outside was darkening to a midnight hue, and Abigail decided to delay her choice until morning. Leaving her safe haven to risk the dangers of the reef during prime hunting hours would be foolhardy. Fate had already sided against her. No reason to tempt it.

Slowly, Abigail crawled away from the door, more aware than ever before of the instruments and gauges stabbing her shins and palms. There was just enough room to rise up on her knees, but nowhere near enough to stand.

After several minutes' battle with her skirt and the sharp gears on which they were caught, she managed to pull herself to the chair, the back of which was almost long enough to hold her entire body. The soft leather was a balm to her torn shins and elbows.

The tide brought evidence of the wreck. The captain's log book came tumbling along the sea floor amid a forest of shattered timber, much of it scorched from the blast. Pages of the journal waved and fluttered, animated by the current. One of her own petticoats drifted by, ballooned out, floating with suspended grace in the attitude of a jellyfish.

The sun sank, and the surface glowed gold. The water grew dark. Then darker. The moon rose, and in the silver gloom a fleet of shadows appeared. Reef sharks cruised in lazy circles, all sharp angles and fluid turns. Hundreds of little fish darted about in search of food, and dozens of larger fish swooped to prey in turn upon them. An eagle ray flew in from the direction of the drop-off, wings graceful as a bird as it slipped through the scene.

At last Abigail closed her eyes, empty after the rush of adrenaline, and she dreamed that she floated up to the moon, swimming in open air.

Abigail woke to a face looking down at her. She moved to demand what the nosy crewman thought he was doing above her bunk, but then she felt the cog digging into her ankle, saw the glass fogging ever so slightly where her sleeping breath warmed it. There was no ship. She was in the pod, and on the other side of that glass was ocean.

There were no men in the ocean. She ground the sleeping sand from eyes and looked again.

There was a man in the ocean. But he was not a man. A man should not have four gills in place of nostrils, nor skin the color of turquoise and algae.

Should she sketch or scream?

The face above blinked with sheer lateral eyelids. Then it drove a rough spear at the glass, directly towards her face.

Abigail screamed, more surprised than afraid. The spear barely left a scratch, and the creature rebounded. It swam back in a loop to press a wide, webbed hand against the viewport. Abigail counted three fingers and an opposable thumb.

She was baffled. Mortified. Fish did not look like men. Fish did not have opposable thumbs. Fish weren't meant to have thumbs at all.

But this one did. It had not only the thumbs, but the face and arms of a man. Its body tapered in a long, spotted tail, a billowing three-finned fluke unlike any children's book illustration she'd ever seen.

She staunchly refused to call the creature a mermaid, though merman might have been more correct. Paintings and folklore pushed her to read the colorful thing without mammalian breasts as male.

Before she had even recovered from her shock, she found her hand reaching for her sketchbook. But she didn't take her eyes off the creature, and he didn't take his eyes off of her.

On the creature's right hand, the hand pressed to the glass, the webbing between the second and third fingers was torn. Tendril-like spines sprouted from the top of his head, curiously similar to hair, and the form of its arms was like a man's apart from the winged fins joining them to the body. And there all similarities ended. The neck was elongated and hosted ranks of cream-ruffled gills to either side. Then, of course, there was that bizarre tail...

Abigail felt like a fish in an aquarium, and her curiosity withered under the heat of rising panic. Trapped. She was trapped, and there was a monster outside her window.

She didn't quite mean to, but she screamed again. The noise startled the creature. He sprang back from the glass again, and this time he swam away, out of sight of the viewport.

She took the opportunity to try the hatch. She hissed as a sliver of broken glass from a pressure gauge nicked her wrist as she crawled over the controls. Just what she needed. Blood to bait the sharks. Abigail's hands shook as she grabbed the lever. How much time did she have? Was the creature really gone? What about the sharks? Should she stop to remove her petticoats before she unsealed the hatch? No. She had to get out of the cage.

All it should take was a few good turns, and she could breathe free air again.

She gave the wheel a good yank. It didn't move. Resistance was to be expected, but she couldn't force the mechanism to turn at all. Maybe it was the angle. Ignoring the pain in her shins, she writhed around to find better leverage.

She tried again. And again.

She screamed and fought with the dead metal, trying to rein in her terror.

Her prison just became her coffin. Each gasp of air was now precious. How many were left? She had no more than a day remaining, and that was a generous estimate. If the rebreather had been damaged in her mad rush across the reef, she would have less.

Her nails broke against the brass handle, and her palms bruised. The most important tools of her trade – her hands – and she was breaking them. A narrow cut severed what palm readers would call her "life line."

Abigail watched dispassionately as blood crept from the slice and spread through the channels of her skin. More blood. It would bring the sharks if she ever escaped the pod, and they would tear her apart. Maybe they'd already had their fill feasting on a crew's worth of corpses. But there were always more sharks. And she couldn't even escape to be eaten.

Her survival instincts gave way to despair. She didn't drag herself back to the throne, but curled up on the machinery and let her tears run free until her curls were stuck to her face and her sleeve was damp. It was a different kind of drowning.

She recognized the urge to anthropomorphize the creature the moment he pressed his hand against the glass. The eyes were soulful, but so were a seal's. The touch made the connection. Marine fauna examined surroundings by bumps and bites. They did not reach out to investigate, and they didn't carry spears.

It was easy to see what one desired in a face, but the actions of a creature told its true nature. The hand was not a perfect facsimile of her own, but the shape was the same, and the last digit clearly operated in opposition to the others. More than the shape was the gesture. The creature had teeth and a tail, but he chose to reach out and touch as he tried to understand the alien object on the seabed.

She was still thinking about the creature when he reappeared. This time, he approached the pod cautiously and spent an hour circling before he decided it was safe to approach.

Abigail was ready for him. She'd tried the hatch again, but it was well and truly stuck. Though the *Selkie* had held up amazingly well during the trip across the ocean floor, the door would never open again. Either the mechanism had been warped by a strike against the coral, or it was simply wedged against the rock outside. Resignation hid behind her scientific curiosity even as it tempered the simmering panic. It was too soon to give up, but too late to keep hope.

She sat on the back of the throne, her sketch book balanced on her knees as she studied the world into which she'd fallen. The creature's fins and eyes took up page after page of notes. She dedicated an entire sheet to capturing the texture of his mottled skin.

Comfortable at last, the creature began investigating the glass he'd struck the day before, going over it with broad sweeps of his strange hands, analyzing the barrier.

He was just human enough that Abigail struggled not to think of him as such. His features compelled a natural response to reach out in kinship, to recognize a compatible mind and call out for aid, but logic told her he was simply another obstacle between her and the shore. Even if he did not willfully attack her – either as prey or competitor – a few playful dunkings would kill her just as surely as an intentional assault. It wasn't impossible that he may see her as she saw him – a distant relative, a potential friend or playmate. One innocent assumption that she breathed through gills, and he would be the end of her.

Abigail couldn't tell if the gleam of sentience in the creature's eye was real or imagined. Did she presume to see advanced intelligence because of its humanoid shape, or was it the same as all other creatures, and in her human arrogance she only dared to consider the possibility of a soul because of the creature's startling resemblance to her own species?

How was she to recognize a concept with a name but no face?

As she thought, she rose closer and closer to the viewport. Her breath fogged on the glass, and an idea struck her. She huffed a few more pants until the portal was well clouded. As the creature cocked his head, she drew a simple star on the pane.

The creature swam up to the glass and pressed a webbed finger at the edge of her pattern. It squeaked as he drew it along, and he blinked, baffled when it left no mark as her finger had. Abigail laughed, and the creature continued his efforts, trying and trying until Abigail wondered if he'd leave a groove. Eventually he stopped, wriggling in confusion. But he didn't leave, he didn't attack the glass, and she had his full attention.

Music soothed the savage beast? What rubbish. Art was the best child of the illuminated mind.

And then she had an idea.

She rapped her nails against the glass, and when her creature looked up, she lifted the sketchbook for him to see. Amid all the fragmented bits of the creature, she had composed a single united image. He was frozen on the paper, tail lifted, ready to fall at any instant, eyes focused on problems Abigail could neither guess nor fathom.

His eyes bulged, and he pressed his face flat to the glass, hands spread flat. His nostril gills were squashed against the glass like a sample between a cover and slide. Pumping his fluke, the creature kept himself fixed there, looking at himself. Then he darted away, casting a bewildered glance at the pod. He swam a quick lap around the nearest tower of coral, returning only to look with greater perplexity at the viewing window. Another lap, and he returned to the glass.

Abigail lowered the sketch to her lap. Did he think it was alive? A child, perhaps? Did he expect it to follow him out beyond the glass? But maybe not. Maybe he wanted her to follow him out. Or this was like a man pacing the room, a simple aerobic action meant to calm the nerves and stimulate thought.

There she went, trying to make him human again.

The creature stroked the glass, and Abigail sat back to think.

It was entirely possible the creature had never seen a human before. From below, a boat was nothing but a tapered shadow. Unless he came very near to shore, what interaction might he have with mankind? Dead sailors from a shipwreck? A woman in a glass case was entirely different from a drowned man's bloated corpse. If he seemed strange to her, she reasoned, she must seem impossible to him.

Even if he was not human, he was more intelligent than any fish. His investigations of the pod showed thought and consideration. The weapon he wielded was a tool more advanced than any mindless animal would build. He seemed as intrigued by her as she was by him.

As she studied the sweeps of his tri-finned tail, he pressed close to the glass, watching the way she moved so quickly but with so little grace. Water turned everything into ballet. An air-bound, bipedal creature such as she must seem incredibly clumsy. And quick.

The sun's roiling diamonds at the bottom of the sea faded, and as dusk approached, the creature left, swimming in the direction of the drop-off. Abigail curled up to sleep and felt the first strain of a headache stretching over her mind. The ocean crushed tight against her thin skin of metal and glass.

Seals came to visit in the night.

Hunting nocturnal schools under a bright moon, they probed the strange pod with whiskery faces, asking questions with teeth and eyes.

Abigail watched them eat and fly through moonbeams in swoops and swirls. She didn't hold their curiosity long, but they captured her half-cognizant fascination as she dipped in and out of dreams. They made it look so easy, like they could breathe water as easily as air, and wasn't she a fool for trying to bring her world with her like a pocketful of light into a dark cave?

For a while, they circled like a mobile in a column of shadows. Patchy darkness rolled over Abigail's face. How long had she been dreaming, to believe in mermen when she saw seals?

She wondered how long they could stay like this, so far from air, and if they would outlast her *Selkie*.

She threw herself at the window to see if the glass was really there, but the skin was too strong for her to breach.

She had only wanted her one day between worlds. She never truly wanted to stay.

Human instinct said when something moved it was alive. That was why, after thousands of years of learning and science, humans still jumped at their own shadows.

The sea was always moving.

Abigail didn't have the strength to try breaching the hull again. She sat still, watching the golden morning glow seep through the blue water as the reef began to stir. It was such a pity her thoughts were loose. They'd broken free some time during the night and refused to come to order in the waking light. A passing dream suggested it was the air. The rebreather was failing. When had it failed? Had it failed already? She couldn't think. Her clever fingers found the peeling spine of her notebook, and she clutched the weathered book, half-convinced her lethargy came from a long swim, that she was drowning in dry clothes.

Was it really morning already?

Her merman would be there soon. He wouldn't abandon her here at the bottom of the ocean. It was such a shame there were no seals.

Her head hurt too much to stay awake. She lay down on her throne and closed her eyes. She was asleep in moments. She didn't even know when she died.

The awkward jellyfish woman was dead.

He pressed close to the glass and saw the terrible color she'd turned, noted how still she was, and knew she wasn't respiring. He couldn't quite understand it. She was safe inside her quartz bubble. But she was certainly not breathing. The rock in his hand weighed heavy. He'd brought it to tether his nets deeper in the reef, but now the tool was turned to a new purpose.

After his startled assault on the bubble when he first found it in his territory, he hadn't tried to break through to the creature within, the creature he knew must be from above, the world beyond his. He hadn't believed she was real until he returned and found her there again. Stories said she couldn't survive in his world. That was why creatures from above never stayed long, maybe long enough for one of the Folk to see them, but then they'd break through the border and disappear into one of the hard shadows.

One breath would kill her, which was why, even in this strange exile, she'd been sent with a bit of her world to protect her.

But it hadn't protected her. Something was wrong, and it was time to take more drastic action. He lifted the stone and brought it down hard on the transparent bubble.

Over. Over. Over. Again. It was very strong.

He was strong as well; he was also patient. After many strikes, the bubble shattered.

He retreated as suffocating billows of air poured out, then entered when there was enough water to breathe. The creature from above bobbed in the water, her long jellyfish fins ballooned about her. He took her around the middle, where he was certain she had no gills, and made for the edge of the world. Cradling her head, he lifted her face above the border. He held her so for a long time, but she had taken in too much of the world, and it had killed her. The stories were true. But she died before he broke through her shelter. What had killed her, then? Had she died of a broken heart, too saddened by her banishment below to endure? It hurt to imagine.

Cradling her in his arms, mindful of her ensnaring fins that flared around them, he took her past the drop-off.

The Truth Beneath the Sands

By A.F. Stewart

In the silence between ageless heartbeats, the man screamed. He scrambled across the stone floor until he cowered in a corner. The glint of the gold treasures he sought surrounded him. From the shadows came a growl and the echoing clank of ancient gears and joints. The air stirred with movement, and the walls crawled with silhouettes cast by the dim lamps of the chamber.

He groped along the wall, ready to run, pleading, "Please, I didn't mean any harm. I don't want to die."

The slow, creaking flap of metallic wings was his only answer...

Wallace Shaw spat desert grit from his mouth and wiped grime from underneath his goggles. He leaned on his shovel, each laboured breath catching in his burning throat. Sweat dripped down his brow, and he adjusted the headscarf protecting him from the harsh sun, trying to find more relief from the elements. Around him, the clank and thwack of tools sounded as the hired workers continued to dig.

Wallace stretched his shoulders as he watched the progress. Mounds of sand dotted the area, the work of three days of excavation. Yet, they didn't seem any closer to finding the underground entrance Carstairs wrote about in his notes.

Where the hell is it? It shouldn't be buried this deep.

A nasal whine broke through Wallace's musings, and he shot a resentful glance at one of his partners, Fletcher Davies, who lounged in a chair under the shade of a tent. "My, my, taking a break, old chap? Where is your stamina?"

Bastard. I'm baking in this heat.

"You're welcome to assist, Fletcher, if you think you can do better!"

The man shook his head and lazily waved a hand. "I would, dear chap, but for this fragile constitution of mine. You're more suited to labour than I am. Upbringing and all that, you know."

Wallace ground his teeth against the insult. Fletcher often threw his lack of status and money back in his face.

You're just a lazy buffoon.

"Come now, don't be so hard on yourself. A bit of good, honest exercise will do you some good. Enoch would pitch in if he were here." Wallace knew that last jab would irritate Fletcher. The rivalry between the brothers always simmered near the surface.

Fletcher scowled, and Wallace felt a twinge of satisfaction, but his partner never moved from his chair. "My brother indulges in all manner of foolish things. Like gambling or keeping low company." Fletcher shot him a smug look. "Such pursuits are why we're here after all. If Enoch hadn't made the acquaintance of your friend Carstairs, you would have never tracked us down for this...excursion."

"Carstairs was no friend of mine. That bastard ruined my prospects." Anger welled at the thought of Jacob Carstairs, rich bon vivant, museum patron, and amateur archaeologist.

Fletcher laughed. "Oh, did I touch a nerve?"

Wallace glared at his smirking business partner. "You know damn well you did." His hand tightened on the shovel handle, the memories of his adversary consuming his thoughts. He moved towards Fletcher, dragging the blade of the shovel through the sand.

A foot away he stopped and hissed, "How dare you bring up Carstairs? You know what that bastard did, smearing my good name with his lies. Telling them I lost my nerve after what happened in Turkey."

Fletcher shrugged. "The man was a bit of a prig, I'll admit, but perhaps he had a point. No one likes a coward, old boy."

"I'm not a coward!" Wallace's voice drew the stares of the workers. He flushed in embarrassment and lowered his intensity. "It wasn't like that. Anyone would have run when the chamber collapsed. I wasn't to blame. It wasn't my fault about the shoddy supports, either." Wallace clenched his jaw, willing his body not to shake. The screams of his colleagues still haunted him and chased his new fear of being trapped underground.

He took a breath, trying one last time to defend himself. "It wasn't my fault. Carstairs unfairly ruined my reputation. You know that's why they relegated me to cataloging. That it was his fault the museum eventually dismissed me."

Fletcher chuckled. "Of course, it was, dear boy. It had absolutely nothing to do with your lack of skill or that spot of thieving you indulged in."

The muscles in Wallace's jaw spasmed. "They owed me!"

Fletcher laughed. "Indeed, dear boy. Clearly, you were wronged."

Wallace closed his eyes. *Why do I bother? Why does it matter to me? I don't even like the man. Why do I care what he thinks of me?*

"But chin up, old boy. Some good came from that bastard and your sticky fingers. Stealing Carstairs' notes and that old French map after he disappeared, quite devious. And very inspired to come to us to finance this dig. Carstairs may have been a crackpot with his scribblings full of prattle about magic and strange mechanical creatures, but who knows, you may return to London a rich man yet. Lord knows Egypt doesn't suit you."

Wallace sighed. *He's right about that. I wish I never travelled to this wretched country. I miss London; the bustle, the noise, the incessant hiss of the steam engines.*

Wallace looked past Fletcher, out over the horizon, his emotions a mix of anger, homesickness, and regret.

This desert is so quiet. I hate it. Wallace shivered, despite the heat. *This place feels wrong. Hell, even Cairo is better than here. I miss the drone of airships overhead.*

Wallace sighed again, wanting to rid himself of his fanciful melancholy, but letting his resentment bubble to the forefront of his thoughts. It comforted him in its familiarity, and he imagined his enmity washing over the sandy expanse that surrounded him, as if he could drown the landscape in his bitterness. Yet, like his colleagues, the terrain only mocked him. It dared him to best it, to wrestle the treasures from within its eternal shades of undulating, weather-beaten brown. Shimmers danced on the sand, a reflection of the unrelenting heat. The sunlight that scorched a man's skin, sucked the moisture from his throat. One wrong move and this environment would kill.

Wallace licked his cracked lips.

Sometimes I think this desert hates me. It's worse at night. Gets so cold you can't get warm. Damn place can't make up its mind.

Wallace hefted his shovel, turned, and returned to the excavation. Fletcher's voice trailed behind him.

"That's the spirit, old boy. Work is good for what ails you. Put your back into it and dig. We'll have this tomb excavated in no time at all."

Wallace glanced at Fletcher again. His hand moved to his hip, and he fingered his knife.

One thrust and he'd be sorry. Bones bleach fast in the desert. Wallace smiled at the idle thought before he sighed. *No, I can't. I still need him. And his brother.*

He thrust his shovel into the desert sand and returned to the job at hand. Yet, he snuck a glance at the sky and imagined himself in an airship, flying away from Egypt as a rich man, his partners left behind.

"He is not worth your time." Hammu, the head worker, nodded at Fletcher. "He would not know hard work if it flew at him like a hawk."

Wallace gritted his teeth. "I know. His type just gets under my skin."

"You need thicker skin." Hammu grinned. "And more patience. You look for quick roads and easy journeys. Life is not like that."

"It should be. It's unfair that posh bastards have all the privilege."

"So life is unfair, is it?" Hammu chuckled. "I watch British airships fly over my country every day and see their false superiority in every word they speak. Even in your words, I hear it. Life is unfair to all. Even to those like Fletcher."

"So I should just take it?" Wallace snorted while feeling a twinge of guilt.

"You should find ways around it. And do not let it fester in your soul. Anger and hate darken the soul, my friend." Hammu patted Wallace on the shoulder. "If you succeed at finding the secrets within the tomb, do not fail at embracing your own virtue."

Wallace looked at him in surprise. "So you think I'm right? That there is a tomb? I thought you were here for the pay?"

"I am, but to see what treasures are beneath the sands as well."

Wariness prickled at Wallace. "What do you know of tombs and buried treasures?"

Hammu shrugged. "I studied with a man in my youth. He taught me many things and many secrets. You may learn them too if your map is true. I only hope you are ready to face them. I like you. I would dislike seeing you fail."

Before Wallace could question him further, the clink of a pickaxe hitting something solid brought their attention back to the dig. Hammu rushed forward, followed by Wallace. A thrill of joy raced down Wallace's spine.

"Did you find something? An entrance?" He eagerly pushed past everyone and peered into the excavated hole.

The worker standing beside him shrugged. "A door, maybe. An archway, maybe. We must dig more to be sure."

"Then dig, man, dig." Wallace scowled and kicked dirt at a worker who hadn't moved. "Don't idle about now! Back to work. Dig, blast you, dig!"

From the tent came laughter and Fletcher's voice. "That's the way. Keep the lazy rabble at the job. Don't let those shiftless people take advantage. Make them earn their money." More laughter made Wallace clench his jaw and back away from the hole as the workers resumed their efforts.

The only shiftless person here is you. You just sit in that tent and bark orders and insults. The world would be better off without you. Maybe I'll just...

Those thoughts trailed off as Fletcher continued, his mocking voice ringing out, "Did you finally find something interesting? Or just another wall?"

Wallace ground his teeth. He wanted to lie, but said, "Perhaps an entrance. They are digging more of it out now."

"So nothing to get excited about then. Not yet."

Wallace glanced over at Fletcher, who smirked at him. The man sipped a cocktail that had been dispensed from his personal automaton valet.

Wallace shifted position, trying to get a better look at the digging, trying to assess the amount of work needed. *Damn, I wish I still had access to the resources at the Cairo Museum. Their automaton workers would have dug this out in a day.*

He kicked at the hard-packed sand, dug a handkerchief out of his pocket, and wiped the sweat from his brow. Sudden tiredness washed over him. Wallace walked over to the water barrel and sipped a ladle of cool, clear liquid, doubts gnawing at his brain. Then a hand fell on his shoulder. Hammu smiled at him.

"Learn to go around, not through. Come, let's help."

They walked back to the excavation.

An hour later came a shout, "We found it! It is a door!"

"What?" Wallace raced over.

Fletcher yelled. "Seriously? You found an entrance?"

Wallace ignored his partner, staring down into the excavation. Below him, clearly visible, he saw the top part of an entryway. Carved into the stone were hieroglyphics; a pair of wings and a peculiar-looking wheel.

Underneath that was a feather symbol.

Wallace peered closer, trying to make sense of the images. He finally shrugged and turned to the workers. "Keep digging and clear all this sand away. We need to open it."

He moved away and shouted at Fletcher. "It's an entrance! We've done it!"

I can't believe it. We're almost there. There's treasure down there. I can feel it.

"Come here, Wallace." Fletcher's whine cut through his thoughts.

Damn him. Can't he leave me alone? Even now?

Yet Wallace resentfully trudged over to the tent.

"What did you find? Is it a tomb? A treasure vault?"

"We know nothing yet. But it is a door. We should be able to enter soon and raid what's inside."

"Good. The sooner the better."

Wallace frowned. "What does that mean?"

"Sit, relax for a moment." Fletcher patted the empty chair beside him. Wallace eyed his partner with suspicion. "Don't look so worried. I just want to talk."

Wallace sat down, resigned to hearing whatever foolishness Fletcher had thought up now.

"Do you really think this is it? What we've been searching for?"

Wallace shrugged. "We'll know soon enough, but I think so."

"I'm actually excited, imagine that." Fletcher smirked and sipped his cocktail, the reek of alcohol filling the air. "I never really bought into this nonsense, you know. That was Enoch's thing, with his…well, far-fetched theories. When you came to him with your map, and Carstairs' notes, he was positively giddy. Carstairs tried to cut us out of the original deal, you know."

"No, I didn't know. You never mentioned that." Wallace leaned in, curious.

"Yes. Enoch was livid about it until you came round with a second chance. Personally, I thought the lot of you were a bit cracked. I mean, they buried all those pharaoh chaps down by Thebes. Why would there be a tomb this close to Cairo, by some insignificant wadi? Not to mention all that other drivel."

Wallace frowned. "Wait, I thought that's why you both joined the expedition. I proved to you there was something here."

"That proved nothing to me; that was Enoch's bugaboo, not mine. He's the one that convinced me to come. I'd rather be in Cairo, but..." Fletcher grimaced. "He's persuasive. Now that you've found a door, though, that changes things." Fletcher rubbed his hands together. "Maybe the old legend Enoch is obsessed about is true. We could actually be rich." Fletcher laughed, then a troubled look flitted across his face. "Speaking of Enoch, he may come back tonight." He held up a letter. "The new workers brought this in yesterday."

"And you're just telling me now?" Wallace tightened his jaw, curling his right hand into a fist.

"There seemed little point. The dig wasn't making any genuine progress, and Enoch's trouble wouldn't have changed anything. Frankly, I thought this was turning out to be another waste of time. But if that is a tomb entrance... well, we may have to rush things a bit."

Fletcher's mechanical valet poured him another cocktail. "Enoch was caught cheating at cards. He evaded arrest, but he needed to flee Cairo. Whether that trouble follows him here, I don't know. But we may need to hurry along our timetable."

"Damn it! This could ruin everything." Wallace slammed his fist against the chair. "I knew that's how he was raising capital, fleecing rich fools, but I thought he was good at it. If the authorities locate him here or investigate our operations, we're done. We're not here with permissions. And bribes will only go so far."

"Which is why we need to get into that tomb and loot the treasure, if there is one, as soon as possible."

Well, we agree on that at least. Gold and jewels would make dealing with those two worth it. With money, I could finally be someone.

Wallace closed his eyes, calculating his options. When he opened them, he stared at the low desert sun against the horizon before replying, "It will take several more hours to excavate, and we still have to open the entrance. It's unlikely we can finish before nightfall. It wouldn't be a good idea to enter the tomb in the dark; we'll have to risk waiting until morning and hope Enoch hasn't put a crashing end to this entire scheme." Wallace glared at Fletcher, who shrugged. "At least our base camp is out of sight of the excavation. If the authorities come, they'll go there. We'll need a lie, a plausible excuse for being out here, to hide the real reason."

"Hmmm," Fletcher swirled his cocktail. "I think I can come up with something."

"Good," Wallace grunted. "We can bring camels out here in the morning. Load any smaller treasures into packs in case we need to move out, either to the moored airship or further into the desert for a rendezvous."

"Excellent thinking. Keeping the treasures mobile for a quick getaway. I like it."

"Plus camels will make it easier to get everything back to camp if Enoch doesn't bring trouble." Wallace closed his eyes for a moment, envisioning the moment he divested himself of his annoying partners. "But this means we can't go back to Cairo and the safehouse you set up."

"Yes, that might be a bit of a conundrum but not entirely out of the question. Your name's been kept out of things. We didn't want your rather dubious reputation muddying the waters. Most of the historical community views you badly these days. Suspicions would have been raised if we made our association public knowledge. So there's no reason you can't go back to Cairo. With a letter of introduction, of course. If the worst happens, you can smuggle the treasures into the city and oversee our arrangements to have them shipped to Alexandria. Then you can accompany them to England by the airship passage we secured. Hopefully, I won't have too much trouble re-entering the city, without the treasures, of course, so I can join you a day or two later."

Wallace tilted his head, disbelief and the first vestiges of greed percolating in his mind. *He can't be that foolish. If I had this letter of introduction, I wouldn't need either of them anymore.*

His fingers unconsciously tapped the chair, and his heartbeat quickened. *I could have it all. No sharing.* He licked his lips and shot a sideways glance at Fletcher. *Perhaps this is actually a blessing. I'd just need a way to delay them, or be rid of them...* Wallace smiled, his thoughts suddenly trailing off into fantasies of bleached bones, before ruminating on possible schemes in the dark recesses of his brain.

He inhaled deeply, keeping his voice calm as he replied, "My handling of the treasure makes sense, I suppose. The less we attract the attention of the authorities, the better."

"Good. Then it's settled." Fletcher sipped his drink. "Now we just have to wait and see how rich we will become."

No, Fletcher. I won't let you take my prize. Not this time. I want it all.

Wallace sat outside his tent in camp, a blanket wrapped around him, staring at the starry sky, musing on the day. The rest of the excavation went well. They got the door unburied and opened it with relative ease, doing only minor damage, even closing it enough to keep out larger animals. Enoch's return didn't bring the authorities, as he had evaded arrest and escaped the city without incident. But the man he had fleeced was the son of an important British diplomat. Enoch would not be welcomed back in Cairo any time soon.

Wallace glanced over at the brothers' tent. *Bastard deserves whatever he gets. At least the excavation is safe, and the fool agreed with Fletcher about letting me smuggle the treasure back into Cairo. Everything's falling into place. I won't have to share anything with those pompous fools. I just wish...*

Wallace swallowed, guilt churning in his gut. It hadn't felt good lying to Hammu, but he needed his help to keep an eye on the brothers and to delay or distract them if necessary. Besides, he wouldn't be involved in any possible killing. Another worker happily volunteered if things came to that.

And it's not as if I have a choice. It might have to be done. I can't have them coming after me. It's survival. I will come out on top this time. No one's taking this success away from me.

Wallace looked up and smiled at the stars. They were finally on his side.

No more worries, no more scrabbling. Money and freedom and finally leaving Egypt.

He went to bed confident the morning would change his fortunes.

With the sunrise, coffee, and food in their bellies, the partners and workers were back at the excavation site. They shoved the door open again, lit lanterns, and sent in two workers to check for safety. At the shout of "all clear," Wallace, Fletcher, Enoch, and Hammu followed.

Beyond the entrance was a short flight of steps carved from stone, then a long passageway leading into darkness. Wallace shivered and hesitated.

A slap smacked against his shoulder with a sting, and Fletcher chuckled. "Buck up. I know you're afraid of being trapped below ground, but think of the treasure."

"Who says I'm afraid?" he growled and pushed past Fletcher, marching down the stairs.

They travelled single file down the narrow hall, the lanterns barely illuminating the gloom. Wallace raised his light to see the walls; they were bare rock, with no hieroglyphs or other engravings.

Odd. I would've expected some decoration. I wonder why there is none.

They had walked about ten feet before the workers leading the way shouted, "Mr. Shaw, sir, you must look at this!"

Wallace barely squeezed past to reach the front, where the passageway widened into a small alcove. Wallace whistled in excitement as he gazed at another door.

"This must be the entrance to the antechamber!"

"Look closer, my friend." Hammu nudged him, pointing to the left.

Wallace gaped as Fletcher and Enoch called from behind him, "What is it? What did you find?"

"A chamber door, but it has a…" Wallace didn't know what he stared at, fumbling with words. "A strange type of lock."

The mechanism resembled a metallic sundial embedded in the stone next to the doorway, with engraved lines and a gold obelisk-shaped needle, inside a tarnished copper circle of gears. On the outside, an attached lever was visible, perhaps in place to turn the contraption.

Fletcher and Enoch shoved past the two workers, who were happy to retreat. Hammu also made way, stepping from the alcove into the passage.

"What is it, what did—" Fletcher gasped as he saw the apparatus. "What is that doing in an Egyptian tomb?"

Wallace shrugged. "I have no idea."

Enoch squawked, "It has to be..." He grabbed the lever. "Let's find out what it does, shall we?"

"Wait!" Wallace yelled.

But it was too late.

Enoch turned the mechanism clockwise, the gears grinding and metal squealing. The walls shook in a shower of dusty grime. But nothing else happened.

Wallace sighed in relief until Fletcher said, "Do it again."

Wallace screamed, "No, stop!"

But Enoch rotated the wheel again, only this time, as he moved it one full turn, something cracked into place. The air in the alcove shimmered, crackling with electricity, and a blinding ruby light enveloped the three partners.

As Wallace blinked away the spots obscuring his vision, he glared at Enoch's dumbfounded face. "Of all the stupid things to do! What if you caused a cave-in or triggered some trap?"

"It worked, didn't it? The door opened..." Enoch frowned. "Where are we?"

A long tunnel led...somewhere. Stale air assaulted his nose, mixed with the pungent stench of dirt and mould. "I don't know. I assumed the antechamber was beyond the door, yet—" Wallace turned, looking for the doorway. Fear crawled like spiders over his skin. "What the hell? The door's gone!" He whirled and frantically examined the walls; a metallic sheen glinted against the stone, the feel a mix of smooth and coarse against his fingers.

Behind him, Enoch whined, "I don't understand. Are we trapped? Fletcher, do you know what happened? Fletcher?"

There was no answer.

Only the echo of Enoch's voice.

Panic spread over Enoch's face. "Where's my brother?" When Wallace did nothing more than stare into the darkness Enoch grabbed his arm. "We have to find him! Find a way out of here. Do something!"

With a growl, Wallace shook off Enoch. He stared down the tunnel, his stomach churning. "We have little choice. We go forward."

Wallace plunged into the tunnel, not caring if Enoch followed him, although the tread of footsteps echoed behind him.

The walls had their own viridescent glow, dimly lighting their way. A few feet past the mouth of the tunnel, they stumbled upon a rotting corpse. Wallace pulled up short and Enoch yelped, the sound putting his teeth on edge. Wallace numbly stared at the pile of decayed flesh and bone.

Not Egyptian. Looks English, maybe American.

The glint of gold on the dead man's chest caught his attention. Wallace bent over and snatched a pocket watch off the corpse.

Even with the dingy lighting, he recognized the trinket. "Carstairs! So this is what happened to you." He kicked Carstairs' body and laughed, relief and joy flooding his thoughts, and slipped the watch into his own pocket.

"Is that what will happen to us?" Enoch's frightened voice abruptly sent a quiver down his spine.

Wallace glanced back. "What? What do you mean?"

"He came looking for treasure, the same as us. Will we end up dead as well? Are we going to die and rot down here?"

"No!" Wallace snapped, any pleasure in his enemy's death vanishing. "No, I'm smarter than him. I won't end up like that." He kicked the body again, then moved away. "Come on, we need to keep searching, to find a way out."

They walked down the tunnel, shadows dancing along the green, glimmering walls. The cool air wafted decay and the faint hint of copper into their nostrils. The only sound, the thud of their footsteps. Fear wriggled in Wallace's mind, threatening his self-control, his every breath quickening, panic seeping closer and closer to the surface.

"Hold up!" Enoch bellowed. "That's light ahead, isn't it?"

A skip of a heartbeat and a surge of hope. Wallace growled, "It is! Come on." He broke into a loping run, Enoch racing to keep up. The two stumbled into an immense chamber, pulling up short when they spotted Fletcher standing in the middle of the room.

"Fletcher!" Enoch pushed past Wallace and rushed to his brother's side. "What happened? I was worried."

Fletcher stared into the shadowed recesses of the chamber and whimpered. Enoch took a step back.

Ignoring the brothers, Wallace gave the room a cursory inspection, gaping at the wealth of the huge treasure room surrounding him. He rubbed his hands and the sight of the gold statues, gems, and other marvels, but his heart sank at the solid walls and nothing resembling a door, a window, or any way out. Marching over to Fletcher, he shook him.

"Is there a way out? Did you find anything?" Fletcher's gaze never moved. Wallace scowled, then gulped as he noticed what captured Fletcher's attention.

A hulking, mechanical Sphinx.

Almost hidden by the gloom, the artificial beast overshadowed its corner of the extensive chamber, a colossus of alloy and ore. Wallace whistled in amazement, drinking in the vision of the wondrous metallic marvel, then hurried forward in manic curiosity, everything else forgotten. He brushed past a mesmerized Fletcher and a flummoxed Enoch until he was inches from the Sphinx.

It sat on a raised stone dais, its polished lion's body in repose, giant paws stretched out in front of the bowed female head. An intricate, riveted headdress encircled its face. The eyes were shut. From its back rose etched, golden wings, tapering to a folded position against its back.

"Astounding! The detail, the craftsmanship. It must have taken years to build."

As he moved closer, Wallace clearly saw the gears at the joints of its limbs, in its neck, and where the wings attached to the back. The bronze body was decorated with unfamiliar hieroglyphs and an ankh was etched into the creature's chest.

"How is this possible?" He ran a finger across the metal of the leg. It felt smooth and warm.

Odd. Shouldn't it feel cool? Especially underground.

Wallace leaned over, trying to get a better look at the gears along the joints, and he noticed a red glint underneath the sphinx's lowered chin. Wallace hauled himself up to identify the new object, standing on his toes and grabbing the paw for balance.

A smile lit his expression in greed and glee. "I don't believe it!" Tucked into a recess on the dais lay a huge ruby, at least the size of his hand. When Wallace reached out to snatch it, he heard a grinding noise, and the head of the sphinx moved.

Wallace jumped away with a screech and backpedaled. He watched in fascinated horror and stomach-clenching awe as the mechanical creature's head straightened upright. Enoch let out a strangled inhalation moved forward. His partner's eyes were wild and his face plastered with a deranged grin. Behind them, Fletcher continued to whimper.

Enoch murmured, "It's true. It's all true."

"What are you babbling about? Do you know something?"

"I never imagined. I hoped, but deep down I thought it was just a story to scare people away. I never dreamed it could be real. That they actually built it." Enoch laughed, hysteria edging his voice.

"What was real? Who built it?"

"The Sphinx of Ma'at. My research uncovered snippets, mentions of the great guardian of truth and wisdom, the protector of some secret temple and the heart of Egypt. What I read told of ancient priests who created a mysterious golden sphinx and imbued it with the magic of the gods. A fairy tale, I thought, but she's real."

"That?" Wallace snorted and waved his hand at the mechanical beast. "Don't be daft. I'll admit it's impressive, but there isn't anything ancient or priestly about it, and magic is faffing nonsense." Wallace grunted. "I'd wager this is an old meeting place of some tinker's secret society; there were plenty of them scattered throughout Egypt a decade ago. Or possibly a forgotten anarchist hideout or a rich man's folly." He smirked at Enoch. "Don't believe in ridiculous myths; that sphinx is merely someone's excessive indulgence."

Enoch shook his head, resentment laced in his expression. "You're wrong."

Wallace sneered. "And you're crazy. But either way, we can still loot the place. There's a ripe little ruby under that ornamental sphinx I aim to have."

A rumble echoed through the chamber, and an indistinct sound, like a growl, emanated from the direction of the sphinx. The creature's jaw shifted, and throaty noises followed. The sounds had the cadence of speech, of the Coptic language, but with distinct differences.

Enoch grabbed Wallace's arm, and they both stepped back, colliding with Fletcher, who whined, "W—what was that? Is—is it talking?"

Wallace snapped, "Don't be ridiculous! It's some sort of degraded phonograph recording. That proves—"

The sphinx glowed crimson. More speech filled the chamber, this time in English.

"Who dares enter the Temple of Ma'at? Do you come to challenge me, guardian of the Heart of Egypt?"

It took a moment for Wallace to realize the mechanical creature *had* spoken the words, and that his notions of the world needed serious revising.

Beside him, Enoch gleefully shouted, "The Sphinx exists! A living mechanical beast created by the ancient gods." He danced around the chamber like a madman.

The booming voice filled the chamber, ending Enoch's celebration. "Cease your antics and answer me!" The sphinx glared at the three of them.

Wallace swallowed and asked, "What is the Heart of Egypt, and why would we challenge you for it?"

"The Heart of Egypt is the 'ripe little ruby' you spoke of. It is power beyond imagining for those willing to undertake the challenge and claim it. Pharaohs have sought it, kings have lusted after it, but only the worthy can possess it."

"What if I don't challenge you for it? What if I just take it?"

"You can try. If you can get past me." The sphinx chuckled, showing its rows of gleaming metal teeth. Wallace took a step back as the sphinx added, "Even if you succeeded, those who try to steal the ruby will face their worst fear realized."

Fletcher suddenly piped up. "What's the challenge?"

"Those who seek to claim the Heart of Egypt must partake of two tests. First, you must divulge your darkest secret. If you pass, you may continue. If you fail…" A tinny chuckle rumbled through the chamber. "There will be consequences." Then the sphinx swivelled its head between the three men, its gears and joints creaking. "You must tell the truth of your heart to win the ruby. Do you think you are honest enough to pass the test?"

The two brothers moved closer to the creature, exchanging looks. Neither seemed eager to speak. Wallace smiled.

Fat chance those two will be honest about anything. This is my lucky day.

He cleared his throat, capturing attention. "Here's my truth. I planned to swindle my idiotic partners out of their share of any treasure we found in this place. I was even willing to have them murdered to keep all the spoils. I decided there was no chance I would share my looted riches with them. They're both spoiled brats who think they're superior to everyone else."

Enoch squealed, "Why you double-crossing louse!"

The sphinx rumbled but nodded. "A dark truth, indeed, but a truth of the heart. Does anyone else wish to challenge me?"

"Fine!" Fletcher shouted, his face red and his body shaking. "I never wanted to come on this forsaken expedition or be partnered with that disgraced failure of an archeologist." He spat at Wallace. "If I acted like a spoiled brat, it's because I was blackmailed into coming. By my brother!" Fletcher pushed Enoch, and he stumbled against the dais. "Sometimes I hate you! You can be such a bastard. I made one mistake, years ago, and you're still using it to control me. I want to be free of you."

"You gibface fool!" Enoch swatted at Fletcher, who jumped back. "That one *mistake* got someone killed! And you're too much of a coward to free yourself from me. Too much of a coward to face the consequences of what you did. To act like a man! You deserve whatever you get!"

"A coward? At least I'm not some degenerate gambler! You're nothing but a slave to the cards. You can't stop!"

"Not true!" Enoch raised his chin, his lips sneering. "I can stop anytime I want!"

A growl rumbled into the conversation, halting the argument. They both turned and looked at the sphinx. It uncoiled, standing upright, towering over the two brothers.

"The one called Enoch has lied. He forfeits the challenge. I will now grant the wish of the human called Fletcher."

The mechanical beast opened its maw. In one quick snap, it bit off Enoch's head. Blood spurted as the corpse collapsed to the floor, and the sphinx casually crunched on bones and flesh, dripping blood from its teeth. Fletcher screamed, and Wallace gagged.

The sphinx turned to the caterwauling Fletcher, its mouth still smeared red. "I told you, silly humans, there were consequences for failing. At least you are free of your brother as you wanted."

"I didn't want my freedom that way!" Fletcher bellowed, but the sphinx only shrugged its shoulders with a loud metallic creak.

"Your brother shouldn't have lied."

"Who cares about Enoch? Who wins the ruby?" Wallace interrupted, ignoring Fletcher's wails.

"That will be decided after the second test. Both you and Fletcher told your truth." The sphinx spat out a few bone fragments and settled down on the dais. "You can both proceed."

"What if we both pass? I'm not sharing with him!" Wallace snarled, ready to reach for his knife.

"Only one can claim the ruby and be rewarded with their greatest desire. There is no sharing. One of you will fail." The sphinx spat out the last piece of Enoch's skull.

Wallace shivered but kept silent. Fletcher shuffled forward to stand beside him, finally stifling his mewling.

The sphinx laid its head on its paws with a clang that echoed in the room, making both men jump. "To determine a victor, your souls must be judged. Pick up the feather of Ma'at." The sphinx nodded to a pedestal where a white ostrich plume rested. "If it remains white, you have a pure soul, and the ruby is yours. If it turns grey, you have sins weighing your conscience, but may still win the challenge. If it turns black, your soul is corrupt and unworthy of the Heart of Egypt."

"Fine!" A shaken Fletcher pushed past Wallace and scurried to the pedestal. "I want this nightmare to end." He snatched up the feather and held it. The colour turned to a sooty grey.

The sphinx growled, "You have passed the test. Barely."

Fletcher put the feather back in place, and it returned to white. He turned to Wallace. "Let's see if you, a would-be-murderer, can do better." He moved away to let his one-time partner have his chance.

Wallace reluctantly walked to the pedestal and picked up the feather. He let it sit in his palm and held his breath. For a moment, it remained pale ivory before deepening to an overall muted grey and settling. Wallace exhaled in relief and glanced at a scowling Fletcher.

"It can't be! A nothing like you can't be better than me!"

With each heartbeat, the feather in Wallace's hand darkened. The edges turned a charcoal grey, spreading across the plume, erasing its purity until it transformed into coal black. Wallace dropped the feather as if it burned his hand and watched it float back to the stand, once more as white as snow. Then he whirled to face the sphinx, terror crawling up his spine.

The sphinx tapped a claw against the dais. "You lose the challenge. You have been judged, and your soul is corrupt. Fletcher wins the Heart of Egypt."

Crimson radiance surrounded the gem beneath the sphinx, and it levitated across the chamber to land in Fletcher's outstretched hand. To the left, the air shimmered, and a great glowing doorway appeared, showing a vision of the desert and their encampment.

The sphinx rose and bowed its head, shining in the reflected sunlight from the portal. "The one called Fletcher may leave this place. The one called Wallace must stay to accept his fate."

Fletcher stared at the sphinx, then his brother's corpse, and then the portal, before turning back to Wallace. "Guess you won't get to kill me after all."

He turned and strode towards the doorway.

He didn't make it.

Wallace's blade sank into Fletcher's back. Wallace scooped the ruby from his dead hand and jumped through the open gateway. A jangling roar followed him through.

Wallace laughed as he exited, the portal snapping closed behind him.

"I did it! I won!" Wallace spun in jubilation, but his joy was short-lived. He was back in the alcove, not in the safety of the camp.

He stared at the flickering lantern on the floor and then down the passageway. "Hammu! I'm back. I did it! Hammu?" His shout echoed off the walls. He shook off the unease. *They must have left. It doesn't matter, I suppose. I made it out with the treasure.* His fingers tightened over the ruby clutched in his hand, and he smiled. *I'm rich.*

Wallace grabbed the lantern and strode down the passage to the entrance. As he neared the stairs, he hesitated.

There's no sunlight.

A shiver ran down his spine.

Sure enough, when Wallace reached the stairway, he found the door shut tight. He climbed, placing the lantern and the ruby down carefully, and shoved at the entrance. It didn't budge. He shoved again. Nothing. He kicked at it in frustration.

What's going on? Why won't it move?

Then Wallace noticed the tickle of sand seeping in from cracks along the edge of the doorway. Fear clawed at his guts.

Hammu couldn't have. He would have waited for me.

He swallowed, the truth oozing into his brain. He wasn't getting out. They had reburied the temple.

"No, it can't be!" The screech of his own voice taunted him as it reverberated along the tunnel. "This can't be happening! I'm buried alive." He stumbled back down a couple of steps, his hands shaking and panic surging.

Soft metallic laughter sounded behind him. "Those who try to steal the ruby will face their worst fear realized."

By the flickering light of the lantern, the ruby disappeared.

Then so did the light.

He was alone in the darkness.

The Pinchbeck Engine

By Daniel Sheldon

Kinsey awoke with a jerk. As she sat up, ribbons of frigid water trickled from her clothing and landed on the mattress beneath her.

Her eyes darted around the dark room. "Grandpa! Grandpa!" Kinsey shouted. "Where are you?" She tossed her soaked blankets aside and slowly lowered herself into the water, gasping as the icy needles of the knee-deep water chewed into her flesh.

Her feet pressed against the floor as a thundering crash shook her bedroom. The window behind her had shattered. Water gushed through the opening and swirled around the room.

The force knocked Kinsey off her feet directly into the twisting torrent. She flung her arms and kicked wildly, but she was no match for the current as she was dragged from her bedroom, down the hall, and into the kitchen. Kinsey yelled out once more for her grandfather before being slammed into the kitchen wall. Not done, the rushing water tugged her unwilling body toward the missing front door.

Kinsey's fingers caught hold of the door frame. "Gotcha!" She yanked herself back towards the house, wrapping her legs around the door jamb. The cascade rushed past her, spilling into the nearby street.

After taking a long, labored breath, Kinsey pushed her damp hair from her face.

A distant, muffled sound interrupted her respite.

"Hello?" she screamed. "Is someone there?"

"—sey?" a voice replied, barely audible over the din of the surging water. "Kinsey?" the voice called out again, closer and clearer than the first time.

She would recognize that voice anywhere. "Grandpa!" she bellowed."Kinsey!… Is that you?" Grandpa slowly floated into sight, struggling mightily to captain a battered rowboat in Kinsey's direction.

"Boy, am I happy you're all right…You *are* all right?"

"Yeah. I'm good."

"Oh, thank God," he sighed. "Let's get you out of there. You must be freezing."

Kinsey nodded. She was a proud, independent teenager, but her Grandpa was exactly what she needed right now.

She carefully released her grip. Bringing her knees to her chest, Kinsey pressed both feet against the door jamb and pushed off, sending herself in the direction of Grandpa. "Where did you get *that*?"

"This old thing?" He patted the hull of his boat. "I was hanging on to a willow across the way and it just floated by. Pretty lucky, huh?"

"Help me up?"

"Sure thing." Grandpa lowered his arm into the water behind Kinsey, scooped her up, and deposited her onto the rowboat's floor beside him. "Let's get to the lab. We can warm up there."

Though they made it to the lab without incident, they couldn't just walk in the front door. Only the top few inches of the door showed above the water's surface. They would have to find another way in.

Kinsey paddled them around the side of the building, stopping as they came to a bank of floor-to-ceiling windows that comprised the lab's back wall.

Grandpa stood up and grabbed the brick opening that surrounded one of the windows. "I'll steady the boat." He nodded in the direction of the oar. "You'll have to do it."

"Okay."

Kinsey rose to her feet and studied the nearest window. Needing to be precise with her effort, Kinsey widened her stance to steady herself. *One, two, three!* She drove the oar through the glass.

With a couple more carefully placed hits, Kinsey cleared the remaining glass from the window's steel frame. Reaching inside the opening, she turned the lock and the spring-loaded window jerked open.

Kinsey pulled herself through the opening and lowered herself onto a metal catwalk. She reached back out the window and shakily ushered Grandpa into the lab.

Thanks to a waterproofing system Grandpa invented a few years back, the entire lab remained bone dry, unlike the rest of town. A square wicker basket, large enough to accommodate one person, sat in the middle of the cobblestone floor. Directly above the basket hovered an inflated gray envelope held motionless by a web of thick ropes attached to the basket at its corners. A work table made from wood and steel butted against the shared wall and acted as a home base to Grandpa's current gadgets.

The ground floor was a mess. Gears, springs, and wires sat in heaps throughout the building. The largest pile stood taller than a horse and spilled across the floor next to a steep metal stairway. A dozen steel steps flanked by an aged brass handrail provided access to the catwalk that circled the workspace below.

After losing her parents the previous year, Kinsey had turned her attention to Grandpa and his gadgets. She always had a natural need to know how everything worked and never hesitated to let Grandpa know. "What are you working on?" or "How does that work?" were Kinsey's go-to phrases. Grandpa never hesitated to answer; he couldn't be more excited to share his gadgets with her. He would explain what this gear did or why that thing turned, and Kinsey hung on his every word. She used parts from Grandpa's castoff pile and tried her own hand at making gadgets. Kinsey was a novice compared to Grandpa but she enjoyed herself nonetheless.

Grandpa was hand-picked by the mayor for, quite possibly, Pinchbeck's most important project. Like clockwork, every year as the seasons changed, the floodwaters would follow. The Wash, the vast peaty swale outside of town, always flooded first. To make matters worse, a large river flowed around Pinchbeck. When the floodwaters of The Wash merged with the river, Pinchbeck never stood a chance. Townspeople were lost, livelihoods were destroyed. Buildings were rebuilt only to be destroyed again the following year. It didn't take long to realize something had to be done.

Grandpa was tasked with inventing a way to divert the floodwaters from Pinchbeck out to the sea.

It took months of planning and research and a handful of failed attempts. However, with Kinsey's help, Grandpa eventually had perfected plans for the Pinchbeck Steam Engine. When built, it would be large enough and strong enough to drain The Wash.

The news of Grandpa's successful plans met with great excitement among the townspeople. Every capable person pitched in to help with the project. Ditches were built to carry water away from Pinchbeck. Pipes were installed beneath the deepest parts of The Wash. An ornate brick building with beautiful stained glass windows was erected to house the project on the outskirts of town. When everything was ready, the steam engine was assembled in place.

The entire town had come out for the unveiling. Grandpa had the distinction of throwing the lever after the mayor gave a short speech. Once engaged, the powerful engine started whirring. And spurting. And churning. Water erupted from the pipes with great force, landing in two separate ditches on either side of the building. One ditch skirted the town to the north, the other to the south. They eventually came together a few miles outside of town where they joined the river, which carried the water out to sea. It was a resounding success, and Grandpa had become a hero overnight.

Kinsey fastened the top buckle of her tweed waistcoat. "Oh, that's *so* much better."

It wasn't uncommon for Kinsey to nod off at the lab when Grandpa was working long nights. She learned early on to keep a change of clothing around for the following morning. At the moment, her foresight proved to be really handy. Under the waistcoat, Kinsey sported a white, long-sleeved linen blouse. Kinsey tucked the excess fabric into the waistband of her black and brown checkered trousers. Kinsey snugged an engineer's cap over her damp, chestnut locks.

Grandpa paced along the catwalk, his arms tightly crossed in front of him.

"Why on Earth did the town flood? The engine has been working without issue for months now." He shook his head in disgust. "I can't for the life of me figure out how this could happen."

"I'm sure we can figure it out."

A voice called from outside the lab's open window. "Hello? Is anyone inside?"

"Stay there, Grandpa." Kinsey pressed her palm against his sternum. "I'll see who it is." She dashed over to the opening and craned her neck high enough to see outside.

"Hello?" The voice repeated, now closer to the building.

Kinsey could just barely make out the silhouette of a small dinghy with two passengers.

"Kinsey? Is that you?"

Unsure of the voice, Kinsey stayed quiet.

"It's the mayor. I have the cobbler with me."

Kinsey leaned out the window and waved the men over. "What do you need?"

"I was surveying the damage, and I ran into Henry. His boat floated away in the flood so he asked for a ride to look in on his shop," the mayor replied. "Is your grandfather with you? We *need* to talk."

"Yes, sir. Grandpa's here. You'll have to come through the window though. It's the only way in."

The two men tied their dinghy to a downspout on the side of the building and crawled through the open window.

"Hey, is *that* my canoe?" asked Henry.

"Never mind that right now. We've got a *really* big problem," the mayor said. "The whole town is underwater, Chester. You assured me this wouldn't happen!"

Chester? It didn't immediately register that the mayor was speaking to her grandfather. His name was Chester, but to her, he was always just Grandpa. Apparently, it didn't register with him either, because all he did was gaze off into space.

"Grandpa?" Asked Kinsey.

He startled, shifting his attention to her. "Huh?…Sorry. What?"

"Chester!" The mayor interrupted. "This is *your* doing. You need to fix this."

"I can fix it!" blurted Kinsey.

"Maybe. But, this is my mess. I'll head to the engine building straight away."

"But, Grandpa! You barely made it from our house to the lab. The engine is on the edge of the bog. You'll never make it. It's the whole way across the river."

Grandpa reluctantly nodded in agreement. "Yeah, you might be right. It's probably too hard for a fossil like me. I guess you'll have to give it a shot."

"Very well then," said the mayor. "It's settled."

"Do you have boots?" Henry asked, pointing at Kinsey's stockings.

Kinsey shook her head.

"Well, we can't let you go like that. Give me a second to run next door. I'll find you something to wear." And before Kinsey could thank him, he disappeared through the window.

As promised, a couple of minutes later Henry crawled back inside with a new pair of leather boots. "Will these work?"

"Oh my gosh! Thank you so much!" Kinsey grinned. She eagerly pulled them on and tied the laces snugly across her shins.

"How do they feel?" Henry asked, a true cobbler.

"Like a glove," she replied as she stood up. "They are perfect!"

Henry grinned. "Well, it's the least I can do. After all, you're gonna save our town."

She scampered down the stairs, Grandpa in step behind her. "I need tools. Can I use your toolbox?"

"It'll be too heavy. But you can take this."

Grandpa handed her a large, well-loved leather tool belt. Wrenches, screwdrivers, and a hammer were affixed to the belt by small leather straps. A copper snap on the end of each strap held the tools in place. A monogrammed pouch attached to the center of the belt held various useful items.

"Wow, Grandpa. Thank you!"

She studied the belt as she rotated it in her hands. It was quite large compared to her. Set to the smallest size it would never fit around her waist. Kinsey slung the tool belt over her head. One end of the belt came to rest on her shoulder, the other on her opposite hip like a bandolier.

"Hmmm." She smiled. "This might just work."

Kinsey and Grandpa scurried up the stairs once more.

"All set." Kinsey hugged Grandpa, crawled through the open window, and stepped carefully into the awaiting rowboat.

"You've got this," assured Grandpa. He untied the vessel and pushed it away from the building.

Kinsey had barely made it past the corner of the lab when she heard voices from overhead. Townspeople were gathered on the rooftops, their eyes trained on the sky above the river at the edge of town.

Kinsey paddled a few blocks down what normally would have been High Street and into Pinchbeck's Town Square. The size of a large city block, Town Square was surrounded by two-story buildings on three sides. The remaining side was unimpeded by structures and provided a beautiful view of the river.

A blinding spotlight shot down from the sky and enveloped Kinsey.

A gruff voice filled the sky. "What do you think you're doing?"

Everything went quiet as the townspeople looked on in astonishment.

The only sound was the subtle sloshing of water as it slapped against the rowboat's hull.

Kinsey raised a hand to shield her eyes. "Who are you? What...what do you want?"

"I'll ask the questions if you don't mind," bellowed the voice.

As her eyes adjusted to the spotlight, Kinsey could make out the silhouette of an airship hovering over the river. She squinted, studying the airship closer. There weren't any obvious signs of life on board. However, a small flock of mallards flanked the aircraft.

The airship's captain hesitated momentarily. Pondering his next move, he pensively ran his boney fingers through a long, stringy beard that dragged along the deck behind him.

"I hope you're not planning to fix the engine," the voice growled.

"Y—yes," Kinsey responded timidly. "Our...our town is in ruins."

"Don't waste your time, little one. I destroyed it!"

The townspeople gasped in disbelief.

"Why would you do that?" One of the townspeople cried.

The airship's captain walked to the deck's railing, finally coming into view of the terrified onlookers.

"I am Fenn, ruler of The Wash! I control it! Everything from here to the sea. And, if I want The Wash to flood, I make it flood. *I* say what happens around here. Not you!"

"But...this is where we *live*," Kinsey replied. "Pinchbeck is our home."

"That is of no consequence to me. This is how it's always been. And this is how it will continue to be. You can try to fix the engine if you want to. But, I am warning you!" He threatened. "If anyone goes near that engine, it'll be the end of you all!"

The spotlight shut off. The airship shuddered forward as the bow rotated away from the stunned crowd.

Kinsey wanted to respond but it was too late. Fenn, his airship, and the flock of mallards disappeared into the night.

A few minutes later, Kinsey pulled herself through the lab's open window. "It's... it's Fenn. He sabotaged the engine!"

"I heard. But, it's our only chance. If we don't get the engine up and running, Pinchbeck will continue to flood every year. So...kiddo, I think you at least need to try."

"But, he has seen me. I'm sure he'll be watching." Kinsey said. "He won't let me get anywhere near that engine."

"So, don't take the boat."

"It's not as if I can *walk*!"

"Well..." Grandpa hesitated. "You can take my balloon!"

"Really? Are you sure?"

"I think, at this point, it's your only option." Grandpa hurried down to his work table and grabbed a copper gas lamp and a pair of navigator's goggles. "You'll need these."

Kinsey pulled the goggles over her head, leaving them to dangle around her neck. Kinsey crawled into the basket and he handed her the lamp.

Grandpa hobbled over to the straps that dangled from the ceiling above the balloon. One at a time, he pulled them. The overhead windows glided along their tracks to reveal the crisp, clear night sky. He untied a series of ropes that secured the balloon in place.

Grandpa turned toward Kinsey. "Well, I guess I'm ready when you are."

"Here goes nothing." Kinsey ignited the overhead burner. With a loud *whoosh*, fiery air started to fill the envelope and the balloon crept skyward.

Kinsey kept her eyes trained on the altimeter. When she arrived at a safe elevation, she cut off the gas to the burner and an eerie quiet filled the space around her. Wind gusts would interrupt the silence every so often, but they didn't make her feel less lonely. Minutes slowly ticked by. This was not going to be a speedy endeavor. so she lowered herself to the floor of the basket.

Without warning, dense, thick fog oozed through the walls of the basket. Kinsey sprang to her feet. The fog grew thicker by the second. Kinsey secured the goggles over her eyes. She snatched the gas lamp with one hand and reached into the leather pouch of the tool belt bandolier with the other.

Kinsey pulled out a mechanical lighter and pushed the lighter's button rapidly. *Click, click, click.* A small orange flame shot from the end of the lighter. She drove the flame into the open door and the lamp glowed, illuminating the basket around her. Kinsey spun around with the lamp at an arm's length. Though aided by the goggles and gas lamp, she couldn't see more than a few feet in any direction.

The risk of crashing in these conditions was far too great, so Kinsey decided she would have to ground the balloon. She carefully set the gas lamp on the floor of the basket, determined not to disturb its flame.

Kinsey reached for the valve cord that hung down through the center of the balloon but it was out of reach. She followed the cord into the envelope with her eyes as the problem quickly revealed itself. The cord was hung up on one of the burner's supports but would be easy to dislodge if she could reach it. Kinsey rose to her tip-toes but was still a few inches too short.

Kinsey grabbed hold of one of the ropes that connected the balloon to the basket's corners. She gave it a firm tug. It hardly moved.

Bringing one of her feet above her waist, Kinsey pressed it against the basket's rim. Pushing off from the floor with her other foot, she wrapped her arms securely around the rope and brought her other foot up to steady herself on the rim. The valve cord hung loosely, now just a few inches from her. Kinsey reached out and grabbed the cord, pulling it toward her body. She wrapped the end of the cord around her hand until it was taut and leaped to the floor, yanking the cord. The parachute valve on the top of the balloon flew open. *Whoosh!* Hot air erupted through the open valve. The balloon shuttered, and Kinsey crumpled to the floor as it plummeted towards the Earth.

She stared at the altimeter and watched helplessly as the device's hands raced around the dial.

60 meters, 50 meters, 40 meters…

Kinsey scrambled to her feet and pulled the lever on the burner. A burst of roaring fire shot into the balloon causing it to abruptly halt mid-air. Kinsey found herself on the floor of the basket again.

30 meters.

Pulling herself to her feet, Kinsey adjusted the burner's flame and the balloon began to fall again at a much slower rate.

20 meters.

15 meters.

She had no idea where she would be when she finally made ground. But whatever the answer, she'd have it soon.

10 meters.

5 meters.

The basket met the Earth with a jolting splash immediately followed by a dull thud. The envelope quietly deflated, blanketing the basket beneath it. Not interested in an aircraft fire, Kinsey bolted up and quickly shut off the burner. Once again, everything was quiet.

After a long, deep breath, Kinsey examined herself thoroughly. No blood. No broken bones. She was a mess, but she was still alive.

Phwit! The gas lamp's flame sizzled and went out.

Kinsey glanced at the lamp on the floor. Dark, murky water spilled into the basket.

"I need to get out of here."

Kinsey grabbed the deflated envelope that stretched across the basket's opening and pulled the fabric towards herself, searching for an opening. After a short while, fog billowed through a gap between the fabric and the basket. Kinsey dropped the gathered fabric on the floor and retrieved the lamp. She reached over the edge of the basket and dropped the lamp softly on the other side. Kinsey pulled her hips even with the rim of the basket and flung one leg over the side. She rolled her weight towards her dangling leg and fell over the side. It was not a terribly graceful maneuver; however, it was effective. Her feet slammed into the unwelcoming water below. Dark, frigid liquid oozed over the sides of her boots, stopping just below the knees.

As quickly as it had appeared, the fog lifted. Kinsey ripped off the goggles and rubbed her eyes vigorously.

Fenn's thundering voice filled the sky around Kinsey. "I warned you!"

She froze.

"I told you not to try to fix the engine!" Fenn disciplined tersely. "Did you think I would not find out?"

"But Pinchbeck?... Our homes?"

"Oh, who cares? Would you *please* quit it with that?"

Kinsey scanned her surroundings, but there was no sign of Fenn.

She stepped away from the downed balloon, struggling against the knee-high muck. A few hundred feet in front of her, a swift current churned through the bog.

Behind her, a knoll peeked out from the marsh. Steep, rocky walls descended from the top of the hill and plunged into the water on all sides. Two majestic willows jutted from the top of the hill on either side of a small wooden gazebo. A stone pathway led from the gazebo to the edge of the knoll before transitioning to a stairway that disappeared into the bog.

Hogback Hill. She knew it quite well. In fact, it was her favorite place to go with Grandpa when they weren't busy at the lab. It made for the perfect lazy picnic getaway. They spent hours feeding the birds and learned everything they could about each other.

"I told you! Everything around here is mine!" Fenn continued.

"You're right!" She yelled, hoping to appease Fenn. "I'm sorry!"

"Do *not* test me! If I catch you again, young lady, I guarantee I will not be so nice."

Once again, everything went quiet.

When she was certain Fenn was gone, Kinsey opened the door to the gas lamp, lit the burner, and secured the lock. She raised the lamp above her head and peered at the knoll.

"If that's Hogback Hill…" She swung that lamp as she pivoted. "And that's the river over there… That means town is that way!"

Her eyes slowly adjusted as she searched the horizon. Eventually, Kinsey could see the light pollution emitted by Pinchbeck's street lamps. Luckily, this meant she only had drifted about a mile outside city limits before crashing. However, it also meant she was on the wrong side of the river. The current was too strong here, but if she could make it to the Old Bridge, she would be close to the engine.

Kinsey slogged through the muck.

She slogged.

And slogged.

The bog was unyielding beneath her feet. Kinsey's muscles ached more with every step. Still, nothing was going to prevent her from getting back to town.

She stopped for a break here or there but never took too long. Everyone was depending on her.

When Kinsey finally crossed into city limits, she was beyond exhausted. It would be so easy to just throw in the towel and make a beeline for the lab. It would be so easy. She was only a few blocks from the Old Bridge but she was *also* only a few blocks from the lab, not to mention a fresh change of clothes. Warm, clean clothes. As tempted as she was, Kinsey knew she couldn't do that. She couldn't let everyone down.

Unbeknownst to Kinsey, she was being watched. Hiding in plain sight, a small flock of mallards scattered about the bog nearby. Their webbed feet dangled like dead weight beneath their bodies, not to disturb the water's surface. Long-stemmed redshanks stood as resolute lookouts throughout The Wash.

Near a small thicket of trees, a single boulder poked above the water's surface. Fenn ducked behind the rock, plotting his next move. He watched Kinsey through a copper spyglass, long ago oxidizing blue-green from use. Moving the spyglass left to right, he carefully followed Kinsey while she negotiated her way to the Old Bridge.

"That little brat. She just won't quit." Fenn grumbled to himself. His knuckles grew white as his bony fingers wrapped tighter around the spyglass. Fenn was livid.

A tiny, timid voice interrupted Fenn. "Can you blame her?"

"Who said that?!" Fenn glowered.

In unison, the redshanks and mallards turned away from Fenn, determined not to make eye contact with the diminutive, hirsute creature. Except for a lone redshank who nervously peered back at Fenn.

"I…I did." The bird muttered cautiously.

"Can I blame her? *Can I blame her?*"

He leaped from his hiding spot and stomped briskly toward the redshank. Stopping just short of the cowering bird, Fenn shook his spyglass violently in its direction. "Of course, I can blame her! She knows what will happen if she crosses me!"

"She's just trying to save her—"

"Quiet!" Fenn's face was crimson. "Your opinion means *nothing* to me!"

Staring down the redshank, Fenn waited as a few uncomfortable moments passed.

"I...I rule The Wash. Everything you see here." He spun around, his arms outstretched, "*Everything* is mine." Fenn paused briefly before continuing, "And...that includes you." His eyes shot back to the redshank. "All of you!"

Not one member of Fenn's audience moved.

"Now, where is our little adventurer?" He whispered to himself as he crawled to the top of the boulder. His tantrum had taken long enough that Kinsey was now just a few paces from the stone embankment of the Old Bridge.

"What do you think you're doing?!" Fenn hollered.

She froze mid-step and slowly pivoted her head, locking eyes on her hairy little adversary for the first time. Fenn crossed his arms firmly in front of his body and arched his back, thrusting his chest outward.

She let out a brief chuckle, stopping immediately once she realized what she had done.

"What is so funny?" chided Fenn.

"I'm so sorry..." Kinsey paused. "You're...you're just so—"

"Small? Tiny? Diminutive?"

"Well, I'm really not trying to offend you, but yes."

"Does it matter? Have you not seen what I can do?"

"I have. And it's quite impressive. You're just not what I expected."

"Go home!" Fenn screamed. "Now!"

"Sir? Mister Fenn?...I *need* to fix the engine. Please, just let me go. Pinchbeck is just a tiny village but The Wash is huge. We don't care what you do with the rest of The Wash, but...our home," she pleaded. "Just please let me go." Kinsey took a small step toward the Old Bridge. Then another.

"Not one more step!"

She didn't stop.

"That is it!" Fenn closed his eyes tightly, raised his arms over his head, and focused on the bog around him. The water started to bubble. Tiny at first, the bubbles grew as Fenn concentrated. Horrified, the mallards and redshanks took to the sky and looked helplessly back at the bog. Fenn thrust his arms toward Kinsey. The bubbling water erupted from the bog, and he hurled forward with a *whoosh*.

Kinsey turned sharply toward the advancing wave. She'd be killed if she didn't find shelter. Her only hope was to reach the bridge.

Constructed of simple stone and mortar, the Old Bridge was hardly an architectural marvel. The bridge did, however, boast shoulder-height stone walls flanking the roadway on either side. At least two feet wide at any given point, the walls stretched the portion of the bridge that spanned the river below.

Kinsey dropped the lamp to her side and trudged through the bog as quickly as she could. Her legs burned from exhaustion as she made her way up the approach to the bridge.

The oncoming wave was almost on top of her as she lunged behind the closest wall of the bridge.

Fenn's rage slammed into the bridge with god-like violence. The crunching clangor reverberated around Kinsey's skull as the wave cascaded over the wall behind her. She shoved her back up against the wall, pulled her knees into her chest, closed her eyes tightly, and cupped her hands over her ears. Kinsey desperately wanted to be anywhere else at the moment, but there was nothing she could do but wait for the assault to be over.

It only took a few seconds for Fenn's wave to destroy the Old Bridge. When the watery onslaught cleared, there were only a few small sections of the wall still standing.

In the distance, the mallards and redshanks scuttled back to the bog. They were immediately gripped by sadness as they inspected the aftermath of Fenn's wrath.

"Where is my nest?" one redshank wailed.

"Where are my eggs?" added another.

"Oh, be quiet!" yelled Fenn.

"But…you destroyed our homes," cried a mallard.

"Don't you get it? None of that matters to me. You can build new nests. You can lay more eggs. That little nuisance *had* to be stopped." A clever smile crept across his face. "And now…she's dead," Fenn bragged.

Fortunately for Kinsey, one surviving section of the wall was the very one she had hidden behind moments earlier. Cautiously rising to her knees, Kinsey assessed herself for any damage. She was drenched, covered in mud, and everything ached. Besides that and a bruised ego, she felt remarkably okay.

More determined than ever, she would fix the engine or die trying. Kinsey stood up, now visible above the broken stone wall.

"Look! She…she's not dead!" shouted redshank.

"She's not?" asked a mallard. The bird located Kinsey by the stone wall. "Oh, good!"

"What?!" Fenn questioned. "This can't be!"

His eyes darted toward where the Old Bridge once stood. "But…There's no way she could have survived that. I killed you!" He shook an angry fist at Kinsey.

Fenn's screams as they hammered throughout Wash as she was readied herself for the task at hand. She untied the gifted boots and tossed them aside. After yanking the stockings from her feet and cinching Grandpa's tool belt tightly around her torso, she sidled cautiously to the edge of the missing bridge and carefully peered at the surging waters below. Retreating from the edge, Kinsey pulled her goggles over her eyes and paused momentarily to find her courage.

"Here goes nothing."

She dashed toward the end of the roadway and plummeted into the raging current. What felt like electric daggers shot throughout her body as the frigid river enveloped her.

Kinsey tried to hold her breath but the numbing shock was too much. She screamed, instantly regretting her decision. Murky water spilled into her open mouth as she instinctually thrashed, searching for the surface. In quick bursts, Kinsey pictured her grandfather. Oh, how devastated he would be if anything ever happened to her.

Realizing this, Kinsey slowly relaxed her limbs and collected herself. After a few moments, Kinsey started to swim.

After a couple more powerful kicks, she peeled through the surface, exhaling forcibly as she met the crisp evening air. She coughed a few times and cleared her throat. Filth poured from her mouth.

"That little brat." Fenn scurried to the top of the boulder. "What does she think she's doing?"

He glared at his foe through the spyglass. "You'll never make it to that engine. There is no way. I won't let you!"

"Wh—why can't you just let her go?" squawked a redshank.

"Yeah. Hasn't she had enough?" begged a mallard.

"Quiet! Not one more peep!" Fenn commanded.

"But…" the mallard replied. "You've flooded *her* town. You destroyed *our* nests. "Don't you think you've proven your point?"

Fenn didn't take his eyes off Kinsey.

He jumped from the boulder, landing in the bog with a splashy thud.

"Hey, little girl," he taunted. "If you make one more move…"

Kinsey leaned her weight forward in the water and began swimming. Her feet fluttered rhythmically below the water and her arms spun powerfully about her shoulders. She was robotic as she glided through the water.

"How dare you! I told you to stop!" Fenn grew more and more incensed with every stroke.

Swimming the river would have challenged anyone on a normal day. Add in the flood water and the feat bordered on impossible. Still, Kinsey pressed on. Her muscles burned, the gelid cold was unforgiving.

"You, stop this instant!" admonished Fenn.

"Please, Mister Fenn…" implored another redshank. "Just let her go."

"That stubborn little madcap has had so many chances to cooperate, and she just won't do it! She brought this on herself." Fenn stomped his foot. "Plus, I don't have to explain myself to *you*! You're just a stupid bird." He pointed a nimble finger at the redshank. "Hell, you're all just stupid birds!" One after the other, Fenn locked eyes with the onlookers.

Once convinced he had made his point, Fenn turned back to his adversary. "Little girl! You give me no choice!"

Two spherical orbs lifted from the bog and stopped just shy of his outstretched hands. He rotated his palms skyward and hurled one of the watery weapons at Kinsey.

Fenn's efforts rocketed through the air, slamming into the river mere inches from Kinsey.

Kinsey stopped swimming and hastily searched for the projectile's source. Fenn was readying another ball of water when she located him.

A second blow crashed into Kinsey's leg. Her knee erupted with pain from the impact but Kinsey would not be deterred.

A few more strokes and Kinsey's foot brushed against a downed tree trunk. She rolled her weight backward, bringing her feet underneath her. The thick, sticky sludge of the swampy floor oozed between her toes. Normally, Kinsey would be disgusted. Not this time. Dry land had to be close by. Waist-deep water rippled around Kinsey as she methodically trudged through the bog. Kinsey was so excited to see land, she forgot she was being hunted.

The marsh exploded a few feet ahead of her. Soggy debris knocked her from her feet.

"Bloody hell!" She sprang up and started to run.

Fenn's final effort spun Kinsey like a top as it ripped across her face. Everything went dark; her limp body collapsed into the shallow water and disappeared beneath the surface.

"Ha! Gotcha!" Fenn bragged.

A nervous redshank turned abruptly towards Fenn, "Is…is she dead? Did you kill her?"

"What do *you* think?" Fenn snapped.

He beamed proudly at his unconscious enemy. "If she's not dead yet, she will be soon!"

"But, she can't die! She just wants to save her home!" cried a mallard.

"Oh, for shame. The poor little failure let everybody down," Fenn teased. "Boo-hoo."

"But—"

"Oh, will you just shut up?!" Fenn interrupted. "All I ever hear from you birds is—"

"No!" the mallard retorted. "I will not shut up. This is *wrong*, Fenn. You might rule The Wash but you don't have to be so cruel. We have followed your lead for too long now…"

"What are you implying?"

The mallard was so incensed that its feathers now stood on end. "I'm not implying anything. I'm flat-out telling you. Enough is enough. We are not going to just sit here and watch you kill her. She hasn't done anything to you or any of us."

The mallard trembled as it glared at Fenn.

Fenn stared back.

No one moved.

Finally, a redshank broke the silent stand-off. "Come on, guys. We're not gonna let this angry toddler push us around anymore! He has destroyed our homes. Let's help her save hers."

All at once, the redshanks and mallards took to the air.

"Come back here!" He shook an angry fist at the betrayers. Small splashes scattered the bog around Kinsey's lifeless body. Redshanks landed first as they encircled Kinsey. They stabbed their long, straw-like legs into the muddy soil and held Kinsey in place as the mallards joined the rescue. The ducks dove into the water beneath Kinsey. Creating a makeshift raft with their bodies, the mallards pushed her to the surface. Thick, murky liquid spilled from Kinsey's mouth.

A redshank looked on nervously. "Is she…?"

One of the redshanks near Kinsey's head leaned down to her nose and listened intently. Kinsey's chest rose slightly as a shallow breath escaped her lips.

"She's alive!" squawked the excited bird. "Let's get her to land!"

In no time, they arrived at the nearby berm and rolled Kinsey on her side.

She sputtered, letting out a loud, garbled gasp. Fresh, crisp air shot into her lungs and she jerked forward, sitting up. Kinsey breathed deeply. In and out, in and out. Fenn hollered, shaking his head from side to side. "How can this be?"

He slowly surveyed The Wash, the place he had ruled over for so long. Great sadness washed over him as he realized he had lost the power he once had. The redshanks and mallards no longer listened to him. He couldn't outwit a teenage girl. Nor could he best her with the waters he controlled. This was the moment Fenn had feared more than any other.

He scuttled up the side of the boulder.

"Fine, little one…" Fenn raised one arm, bringing his wrist above his shoulder. He pressed his thumb to his middle finger. "I know when I've been beaten!"

Kinsey and her rescuers turned sharply toward the angry little man.

Fenn snapped his fingers.

Poof! A fine mist fell softly into the bog below the boulder.

Just like that, Fenn was gone.

Kinsey couldn't believe her eyes.

Her feathered companions began wailing and cooing in some kind of avian celebration.

Brushing herself off, Kinsey stumbled to her feet. She clutched Grandpa's tool belt, still wrapped around her torso.

She popped open the monogrammed pouch. To her astonishment, everything was right where she had left it.

Kinsey ran to the top of the berm. She had never been happier to see a dusty road in her life.

She turned back to the redshanks and mallards at the water's edge and waved.

"Thank you so much for your help! You saved my life!"

With Fenn no longer standing in her way, Kinsey was able to get to the engine in no time. Once inside the engine building, she immediately got to work. A few hundred screw-turns and a couple of replacement parts later, Kinsey pulled the lever to engage the engine. Just like when Grandpa had pulled the lever at the engine's unveiling, it whirred and spurted and churned. Water shot into the drainage ditches. It wouldn't take too long before the Pinchbeck would be back to normal.

Something South of Human

By Thomas Gregory

Ahead of me, a gang of monkeyboys waited in line, construction types with an affinity for zipping simian DNA into themselves, fresh off the job site, their neanderthal brows creasing as they laughed at a dirty joke. I watched as they entered their individual gene pods and received all-in-one unzips, injecting them with the genetic instructions for pure human and the activating catalyst in a single treatment. One by one, the construction workers went in part ape and came out moments later pure human beings, barring any unintended genetic remnants. That was the risk you ran by zipping on a regular basis.

Most people were weekenders. Put on some dolphin DNA for a day at the beach or dress up in feathers and scales for a night out. Then there were the workaday types, guys like the monkeyboys who regularly zipped for their jobs. Like a miner chancing black lung, they got paid for putting their genetic material at risk. A lifetime of daily zipping, and you were bound to see some side effects. If they were lucky, they might end up with a little extra body hair and a banana fetish by the time they reached fifty. There was an equal chance they'd end up with increased aggression, territorial behavior, or permanent physical deformity.

Then there were the addicts. A zip addict could come from either group. They started out as weekenders or daily zippers who decided they liked who they were zipped more than when they were pure humans.

So they just kept zipping.

And zipping.

And zipping.

Eventually their DNA was so scrambled even the best gene pod couldn't bring them back. They were left as sterile chimera, second class citizens stuck with the mark of their shame. Outcast.

I had more in common with the weekenders than I did the construction guys ahead of me. I only zipped when the job required it to even the playing field. I hated zipping, hated the way it made me feel after. I had to keep away from people for a clean week afterwards. But I wasn't afraid to use it as a tool.

My turn came up, and I entered the pod. It smelled of the sterilant they automatically sprayed between customers. Somewhere, a Ziroco computer scanned my ear tag and registered the shiny new private contractor clearance they'd furnished me with when I signed on to the job. Your average zipper only had access to traits that were generally accepted as "safe," ones you'd have a hard time using to weaponize yourself. That didn't mean the genetic traits didn't exist if you could crack a gene pod control system or, like me, you had special Z/C access.

I already had an idea of what I'd need to work, but when the gene catalog came on the screen, I found myself overwhelmed by the selection I'd been given. Ziroco must have wanted their property back pretty badly to open this many doors. I picked out some traits I'd used before, tiger eyes for intimidation and night vision, scent receptors from a black bear, and bioluminescence from a lanternfish. Then I added on a few extras I wanted to try from the wider catalog. Rhino hide. Ampullae of Lorenzini from a great white. Retractable claws from a caracal. A few other things that I wanted in my toolkit just to have them. The rhino, luminescence, and one or two of the extras I had separate catalysts run for. The rest was put into an all-in-one. The spinal arm unfurled from the top of the pod, and I stepped back, snugging it against my back. The moment the surgical steel arm was properly positioned, I was rewarded with a dozen fine needle pricks coupled with a low voltage shock of electricity that ran from needle to needle all the way up to my neck.

When the machine had finished, the arm retreated into the ceiling, and it spit two small catalyst beads into a slot beneath the gene catalog screen. They looked like two fluid filled Jujubes with thumbtacks glued to one end, red for the rhino hide, green for the rest of the dormant DNA.

I exited the pod, tiger-eyed and ready to work. Ziroco had already given me a lead on their property. Bollard Moreo. Bolly. He was a fence and a go-between for hire who made money off of his reputation for professional neutrality. I already knew where he lived. If I didn't know how this business works, I'd have called it easy money.

Bolly Moreo's apartment had originally been tenement housing way back. At some point, gentrification had taken hold, and it had gone from tenement to mid-priced condominiums. Now it looked to be on a slow, inevitable slide back to its roots. But it wasn't there yet. I knocked on Bolly's door, halfway up the building. I'd cased the outside briefly before I came in. Mildly stupid setup. A difficult escape going from balcony to balcony and no fire escape, but not impossible. A young woman opened the door. She was slight to the point of twigishness, her straight brown hair fell to her waist and freckles dotted one side of her nose.

"Hello."

"I'm looking for Bollard. I'm a work acquaintance?"

She closed the door and undid the chain, then opened it again. "Come in."

The apartment had been done up in the kind of 70s retro décor that had gotten fashionable in the last few years. It reminded me of the set from *Good Times*. The woman went to get Bolly. While she was out of the room, I looked at one of the pictures on the sideboard, a selfie she'd printed out, Bolly's arm wrapped around her shoulder, his goat-like face in a wide grin, mountains in the background. Funny, I never expected him to have an old lady.

A bear has better scent receptors than any other mammal on Earth. I could smell the gun oil well before she came back with the shotgun, already rolling forward before the blast, swiping it from her hands and jamming it into her shoulder. I thought I felt bone crack, but I wasn't sure. Either way, it had to be painful, even before I knocked her legs out from under her and she landed on it. I tossed the gun away and pinned her by the wounded shoulder.

"Goddamn contractor shit tick," she spat, gritting her teeth. "You're a parasite, you know that?"

"Where's Bolly?"

"Bollard's not for sale."

"Bollard's always been for sale." I let the claws show on the hand that wasn't busy pinning her down.

"He's just trying to help."

"Lady, I don't care. I'm just here to get back what's not his."

"It's not the Z/C's either."

"Look, Bolly knows how things work. Sometimes you get caught. We're just two guys working different sides of the same line. Tell me where he is so we can all go home safe, himself included."

She laughed and spat at me.

"You might as well just keep hitting because I'm not telling you. At least you'll get to feel like a big man."

I released Bolly's old lady and stood as she tried to prop herself up on one elbow.

"I'll tell him you're looking for him!" she yelled as I walked out of the apartment, leaving the door open for someone to find her.

Down on the street, I began to shake, chills taking over. Like I said, I don't like how I am when I'm zipping. I walked down the street to the hourly to rent a room and a cold shower. A girl with eyes like a Siamese asked if I wanted a good time; she had a room all picked out. I told her all the good times were gone. This was what's left.

Up in my rented room, I stood in the shower and thought about my next move. I'd failed to give Bolly enough credit for being prepared. Chances were his old lady was already on her way to contacting him, but I was in no mood to tangle with her again. I needed to explore alternative avenues. I needed to talk to Siouxsie Medusa.

She was finishing the last part of her set when I walked into the Fistful of Eights, already naked except for the porcelain doll's mask that was her trademark. No one knew what she really looked like under the mask except for her eyes, green and serpentine. There were plenty of theories, though, in circles on both sides of the line, that she was a chimera, that she had serious scarring from early zipping technology. Like Bolly, she worked both sides, but where he trucked in neutrality, Siouxsie was an information broker.

I went to the men's room while she finished dancing to avoid having to buy a drink I didn't want. It smelled of cherry urinal cake and misplaced want. The ice in the urinal crackled as I emptied my bladder. She was waiting for me when I came back out, dressed in a silk, cherry blossom-print robe.

"James."

"Su."

"Business or pleasure?"

I narrowed my eyes at her. In all the years I'd used her as a source, I had never stayed to see her dance.

"Business, then." She smiled behind the mask. Probably.

A man will tell a sex worker more than he will his bartender, much less his priest, and they don't have the ennui of the former or the imperative towards secrecy of the latter. That and a talent for sorting the wheat from the chaff and knowing who'd be interested was what made Siouxsie such a valuable and successful asset.

"I'm looking for someone telling against a take from Ziroco. Bolly was the handler, but he's gone to ground."

Siouxsie stared at me for a moment through the mask, not saying anything, then shook her head. "Rector. In all the years I've known you, have I ever given you free advice?"

"Not to my knowledge, no."

"Then take it as a mark of how serious I am about this that I'm saying it without the upfront. Let this one go. Square it with Z-co however you do that. Give them their money back. With interest if you have to, whatever. But don't follow this to where it ends. You won't like where it puts you."

"Those aren't the kind of people you square with, you know that. So be elaborative." I slid an electronic envelope, one that would credit a not insignificant sum into whatever account Siouxsie chose across the table. She stared at it for a moment.

"That gray hat of yours is going to start looking real black if you don't take my advice. If you want more than that, you'll have to ask someone else. Maybe ask the Z/C who stole their property in the first place. Bolly's just the middleman; that's all he's ever done."

"They were button-lipped about it. Too much proprietary information involved. I'm just doing the hunting. Pickup's on them."

"Then I guess they're not really that attached to what's theirs after all." Siouxsie stood, tightening her robe around herself. "See you around, cowboy."

So that was me, out of leads and out of ideas. I pocketed the e-velope still sitting on the table and made for the outside world. You know that old Chandler trope that says "when in doubt, a man walks in with a gun?" Well whoever'd been scripting my life of late must have been bereft because I had three waiting for me in the alley outside, all of them mandarin collared, Aryan, wearing Society for the Human Species pins. Body purists. Just what this job needed. A metal lump pressed in my back.

"Move. There's a van down the block."

"Yeah, yeah, not my first time having a gun in my back." I suddenly wished I'd put that rhino trait in the all-in-one instead of saving it for later. Next time.

The S.H.S. trio marched me toward a catering truck a few doors down from the Eights, the engine already running. Behind me, I heard the stage door open and the quick *zik-zik* of very illegal ribocidal rounds headed in our direction. The S.H.S. heavy at my back cried out as his gun arm withered and decayed, the ribocide starting a fire in his cells, breaking them down at a genetic level.

The cassowary, a flightless bird found in Australia and New Guinea, grows a rigid casque from its bill to the top of its skull, used, among other things, for battering its way through the dense underbrush. On a human, it's not hard to conceal beneath a knit cap, and taking a shot from one is like getting hit in the face by a bowling ball wearing a steel helmet. I took my shot and whipped the street-side muscle around, cracking my skull against the bridge of his nose and trusting that the continued fire from the alley would keep the other two occupied. The heavy howled, clutching his face. The smell of blood filled my nostrils, overwhelming my senses for a moment, long enough for the heavy to slide a knife from somewhere and come at me again, hate outweighing pain.

"Animal filth!"

The *psst* of gas said he'd released a smart viral cartridge programmed to do who knew what to anyone he drove the blade into. I didn't have the patience to dance. The moment he came in to attack instead of backing away I moved to close the gap and the claws came out, one set into the tendons of the arm, and the other across the right side of the face. This time the heavy went down. I moved to break for the street but 30,000 volts from another body purist in the van had other ideas. I went down on the dirty pavement, right next to the bloody S.H.S. creep, watching Siouxsie weave her way down the alley still laying down fire as I blacked out.

Gene dreams filled my aching head. One of the forest reclamation states, fern-ridden, dense, and damp, and hot. The vicious, uncaring web of predator and prey, and something bigger, darker than me, breathing, making me, making the predator fear, running away into the safe embrace of shadow. *Run, little hunter, always something bigger and meaner and sharper than you, something hungry, so hungry.* Burrowing down, belly still empty, as far and as fast as I could get before the thing clutched at my hind legs, dragging me back, back, closing my dreamer's eyes against the light.

I'd been stripped of my jacket, along with the catalyst beads in the pockets. Likewise, my hands had been taped together, fingers and all. They'd anticipated the caracal trait I'd loaded. The S.H.S. had stuck me in a closet somewhere. Not deep enough to stretch my legs completely. Crawlspace hatch on the ceiling too high to reach. Boots still on. Legs similarly taped together. My chest ached. The heavy with the knife hadn't managed to stab me cleanly, but the dried blood and the tear in my shirt said he'd scratched me at least, and that was enough for whatever smart viral load the blade had been dosed with to get to work. The wound already looked puckered and angry. Likely a fast-acting form of rabies+ based on the design of the knife. Not cheap, but not hard to get hold of on the East Asian surplus market. The average rabies virus has an incubation period of at least a month in human beings. Weaponized rabies+ caused symptoms within hours and death within a day or two.

When trapped in a strange and enclosed location it helps to have a sixth sense available, and I cannot stress enough that one should make use of it. Case in point, ampullae of Lorenzini found in several sharks and eels gives a sensory input based on prey's electromagnetic fields. As mediums go, water gives it a wider range, but it's not entirely useless on land. Three warm bodies outside the door. Two standing, one curled up on what I expected was a bed. I wasn't alone in my situation. They'd grabbed someone else. I hoped to hell it wasn't Siouxsie. Hot adrenaline surged, urging me to break out quick-time, and I had to force myself to breathe before the hormones loaded with the DNA zipped into my body got out of hand.

Breathe. Plan. Act.

A cranial ridge isn't the only thing the cassowary has going for it. They're better known for the razor sharp talons on their feet that are more than capable of killing, and certainly capable of cutting through the tape currently binding my hands with ease. There's a reason I keep a set of boots a size or two larger for work. Sometimes you've just got to account for extra parts when you're going to hack your own DNA. Off went the boots with no small amount of effort. The two bodies on their feet outside were too busy shaking down the third to hear my movements.

"I am going to ask you a series of questions, if I may? I would very much like it if you answered them. If I am pleased with your answers, we'll put you back where we found you, is that understood? Good. Now, where is the sample?" The response was indistinct, but the voice was definitely feminine. "Where is Mr. Moreo?" The body on the right was leading the questions; the one on the left doing the manhandling.

"Call Mr. Moreo." The questioner threw something small with its own electromagnetic field at the figure on the bed. They were on to Bolly just like me. The gene-purists and I were after the same package, only they had a near religious fervor about it, and that will trump money as a driving force every time. It will also make you sloppy.

The tape around my wrists and legs was off by the time I finished the assessment.

Two ways to leave, up or out. Up or out.

Up, then.

I felt the wrong step as I made it even as the ceiling beam creaked. Everything below stopped.

Down and out.

My mother was a dance teacher. I can still hear her chastising her students for not pointing their feet. Didn't take much to terrify those eight-year-olds. She was so disappointed I was built more like my father than her. If she could see me now.

Down and out, straight through the ceiling, cassowary talons plunging into the muscle's neck, caracal nails digging into his scalp as I pulled him down, taking no small amount of flesh off with me. Bandages across his cheek and nose from where I'd gotten him earlier on the street. Bad day. I felt the prisoner lash out at the questioner and kick again, cracking bone. My bear nose made everything smell of blood again, coupled with sweat and the muscle's soiled pants.

"You've got to be shitting me."

Bolly's old lady weighed how much she wanted to get away against how much she wanted to go at me with the taser she'd grabbed off the floor. Part of me wished it actually had been Siouxsie they'd grabbed. She disappeared back over the bed, and a moment later, after kicking the questioner again, tossed my jacket at me.

"Cover up. That's a lot of blood."

"What's your name?" I asked, following her out of the bedroom.

"Von."

"You can fight?" I eyed her thin frame.

"Worked for a corporate security corps for seven years before someone infected me with nutrient blockers. Yeah, I can fight, shit tick."

"I meant right now."

"Shoulder's still tweaked. Thanks for that."

"I'll be sure to let you shoot me next time."

"Yeah, good thing you don't throw down as hard as you think you do." I edged to one of the papered over windows, peeling back the covering. "You know where we are?"

Outside, a planned neighborhood that would never leave the construction phase, skeletons of buildings standing like tombstones to the failed development syndicate as far as the eye could see.

"Marshall's Grove, I think. Place is littered with dead subs. Nobody around. Makes sense. The van?"

"Can't see it. Driveway must be on the other side."

"Right. Can't say it's been good to see you again." Von made to leave me behind.

"Where's Bolly?"

"Don't start."

"Von. These people will kill him. I won't. Now we've got a better chance to protect him together." Her finger went to the stun gun's trigger as she again considered shooting me. "What the hell did he come into that the Z/C and S.H.S. are both after him?"

"Her name…is Zillah."

"Are you telling me Bolly kidnapped someone?"

"No. Yes. Sort of. A friend of Bolly's works for the Z/C. He broke her out, but things got too hot, so he handed her off to Bolly before they took him out."

"What's so special about this girl?"

"She's a chimera."

"So what?" Behind us the questioner crawled out of the bedroom and down the hall towards us. Von ignored his whimpers for help, pointed the stun gun at him, and fired.

"She was born that way."

"Bullshit."

"You think the Z/C and these S. H. S. jerk-offs are after Bolly for money? Just how long have you been doing this recovery gig? Shit."

"What?"

"Keys." Von stalked back down the hall. She zapped the questioner again, putting a boot to him for good measure before prying the van keys out of his pocket.

"These assholes want Zillah so they can prove to the world that zipping is dangerous to the human species, that it's changing us, and that we need to stop using the technology or we're screwed. Z/C needs her so they can keep that quiet."

"And Bolly was helping keep her from both of them."

"Yup."

I felt around the pockets of my jacket for the catalysts once we got in the van. I pressed the rhino hide load against my arm and sat back waiting for the change to come while Von climbed behind the wheel. My head hurt, either from hitting the pavement outside the Eights or whatever my human scratching post had put in me.

"So where are they?"

"I don't know. I wish I did so I could warn them, but we agreed it would be safer if Bolly didn't tell me until they were already out of town." Von jerked the van down the driveway and into the empty street. "If you were trying to smuggle the world's most valuable chimera out from under Ziroco's nose where would you go?"

"Me? I'd make a deal with the devil."

The thing about becoming a chimera is that the marks it leaves don't always let you persist in everyday society. Sometimes you just stand out too much. Sometimes your needs, whatever they may be, are too much for the rest of the world to be bothered with. Sometimes the panicked attempts to stop the genetic damage that's already been done leaves you worse off than before. For these castoffs and dropouts of the world there was Malphas Killdevil and the Enclave. Killdevil had been where they had been, suffered as they had suffered, and had opened his arms to the unwanted, the outcast, the all too alien. Of course, the jury was out as to whether it was out of some sense of solidarity or purely self interest, and a loose connection to old Russian mob-state apparatus didn't help matters. Regardless, for a chimera who found himself in a certain sort of trouble or desperation, Killdevil was a reliable option. I told Von to head to the old Northern Tunnel near Yessler Terrace and closed my eyes.

The Enclave had been built up in the abandoned rail tunnel under downtown, a mile-long stretch that had become their own and that no one had yet been able to dislodge them from. Something that looked like a man-sized tardigrade was posted up in front of a barrel fire outside the boarded tunnel mouth, engaged in shoving fistfuls of peanuts into its snout-like orifice. The grotesque absurdity of its appearance out in the open made the tardigrade feel like a distraction, drawing our attention from a more alarming doorman watching from the wings as we approached.

"Offerings?" blurbled the tardigrade.

"Offerings?"

"Gene material. She's useless." He gestured to Von. "But you maybe got something." The tardigrade slurched close and started going through my pockets with several appendages at once until it found my last catalyst bead. "This'll do," it snorted, hiding the bead in its fleshy rolls. "Devil's in the caboose."

I don't know why I expected a shantytown beyond the tunnel doors. Killdevil's underground Island of Misfit Toys was more like a frontier settlement built into the sides of the tunnel. Desperation had given birth to a half-semblance of life, and Killdevil and his people had made the most of it. Heads turned as we passed, headed for the tunnel center where the back half of a commuter train had been abandoned, now sitting in the middle of a network of power lines that made it look like a great aluminum serpent caught in a spider's web. The curtains were drawn on all the windows of the caboose, but the lights were on inside. A girl with the legs of a pronghorn and the jeweled wings of a dragonfly leaned over the car's back railing.

"Offering?"

"I left it at the door."

The girl mounted the railing and buzzed down to us, getting up close to my face.

"Door offering gets you in the door. You want to see Killdevil, you bring an offering for him too. Nobody educated you on the importance of gifts?"

I could feel Von getting twitchy behind me.

"I'm looking for Bollard Moreo. He might've had a meeting with Killdevil. This is his wife."

"Wife, no wife, you..."

"Let them in." Killdevil's voice came from behind the curtains of the train car. The pixie-goat took a step back, glaring at Von with eyes like flint as we passed.

The train car had been completely gutted and rebuilt to serve as both throne and war room for the Enclave's lord and master. Its appointments, while not lavish, were ones of taste and refinement among the frontier trappings outside.

Killdevil sat in a plush velvet high-back chair at the opposite end of the car smoking a rotten-smelling Russian cigarette. Smoke wreathed his head as it was expelled from the blowhole between his two spiral addax horns. "Sorry. It's difficult to operate a barter economy when you don't produce anything, so we trade in what's valuable to one another."

"Genetic material."

"Yes. Drink?" Killdevil offered us shot glasses full of something translucent and gray that went down like napalm and tasted vaguely like dirt. "We make it from the mushrooms that grow in the steam tunnels below us." Killdevil finished his own glass. "Let us say, for sake of argument, that Bollard did contact me about something that I would be greatly interested in protecting."

"Let's say that."

Killdevil answered my interruption by standing up from behind the table on six octopodal tentacles and propelling himself across the room at alarming speed. Each of the tentacles ended in a dexterous monkey-like hand, one of which took Von's chin between its thin fingers.

"Why would I give you, a recovery agent of note, the first mote of information about it?"

"I'm his wife," Von replied before I could.

"I don't know you from Eve, my dear."

"I'm done," I said, and it was true. I was done after this, exhausted, and

Killdevil could see it in the redness ringing my eyes, the exhaustion that had set in when we left Marshall's Grove. "I'm out. Z/C gets their money back, and I go away. But I want to see this through, understand?"

The tentacle hand released Von's chin. Another passed his cigarette off and to his lips. The blowhole exhaled smoke again as he weighed us silently.

"Bollard arranged a meeting. He wanted me to help him get the girl out of town, but he never showed. Either he got picked up or he went to ground."

"Ziroco could have called me off if they had him, and S.H.S. wouldn't have bothered picking us up if they didn't think we were on to where he was hiding out."

"So he's still out there somewhere," Killdevil reasoned.

"Maybe. I need to make a phone call."

"Does this look like a service station to you?"

I ignored the jab. "If I can find the girl, can you still get her out of town?"

"Yes." The chimera paused. "Do you know what this child is, Mr. Rector? This," Killdevil gestured, sweeping a hand in front of his body, "says that we can be denied a job or a place to live. It says that we can be beaten by the police without consequence. It says that we don't count as people anymore because we did this to ourselves through our own predilections, our own addictions. But that girl makes us people, instead of just gene-junkies. Instead of something south of human."

"Is there anyone who doesn't want a piece of this poor kid?"

Killdevil puffed again. "There's a service offshoot about 200 feet down. Phone's in there. Don't run up the bill."

I left Von in Killdevil's rail car lounge and hiked farther into the tunnel. In the dim, string lamplight, something dog-headed passed through the shadows. The phone was where Killdevil had said. I placed a call to the Aces and Eights to let Siouxsie know I was ok. After giving me some shit, the bartender finally put her on.

"Siouxsie, it's Rector. I'm alive." Siouxsie was silent on the other end. "I know about the girl. Listen, I'm not going to turn her over to Z/C."

"Bollard's dead."

"What?"

"They found him floating in the sound. Tide brought him back in last night." I wiped my face with the palm of my hand, coming away sticky with sweat.

"How long has he been floating around out there?"

"A few days maybe? My…friend at the coroner's wasn't sure. You should come in. There's more, but I can't give it to you over the phone."

"I'm with Bollard's wife, Von." On the other end of the line, Siouxsie hesitated.

"Bring her with you.

"You sure?"

"Yeah."

Something wasn't right. I didn't need to be zipped to know that.

"All right. I'll see you soon."

"Rector. I'm glad you're ok."

"Yeah. Thanks for the backup."

I hung up and considered my situation as I walked back to Killdevil's train car. If Bollard had been dead all this time, why had Ziroco sent me after him as if he were alive? Why had the S.H.S. asked after him when, between them, they were the most likely to have killed him?

The dog-headed chimera stopped me in my tracks, putting a clawed finger to her lips before pointing at Killdevil's car. I could see someone pressed against the curtains inside. Doghead gestured under the railcar, and I nodded as she shimmied under before making my way to the back end. Cordite drifted on the wind from outside, and the aluminum and steel body of the train car was playing merry hob with my shark-like sixth sense. A moment later someone cut the lights, and the world was suddenly ending as Doghead came up from whatever service hatch was underneath. A muzzle flashed, and Killdevil screamed in pain or rage or both as his pixie winged protection detail gave their unwelcome visitor the bum's rush out to the car's back railing, below which I was waiting. My job had never called for me to play the bogeyman under the bed before, ready to drag someone down by the ankles. First time for everything.

I didn't get my first good look at Killdevil's uninvited guest until I was already on top of him. Damned if that shrivel-armed bastard Siouxsie'd shot hadn't caught up with us. One Arm tried to use the moment of recognition, but this time I was ready for the attempted knifing. The blade tore through my jacket and glanced off my arm as I rolled off him, thankful for the rhino hide this go-round. One Arm fought his way back to his feet, not yet used to righting himself sans the extra limb, and looked for a way out as we squared off again.

"Where's Bollard Moreo?" I threw at him as I started circling, trying to put myself between One Arm and the tunnel entrance. I knew the answer, knew he didn't, and I hoped it would throw him for a moment. Confusion and a sneaking suspicion that he was in over his head crossed his face.

"We don't know!"

Behind One Arm, I could see the tardigrade lying in the doorway.

"So what, you clowns are going to take Ziroco out in the court of public opinion by parading around a gene-twisted little girl? Genie's already out of the bottle. Zipping's the way of the world now."

The twitchy bastard suddenly caught on to what I was doing, swinging wild, trying to keep me at arm's length. One Arm tried to get in close enough to plant the knife in my gut, putting so much focus on doing so he failed to notice Von until she put the gun he'd dropped in the train car to the back of his head and pulled the trigger. He deflated more than fell, somehow looking even more surprised than he had when his arm shriveled away. A black, animal hunger inside me suddenly gave way to nausea.

"Come on," Von said. "We're leaving."

"Oh yes, just leave this here," Killdevil shouted. One of the monkey paws was clutching the shoulder where he'd been hit. "I can promise you, Rector, the girl will be safer with us than anywhere else!"

Von stepped over the tardigrade on her way out of the tunnel. Outside it had started to rain as we trudged back to the van; not yet one of those summer downpours that cleanses everything and makes the world feel clean again. Still too cold.

"What now?" Von asked.

"I don't know," I lied. "When was the last time you saw Bolly?"

"Last week. Tuesday, I think. Christ, I don't even know what day it is anymore."

"He's dead. Bolly's dead."

Von stopped, and I saw her flinch.

"How do you know?"

"That phone call I made to my friend. His body washed up in the sound last night."

"God damnit, Bolly. Why couldn't you just stick to the plan? We take the girl and skip town, the three of us." I don't know why, but something made me reach out to touch her arm. Von shrugged it off. "Someplace you can see the sun. The three of us."

"Come on. I have an idea. We're going to see my friend. Hey." Von looked my way. "I'm going to help you finish this, ok?"

The rabies+ was finally starting to go to my head, but I was still clearer than I expected Von was for the moment. I climbed behind the wheel before she could. She handed me the keys, and I turned the van towards downtown.

By the time we stopped to buy a plastic gas can and a gallon of unleaded, I realized I'd started to feel feverish, staring out the windshield at the rain while Von paid, my throat tight, unsure as to how long I'd felt that way. Twenty minutes later we were headed for the Eights on foot while the van blazed away in an alley behind us as the sun rose over the city.

"You don't look so good," Von said.

I took a look at my reflection in a blacked out window. My eyes had gone from red to dark, almost bruised looking, but the casque kept sweat from pouring down my brow. There was a warm numbness in my legs.

"Knife was dosed. I'll be fine." She could tell I wasn't. "We do this first, then find a medic." Von put an arm around me to keep me from staggering as we walked the last few blocks.

Siouxsie had left the door unlocked for us. Only the purple ambient lighting under the lip of the stage and the red neon dragon curling around the back of the bar were left on to illuminate the room.

"Your big source is a stripper?" Von balked.

"Is that a problem?"

"No. Not what I expected, that's all."

The dressing room was tucked down a short hallway behind the stage, hidden behind the lighted filament curtains the dancers entered and left through, just a waterfall of plastic threads now that it was powered down. The door was protected by a punch code lock, I suspected as much to shield Siouxsie from her black market information clientele as from a lascivious rowdy.

"Siouxsie, it's me. I've got Bollard's wife here with me."

Someone moved inside and disarmed the door. Siouxsie still had her mask on, though she'd traded her robe for street wear, loose hakama trousers and green flight jacket over a dark muscle shirt. She closed the door behind us and sat at a dressing table against the wall. The very illegal ribocide gun was laying in an open drawer on her left as she faced us.

"Is it true? Is Bollard dead?" Von asked.

Siouxsie looked at me, and I nodded. "Tell her what you told me."

"I'm sorry. They found him last night floating in the sound. He got tangled up in a loose garbage patch. He's been dead a few days at least."

"How?"

"I don't know. My friend at the coroner's only had that to give me."

"Well, find out," Von demanded.

Siouxsie stood. "Listen, you, I'm not a goddamned crystal ball." It was hard to tell behind the mask and slit pupils, but it felt like Siouxsie stared straight through her, as though Von wasn't even there, before turning back to the table. I suddenly felt my legs wanting to give out, and had to lean myself against the door to stay upright.

"What were you going to do, you and Bolly?"

"Take the girl. Leave the country. Out of Ziroco's grasp, not that it's your business."

"And you, Rector? Did you mean what you said? About not turning her over?"

"Yes, but it won't matter if we don't know who's got her."

We both went silent. Von's eyes went wide.

"You know where she is, don't you?"

"I know where she is," Siouxsie said quietly. Both she and Von tried to draw down on each other at the same time, Siouxsie going for the drawer and Von reaching for the pistol she'd lifted from the S.H.S. clown at the Enclave.

Von was faster. I was closer. I slashed her hand, and the gun fell. I followed behind, hitting the floor hard, my legs finally deciding they'd had enough. Not to be outdone, Von grabbed at Siouxsie's wrist, pulling her into an arm lock and driving an elbow into her temple, shattering the porcelain mask. That the face beneath turned out to be perfectly human was a surprise I didn't have time for as Von put Siouxsie between us, and I grabbed Von's fallen pistol.

"Just tell me where the girl is," Von ordered. "You go home. I go home. One of us is rich at the end."

"Is that why you killed Bollard?" Siouxsie asked. Her lip had been split by the shattered porcelain, blood mixing with spit as she spoke. "He was going to do the right thing, but he didn't think he could trust you not to sell her back to Ziroco, so he hid her. I guess he was right."

"Bolly and his stupid hustles. We'd both be out if he'd only listened. Especially once the Z/C thought those gene purists were going to buy her if they didn't." Von gave a desperate smile. "Come on, Rector, you and me, we'll get the kid, split the money. Enough sunset for both of us to ride off into if you make it to a hospital in time."

"She's a child," I protested.

"She's a payday."

Siouxsie craned her head to look at Von and spat. Von screamed, releasing her and clawing at her own eyes. Cobra venom. Turned out her eyes weren't the only traited thing about her. Behind me I heard the *zik-zik* of Siouxsie's ribocide gun, in the hands of the doe-eyed adolescent who'd been hiding behind her dressing screen, her skin shifting from the camouflage pigments that had hidden her like a cuttlefish to something resembling baseline human. Her black upturned fox nose, rimmed by red fur twitched as she panted, watching as Von's veins turned black, the ribocidal rounds going to work where she placed them, directly in her heart. I didn't want to know what it felt like, her heart shriveling in her chest. Siouxsie took the gun away and turned Zillah to face me as Von fell.

"You had her the whole time?" I asked.

"When the S.H.S. showed up, I thought they were here for her, not you. Sorry."

I looked at Zillah. "Here I thought she liked me."

"Come on."

"No." I waved Siouxsie off as she tried to haul me off the floor. "Someone's got to clean this up." Reaching into my jacket, I dragged out the electronic envelope, turning my pocket out in the process. "This'll get you started. I'll call Ziroco when you're gone. She killed Bollard." I nodded at Von who was, by now, deceased. "The girl died trying to save him. They'll waste time dragging the sound. You'll have a head start. If you're lucky they'll assume the body washed out to sea, and if I'm lucky they'll waste a bunch of resources saving my ass, better than I'll get at any hospital." Siouxsie looked at the envelope before pocketing it.

"You know that gray hat of yours, Rector? It's looking real white right now."

So that was me. Alone, burning up, and burned out on a strip club floor, watching Siouxsie and the girl walk away, feeling…pretty good about myself actually, at least, for however long I had.

Yeah. Maybe the good times were gone. But what was left, sometimes that wasn't so bad either.

Sacrifice

By Phoebe Darqueling

Northwestern Bulgaria
July 1995

Brian Jeffries checked the knots for the third time. The gnarled, ancient tree would support his weight, but an untidy knot could spell the end to his expedition before it even started. Making all his preparations under the cover of darkness didn't make it any easier. He was a competent enough climber, but the words of Dr. Evans had made him more skittish about making this attempt to rappel down the cliff face than he'd like to admit.

"Don't believe what you see in the movies," Evans had sneered that morning. "Archaeology isn't about swinging around on a whip and outsmarting booby traps. It isn't about glory. It is about patience and diligent study."

The old man had pulled out a fresh pack of cigarettes and knocked it against his shoe-leather hand to settle the tobacco. In truth, he may not have been all that much older than Brian's parents, but years spent baking in Mediterranean sun early on in his career had given him a muddy tan that never changed. That and his general get-off-my-lawn crankiness made it impossible to think of him as anything other than old. But he was a reasonably well-known scholar with a reasonably well-funded project, so when it came to choosing a dissertation advisor, it was a no-brainer for

Brian.

Evans had ripped the Marlboro Silvers open and held them out to his student, but Brian wasn't a smoker. With his cigarette bobbing precariously at the side of his mouth, Evans had continued. "It was hard enough to get this permit. And you think we've got insurance to cover you if fell? Do you think I'd ever be allowed to bring students on a dig again? I'm not risking my reputation, my career, on you and this stupid stunt you want to pull. Get back to work."

Twelve hours later, Brian held his flashlight in his teeth as he adjusted his harness, diligently pulling every strap taut and threading them back through the D-rings so they couldn't come loose. Evans may not have had any faith in him, but Brian knew better. He was careful, meticulous. Okay, sure, rappelling like this should technically only be done with a partner. The professor's lack of vision was forcing him to do without. The hole in the stone above the site had been calling to him all summer, and he'd be damned if he didn't take a look inside before the season ended next week. But that didn't mean he was the idiot his mentor made him out to be. He was probably smarter and more capable than Evans, in fact. The bitter professor was holding him back. The old guard never liked to make room for the new.

Crickets were his only company as Brian flicked off the flashlight and pulled on his gloves. He picked up the coils of rope—one main line, one safety line—and threaded them out behind him as he approached the edge. The few Roman Era walls that were visible on the surface that had brought them to the site in the first place were a rough, dark stone, but the cliff was made up of a milky gray limestone that caught and reflected the moonlight. Of course, making this climb would have been better during the day, but he assured himself it was plenty of light to see by. The top of the cliff had to be at least 80 feet high, and the cave was maybe 30 feet below him. He could have climbed up from the bottom, which would have been safer, but hammering in the stakes would have no doubt roused someone in the camp. This had to be done quick and quiet if it was going to be done it at all.

His eyes needed a minute to adjust to the darkness, and he took that minute to peer down the rock face and plan his route. With the aid of the rappelling ropes, going down would be far simpler than going up, but a whole summer wielding a pickaxe and shovel had made him stronger than he'd ever been before. Evans was right about one thing; real archaeology wasn't anything like the movies and video games he'd grown up with. It was slow, grueling work done by the young while the old sat in the shade and pointed this way and that with a nicotine-stained hand. Lara Croft and Indie had never endured such indignities.

"Now or never," Brian whispered as he turned his back to the abyss.

The weathered stone beneath sneakers was slicker than it looked, but within a few sweaty minutes, he was standing on the lip of the cave. The size and nature of the entrance had been difficult to assess from the ground, but now that he was standing in it, he was more certain than ever that this was no purely natural phenomenon. He ran his palm over the pitted surface of a column carved right into the living rock. At its apex, his fingertips snagged on a triangular corner, though most of the pediment had been worn away by time.

"A temple?" he wondered aloud. "Up here?"

The moonlight only reached a few feet into the cavern, so he wriggled his flashlight free of its holster on his belt. Next time, for there would surely be a next time, he'd make sure to bring a headlamp. At present, he had to settle for the thin ray of light to penetrate the gloom. After tying off his ropes and tugging the harness into a more comfortable position, he set off into the tunnel.

The inside of the temple had fared far better than the outside. The floor had been paved with an intricate mosaic depicting all manner of crops. Porphyry bunches of grapes mingled with vines of malachite and glass. He walked over countless, flat bundles of freshly harvested wheat and intricate stone baskets of fruits and vegetables. The walls were covered with elaborate paintings even grander than the floor. On closer inspection, he could see that they had been done onto plaster. They should have been cracked and decayed at best, or in pieces littering the ground at worst, but their unblemished hues were just as bright as the day they'd first been applied. Terracotta figurines ranging from the size of his pinky to the size of his arm were lined up along the floor and placed in niches carved into the walls as offerings.

The condition of the temple was so pristine that Brian's heart sank. It couldn't be millennia old. Someone had to have done this as an homage to the area's Roman heritage. There's no way it could be authentic. Time would have had to completely stand still within the cavern to preserve things like this. Perhaps it was an abandoned attempt at a tourist trap, though he doubted the average tourist would be keen on the route required to enter the temple.

Despite his misgivings, he stepped back to get a fuller view of the nearest fresco. A shrouded figure stumbled toward the cavern's interior under the violence of an angry mob. Brian recognized the trappings and symbols associated with Jupiter, Juno, and a handful of other deities. Which meant the man they were beating was likely their father, Saturn. As he was famously known to have eaten them, their anger was not unreasonable, but he'd never seen a representation like this before. His expulsion from Mount Olympus was always presented as a clean, orderly affair, not something committed with snarling faces and clubs.

Brian moved on to the next painting. Saturn, his face still obscured by an increasingly ragged cloak, was dragging himself across the countryside. Wheat sprang up from the trail he left in the dirt. In the third painting, a man with two faces, presumably Janus, was helping Saturn to his feet. There had to be at least a dozen of these frescoes detailing the life of the outcast god and his acceptance into the Roman pantheon.

He was so enthralled with the artwork that Brian didn't realize he had reached the end of the tunnel until he knocked into something solid. His flashlight fell from his hand in his shock, and as he moved to retrieve it, something thin caught on his forearm and sliced into his flesh. It was so sharp that he barely registered it, like a razor through tissue. Only the ruby droplets splattering to the ground in the beam of the flashlight told him he'd been cut at all.

He retrieved the light and shined it into the final alcove. For an embarrassing moment, he thought the statue standing there was a living person, and he started to apologize to them for the intrusion before he realized his error. Good thing Evans wasn't there to see him babbling at a stone man.

Though made of painted marble, the amethyst cloak draped around the body of the figure as if made of a heavy velvet. If there had been even a hint of movement in the stale air of the tunnel, Brian would have expected to see it shift in the breeze. Like the paintings, the figure's face was completely hidden by a hood. He peered up under it, and was puzzled to find that the sculpture had no face at all. The rest of the temple was dripping with detail and fine materials, but for some reason the artist had not bothered to finish it. Based on the faceless figure's posture, it was gazing down at what it held in its outstretched hands.

He shifted the light and found the source of his cut. The bronze blade of a hand scythe glinted at him, balanced on the palms of the statue. He had knocked it off kilter, and said a silent prayer of thanks that he hadn't actually sent it hurtling to the stone floor to dent or shatter. It was probably about a foot and a half long, not including the handle.

His slack-jawed awe morphed into a smug grin as he examined the artifact. "Nothing to find here, eh Evans?"

The scholarly part of Brian's brain noted that when artifacts of this type were generally found, they were rusted out chunks of iron. That meant this object, if it was authentic to begin with, was more than likely ritual in nature rather than employed as a proper tool. The inner edge of the curved blade was certainly sharp enough that it could have been used for harvesting, but the outer edge added weight to his theory. From end to end, the blade was covered with evenly spaced grooves, like the markings on a ruler. These tic marks had been inlaid with delicate stone shards of various hues and no wider than the tip of a sharpened pencil. There was an enigmatic, narrow channel below the markings, as if something could be set into it that could slide from end to end, but he saw no indication of what was meant to go there.

Try checking the ground.

He shrugged. It was certainly worth a look. Brian was on his hands and feeling around the feet of the statue several heartbeats before he realized that the thought had not been his own.

He scrambled away, falling onto his back. This time when he shined his flashlight onto the statue, the hooded figure was no longer looking at the scythe, it had turned its hooded face to Brian. The flat, lifeless stone now shifted and changed. One moment, the fine features of a young boy regarded him, only to be replaced by the crinkled visage of an old man the next. It clutched the handle of the scythe in a hand both youthful and ancient at the same time, and it pointed at a place a few feet away from Brian with the other. The statue's mouth never moved, but its next words resonated clearly around Brian's skull.

A little to the left.

Brian could do little more in the next seconds than blink numbly at the figure with the dizzying array of faces. Then, he was on his feet and sprinting for the entryway as fast as his legs would carry him. The figure was either finished talking to him, or the blood that rushed through his ears blotted out its words.

The harness bit into his skin and was likely leaving bruises with every step, but it did nothing to slow him. Brian's hands shook so hard, he was almost unable to clip back in to the waiting safety rope. Blood trickled in rivulets from his stinging wound as he made his hasty ascent. A few minutes later, he was lying on his back in the dry grass at the top of the cliff and gasping for breath.

"Find anything good?"

Brian twisted around to his belly to follow the sound of the voice. Unlike the one he'd just heard within the temple, this one was both familiar and dripping with sarcasm. Evans was seated among the roots of his anchor tree, the dying embers of a cigarette illuminating his face. Based on the number of butts strewn around him, he'd been waiting for quite some time.

"Professor, I—"

"Did you find anything?" he repeated coolly, holding up a canteen.

Brian's limbs were heavy with exertion and fear, and he half walked, half stumbled his way over to his mentor. He took the proffered canteen and took a long pull of tin-flavored water.

Evans stubbed out his cigarette. "You're hurt." Coming from someone else, the words could have been a sign of concern, but when the professor spoke, the subtext had a decided I-told-you-so quality to them.

Brian glanced down at his cut, then splashed it with water. "It looks worse than it is."

The old man arched one of his caterpillar eyebrows. "Well?"

For a moment, Brian was going to let the whole story spill out of him. After all, he'd been right and the professor had been dead wrong. If they could be authenticated, the paintings below their feet alone were worth an entire book. The scythe could be a career-making find. But there was no question; it wouldn't be Brian's career that would be made. It would be Evans's. That's how this worked.

"You were right," Brian lied. He focused on screwing the lid back on the canteen to avoid meeting his supervisor's eye. "It was a natural cave. Nothing in there but an old stork's nest and some very angry bats."

The old man nodded knowingly. "I hate those things. Rats with wings." Evans held out his hand for assistance, and Brian helped him get to his feet. He groaned all the way up. It was only a matter of time before he retired, then the temple and all its wonders could be Brian's. The old man gave his protégé an irksome grin and grunted. "I was wondering what had you so spooked."

The strange voice of the statue echoed in his mind for a moment, and Brian forced himself to chuckle. "Yep. Took me by surprise."

Evans jerked his thumb over his shoulder. "You can get your gear in the morning," he said as he brushed away stray pieces of grass clinging to his pants. "For now, let's get that arm patched up."

Brian nodded and made a noncommittal sound. They didn't speak for the ten-minute walk back to camp. For his part, Brian was too caught up in the events of the past hour. Evans was probably just out of breath.

Once they were outside the first aid tent, the old man said, "I trust that's the end of this nonsense. You've learned your lesson?"

"Yes sir," Brian replied. "Not another word from me."

June 1996

Brian didn't dare to return to the temple again that season, but when the next year rolled around, he came prepared. He'd picked up a job in a coffeehouse in addition to his Teaching Assistantship in order to afford an upgrade to his climbing gear, complete with spike-toed shoes to replace his sneakers. The most important new accessory was a digital camera with a good flash. He couldn't get any of the really nice ones with a big memory card, but being able to take and store ten photos at a time would give him plenty to study.

Evans had doubled his staff this year, bringing the total to eight. Half of them were grad students like Brian (which was a fancy way of saying "unpaid laborers"). There was also someone to draw the walls and someone to draw the maps, and a camp cook. The heavyset Bulgarian woman didn't speak any English, but if her girth were any indication of the quality of her food, Brian figured it would be a step up from last year's army rations.

After several trips up and down the hill between their camp and the trucks, they had everything unloaded. There were roads of a sort that got them in the proximity, but any trace of the ancient roadway that would have led people to the site had been covered up long ago. On the route in, the Balkan Mountains could be seen as foggy masses in the distance. In the shade of their valley, everything was green at the beginning of the season, but baked to a lifeless brown by the end.

Brian and an Australian student named Charlie were assigned to set up the tents. The new guy was every inch the stereotypical surfer dude, right down to his flowered shorts and sun-kissed skin. Brian, on the other hand, was like the poster child for academia—smallish, bespectacled, and forgettable.

He slathered on sunscreen to keep from repeating the terrible sunburn he'd picked up within the first days of last season. Mornings and nights there were cool, even crisp, but by midday, summer always asserted itself with a vengeance.

Brian's mind and gaze kept wandering up to the cave in the cliff as they worked. It was tall enough to catch the sunshine for most of the day, but in the evening hours it would be painted with the rosy hues of the western horizon and the setting sun. Though the dizzying face of the statue still sometimes invaded his dreams or flashed before his eyelids even during the day, he'd managed to convince himself in the intervening months that the voice he'd heard was a result of a tricky echo or perhaps losing blood from his gash. The strange face had come of the play of shadows as he cast about his flashlight beam, too many horror movies, and exhaustion from the weeks of hard labor in the trenches. Nothing more.

A cheerful voice interrupted Brian's thoughts. "What should we expect to find here?" Charlie asked.

"We've found some pot sherds here and there. But so far, we've only been focused on the walls and even around them we only made it down a few feet," he replied, grimacing. "Which of course we had to fill back in at the end of last year. So, the first order of business will be digging it all out again."

Charlie pounded in a stake with a stray rock, then wiped the perspiration from his thin excuse for a goatee. "That won't take too long though, will it?"

"No," Brian admitted. "The soil will be loose. Just a few days probably. Then the real work begins."

The blond snorted, then pulled the loop of the tent line over his stake. "What's your focus?" he asked, twanging the strap to make sure the stake held. "Have you settled on a dissertation topic?"

"The cult of Saturn."

"Really? And you're *here?*" Charlie moved to the next corner, his look of incredulity clear even in the shade of his wide-brimmed hat. "Shouldn't you be in Italy for that?"

"Hey, this might be the ass-end of nowhere now, but clearly the Romans did make it this far." Brian swept his arm to encompass their clearing and the surface ruins. "Just because no one has found any temples to Saturn here yet doesn't mean I won't find one." He had to fight down the urge to reveal his find to the Aussie just to show him up, but he had to keep it to himself long enough to check it out again.

Charlie had crouched down with the rock poised to hammer in the next stake, but he lowered it at the defensiveness in Brian's tone. "All right, mate. No offense. All I meant was, given our proximity to Greece, I was just thinking you might be more likely to find references to him as 'Kronos' instead, that's all."

Brian mumbled an apology and picked up the next bundle of canvas and poles. He turned over the scenes painted on the temple walls. It was definitely the story of Kronos and the Olympian gods, but he was dressed as the Roman Saturn. He would need to do a much more in-depth study of the cross-pollination between the two. Maybe the library had a translation of *De Natura Deorum* he could use. His Latin was fair, but translations were always easier. Why not use shortcuts when they presented themselves?

They worked for a while in silence as he assembled a mental bibliography. Brian was eventually pulled out of his daydreaming when Charlie's unsuspecting thumb got in the way of his makeshift hammer. He let loose a string of cursing, or at least Brian assumed it was, but the accent and his anger made it hard to understand.

The other man's mood was considerably darker than when they began their task, and Brian didn't want to start the season off on the wrong foot. He asked, "What about you? What do you study?"

The other man grinned. "Baths, mostly. No shortage of them in the empire, right?"

"They did love a good bath. Probably more than anyone in history."

"Speaking of which," Charlie said, rising to his full height. "Where do we get our water around here?"

Brian jerked his head over his shoulder at a ramshackle shed. "There's a well. But don't get too excited. It's only 19th century. Probably from the Turkish occupation."

"A shame, that. But who knows? If there's a water source now, there could have easily been a bath back in the day. Maybe we'll both get what we want. If I'm remembering my Myth 101, the gods spent a lot of time bathing with the nymphs, didn't they?" Charlie pumped his bleached eyebrows a few times. "Lucky bastards."

Outwardly, Brian laughed with his new colleague. Inwardly, he made a note to check the paintings for any references to the female water and tree spirits. He shielded his eyes as he looked toward the sky. The sun was still a painfully long time away from setting, and he already had tremors of anticipation coursing through his body.

After another hour, he and Charlie had the camp set up and Evans gave them their next task. Dinner was served fireside. The juices of the kofte balls and bell peppers dripped through the grill and sizzled into the flames, adding a counterpoint to the fresh, green smell of the Bulgarian landscape. Charlie pulled out a guitar and sang a few songs, but one by one, people went off to their cots for the night.

Brian doused the flames and stirred the ashes before retrieving his carefully packed gear from his tent. He'd gotten in a few practice sessions at a climbing gym here and there during the school year, which made both his setup and descent faster than last summer's climb.

Once inside the cavern, he could see the cave wasn't nearly as dark as the last time he'd visited. The sky outside was awash with stars, but the tunnel and its various decorations were clearly visible even after he turned off his headlamp. There was no sign of torches or any other light source; it was more like it was afternoon inside and midnight outside. The light was somehow confined to the cave itself. There had been no indication of it from the top of the cliff.

Brian swallowed roughly and peered down the length of the temple. The hooded statue stood like a sentinel forty paces away, the scythe once again balanced across its palms. If it were possible, the far end of the tunnel was actually brighter than the mouth. He held the figure in his gaze for a full, heart-pounding minute, but when it gave no indication of movement, he started the task he'd come here to do.

With only enough memory space for ten photos, he'd have to be strategic.

In order to get a full fresco into a shot, he had to press his back against the opposite wall. He chose a few that were the most compelling, then did his best to capture the floor mosaics and the votive figures. Then he used a pen knife to prise up a few of the edge tiles and take a sample of the plaster. He rolled it around in his fingers and squinted at the white and red powder. It certainly resembled the plaster they'd unearthed down at the main site in terms of texture, but those pieces had been little more than pebbles.

I wish you wouldn't do that, Brian.

Brian froze. He was so engaged in getting the best photos possible, he hadn't even realized he had ventured only a few paces away from the statue. The voice was as inconstant as the face had been, ancient yet youthful, but it also carried a weary sort of affection. He risked a glance out of the corner of his eye, and the figure had once again taken the scythe up in one hand. The other was on its cloaked hip, which jutted out slightly in a gesture of frustration.

Brian's mouth became impossible dry, but he managed to croak, "I'm sorry."

Don't worry about it. The statue relaxed its posture. *I can fix it easily enough.*

The figure shifted its grip on the scythe and touched one of its stony fingers to the blade. In what had been the naked, shallow channel on Brian's last visit, a piece of lapis lazuli had been slid into place. The part of his mind that was fascinated rather than terrified recognized it as the shape of a Roman thunderbolt. It looked much more like a bundle of grain or an abstract flourish than the classic zigzag of children's drawings, but he'd seen it on enough coins to know what he was looking at. A spark leapt from the finger of the statue as it came into contact with the stone, and Brian's hand was empty. He dropped to his hands and knees to examine the spot he'd taken up the plaster, and it was as smooth and perfect as ever.

That's better.

"But…what…how?"

You know how.

"No, I don't." Brian got back to his feet and regarded the statue sheepishly. "How did you know my name was Brian?"

Though the features on the face continued their permutations, he could read an expression of contemplation in them. Then, it gave him a knowing smile.

Ah, of course. You haven't properly met me yet. Forgive me, I can't always keep the order of these things straight. And I've been asleep a very long time.

"But you've met me before?"

Yes. Many times.

"When?"

I've been expecting you.

"What, I was like, prophesized?" Brian laughed. "Yeah right."

The statue made a disgusted sound. *Prophesies are guesses. I knew you were coming.*

Even though he had a creeping suspicions that he already knew the answer, Brian asked the next question anyway. "Who are you?"

I have many names. It makes no difference to me what you decide suits your purposes. The statue sighed. *But if I remember correctly, you prefer to call me by the same name as those who built this place to honor me. Which makes me Saturnus in your eyes.*

"This is incredible!" Brian began to pace and mumble to himself, all of his fear subsumed by the rush of curiosity. His feverish steps were halted by Saturnus's next words.

Thank you for waking me.

"Waking you?"

Saturnus gestured at Brian's arm and the white, raised flesh of his scar.

The sacrifice was most welcome after all these years. The flesh at your fireside was also nourishing. I am still very thirsty though.

Brian twisted at the waist to retrieve his canteen to share with the strange stone man before him, but Saturnus stopped him with a gesture.

No, not water. But if you could provide a calf or some other creature at my altar, I would be most grateful, and I have many gifts to bestow. Calves aren't my favorite, of course, but I am so very thirsty. Anything will do for now. We can work up to more later.

The archaeologist's brow furrowed. "We haven't found an altar. Not yet anyway."

It's at the base of the stairs. Can't miss it.

He shook his head and indicated his harness. "There are no stairs. I had to climb down here from the top."

The statue blinked wise, old and naïve, young eyes at him a few times, then it let out another knowing sigh. This one had the ring of sorrow. *After the earthquake, then. Pity. I am barely capable of more than a spark these days, and I must remain in this single form. I brought in enough sun to see by, but oh! I wish I could walk among streams of time as easily as I did in my youth, when my worshipers were myriad. But I know, my time will come again.*

"Is that what you did there?" Brian asked, his eyes darting to the solid wall of plaster. "You manipulated time?"

Yes.

"Can you do it again?"

Saturnus's expression became as hard as the stone it was made of. *I am not some bear made to walk on its hind legs for your amusement.*

Brian raised his hands in appeasement as he took a few steps toward the statue. "No, no. I know that. That's not what I meant. I'm sorry. This is just all so fascinating! What an incredible power to possess."

The statue preened a little and stood taller after the compliment. *It is rather incredible, isn't it?* It proudly held out the scythe for Brian to examine. *I made it myself. Well, okay, maybe not all by myself. Hephaestus helped. He didn't know he was helping out his grandpa at the time of course. The concepts, though, those were all mine.*

The scholar took the shining implement into his ginger grasp. It was heavy, but also perfectly balanced. "What is the significance of the thunderbolt?"

Saturnus became resigned again. *That's what it takes to power it. But as you saw, I can't quite muster one these days. Manipulating sunshine isn't too difficult, and your blood helped me this time. I might be able to manage a little shower if I really put my mind to it, and a spark here or there, but as my worshipers fell away, so did my power.*

"I thought that thunder and lightning were your son's purview…."

And where do you suppose he got it from? The statue scoffed, then placed a perfectly crafted hand that was both liver-spotted with age and the smooth flesh of a child to its sternum. *Dear old dad, that's where. But time, I kept the secrets of time to myself.*

Brian lifted the handle closer to his eyes to take a better look at the disk. It could be spun and clicked into place, which must indicate the season on an astrological level. As he inspected it, he realized there were three more dials set into the first, making it a series of concentric rings rather than the solid disk he had originally thought it to be. "Days, hours, and minutes?" he asked. Then he drew a finger across the inlaid notches on the blade. "The years?"

Saturnus nodded eagerly. *Good. I thought I remembered you were clever.*

"And if you could make a lightning bolt, you'd be able to use this to go anywhere...er, 'anywhen' you wanted?"

Not exactly. As you can see, there is a finite number of years to choose from. Though time is infinite, my device is finite. One can make a series of jumps, I suppose, but much of this world's history is rather boring. And the farther I get from my worshippers, the less power I have to gather the bolt to return.

Brian adjusted his glasses. "Tell me, does it need to be an actual lightning bolt from you to make it work. A magical one?"

There's nothing "magic" about lightning, my boy. The statue's tone was mildly condescending, which made it especially strange as it came from the mouth of someone incapable of growing a beard. The features shifted, wrinkles from a thousand bouts of laughter folded at the corners of cracked lips. Saturnus waved in the vague direction of the sky. *One just has to blow some clouds around and the particles in there do the rest. It's not rocket science.*

"You're telling me you know about rockets? No, never mind. Time travel. I get it," Brian replied. "But let's say a person can't move clouds around at will. Could he use some other source of electricity?"

Yes, you did. Do. Will. The figure rubbed his face as he considered, then settled on repeating *Will.*

Brian remained in the temple for several hours of polite conversation with the statue. Though Saturnus did not know the name of Brian's power source, a quick game of twenty questions gave him an idea of what direction to go in. He also got straight answers about the past history of the area and some muddy points of historical curiosity on the Romans in general, but Saturnus was either unwilling or unable to say too much about what the future would hold. Perhaps that is what it meant about the device's power being finite.

For its part, the statue was very interested in the events of the past fifty years or so. As he had a particular interest in agricultural practices, he pressed his new acolyte on questions of GMO crops and the use of pesticides. Brian was woefully underinformed for the stone god's taste, but he promised to look into it. Saturnus got himself muddled occasionally when it came to when he was in the timeline, like when he asked about something called a "Shakira." Once they determined that the issue was with the flow of time rather than Brian's lack of pop culture knowledge, Saturnus assured him that it would be worth the wait. Eventually, Brian was dismissed to allow the statue time to rest.

He made it back to camp about an hour before the Sun rose. Despite the lack of sleep, he was so buoyed by his experience and the promise of traveling through time that he rose at the same time as the others with a wide grin on his face. The one question Brian had asked about the future that Saturnus had been willing to answer was about whether or not he told anyone else about the temple. The statue assured him that it and all its wonders remained Brian's secret to the day of his death. And who was Brian to argue with a god? So he kept his mouth shut.

The lack of sleep caught up to him by midafternoon, and as he rested in the shade during their break, his mind turned to the question of a power source. The object in question was small enough he'd be able to carry it with him without too much difficulty. It obviously had to be something electrical, and Saturnus's description of the black coating sounded a lot like plastic. Out here amongst the pastures and streams, there were plenty of tumbledown farmhouses, but not much in the way of Radio Shacks. He was gathering the courage to ask Evans if he could take one of the trucks into town on some fake errand when he realized the truck itself could offer an answer.

So it was that Brian found himself dangling over the cliff face that night with a forty-pound car battery and its jumper cables in turn dangling from him. He slipped a few times on his way down, but eventually made it to the mouth of the tunnel unscathed.

Welcome back. I see you found it.

"I'm glad to hear it," Brian replied, hefting the battery and making his way toward the statue. "I was starting to doubt that dragging this sucker around was going to be worth it."

Shall we begin?

He grunted his agreement, and Saturnus talked him through adding the jumper cables to each end of the scythe. There was a brief discussion about precisely when he would like to travel, which was slowed by the fact that Saturnus had no use for temporal reference points such as "BC" and "AD." Eventually, they settled on the second year of Trajan's reign, which would put him at the height of the Roman Empire.

Brian held onto the grip and eyed the apparatus warily, the clamp of the red cable poised over the blade but still open. "Am I going to get shocked if I do this?"

I imagine it will be little uncomfortable. Especially when I do this.

The statue closed one painted hand over the thunderbolt stone and the other over the clamp. As metal came into contact with metal, a jolt of electricity shot through Brian's body. His back bent into an involuntary arch, and a shriek was ripped from his throat. He tumbled to the floor at Saturnus's feet.

When he regained consciousness, Brian was a heap on the floor of the temple. He blinked around the gloomy interior, which was lit here or there with oil lamps. His head buzzed as he sat up, and as he ran his hand through his hair, he had the distinct impression that it was standing several inches from his scalp.

Hello there. And who might you be?

The voice was the same as before, undulating between old and young, but when he looked up to speak to the statue, there was nothing standing in the alcove. Brian shifted his position, and a hooded man was standing on the mosaiced floor who had not been there a moment before. Like the paintings, his face was completely obscured, but Brian also had a sense that the shifts were not so rapid as in his own time.

"Saturnus?"

The statue spread its arms wide, palms facing the ceiling. It did not bow exactly, but it inclined its head a fraction. *I see you know me. And you are?*

"Brian."

Welcome to my sanctuary, Brian. That is a very odd name. Where does it hail from?

He struggled to his feet. The scythe and the car battery were in a tangle of cables on the floor. Brian did his best to tame his unruly hair in the presence of the fully manifested god as he answered. "I'm not sure. Ireland, maybe?"

I am not familiar with the Land of Ire, thief. It rings of trickery.

Saturnus's words were not said in anger, but Brian's hackles rose. "Whoa, wait a second. I'm not a thief!"

The men of Ire must be very strong. That is not meant for mortals' hands. What is done with thieves in your land, I wonder?

"You're the one who told me how to use it. Practically insisted that I did. I don't think I had enough juice to get here without your help, in fact."

I?

Brian motioned at the empty alcove. "Some version of you, yes. I swear. I am *not* a thief."

Interesting. And what do you plan to do now that you are here?

"I'm a student of this time. I want to take a look around, that's all. Cross my heart."

A scholar? The hooded man brought his hands together and interlaced his fingers. *Well, don't let me keep you from your studies.*

Brian folded into an awkward bow and thanked Saturnus with a string of flowery oaths and tributes to his greatness. The young archaeologist gathered up his ungainly time travel equipment. There was no obvious hiding place for it and his harness, but rearranging some of the votive figures in a dark corner gave it some semblance of cover. He gave the hooded man a wide berth as he passed it, eager to explore the world outside. He'd made it to the threshold when the god made one last comment.

I trust, Brian of Ire, that you will not return without making an offering. The altar is—

"At the bottom of the stairs," he said, excitement bubbling out of him. "Can't miss it."

Outside of the temple door, a massive stone staircase meandered down the cliffside, snaking back on itself three times in the process. Though he had seen the statue in his own time turn back the clock, there was some part of him that remained certain this was all just some wild dream. Now that he stood on the first landing and surveyed the landscape, there was no room for doubt.

In the valley below, the terracotta rooftops of a city complex stretched out into the distance. The buildings were arranged along an east-west axis, with the cliff making up the western end and a grand city gate at the other. The wide boulevard was home to foot and animal traffic, mostly donkeys laden with goods but a few horses and carts here and there.

Brian took the steps two at a time and was lucky not to have tumbled down the final bend in the staircase in his frenzy. A smallish structure, littler more than a roof held up by a series of pillars, stood at the bottom of the stairs. The altar was clearly visible, and like the full-fledged temple above, votive figures were left around it. He made a vague note of it as he passed into the street.

Based on the lack of graffiti, many of the buildings were fairly new. Which made sense, in the second year of Trajan's reign, this area had only been under Roman control for about fifty years. Even in that short amount of time, this complex had already expanded out to meet the walls.

As astonished as Brian was by what he was seeing, the people he passed were equally confused by the young man with the second set of glass and wire eyes walking amongst them. Those who did not stop and stare at him outright made sure to keep their distance. Most of them were in the typical tunics and simple, draped gowns he knew from frescos and literary evidence, although he did spot one toga-ed politician of some kind flanked by a pair of soldiers in their distinctive capes entering one of the larger buildings. His slave followed close behind.

Eventually, he realized he was drawing so much attention that Brian decided to go back to the temple. He noted every nook and cranny as he went and did his best to overlay what he could see over the mental picture of the valley as it existed today. A block or so away from the foot of the stairs, he turned a corner and nearly laughed out loud. A bath complex as grand as any of the ruins he'd seen dominated the street. Charlie would be thrilled.

He remembered his promise to Saturnus to make an offering on his way back, but didn't have any of the local currency to spend. He tried speaking to a few people, but either his Latin was worse than he'd realized or they were speaking some local language that was completely opaque to him. After digging around in his pockets, he was able to produce a pack of gum. His grunted and pantomimed explanation of its use was not nearly as interesting to the baker as the shiny foil, but it was enough to get him a loaf of bread to leave on the altar.

When he huffed and puffed his way back to the cave, the hooded god was waiting for him.

I prefer meat. Or blood.

Brian winced. "Yeah, sorry. That was the best I could do. Or…wait. Hold that thought." He went to the corner where his gear was waiting and picked up the scythe. Saturnus looked on while he ran the sharp side of the blade across the pad of his thumb. A few drops of blood beaded on the cut, then much to his shock, rose into the air. They drifted toward the figure, then disappeared under the hood.

Yes. That will do nicely.

Brian put the cut to his mouth and sucked away the excess. It might make his climb up a little more challenging, but the gift he'd just received was worth more than a little discomfort. "I think I'd better go. For now, anyway. But I'd love to come back, if that is all right with you?"

That is acceptable.

"Awesome. I really appreciate it! You have no idea what this means for me." Brian shimmied back into his climbing harness, then reconnected his battery to the disk on the grip of the scythe. He heaved the battery and the scythe over to the unmoving figure and held out the apparatus. "I think you're going to need to help me out. If you don't mind, that is."

The statue regarded Brian and his request for a few heartbeats, then he placed his hand onto the blade. Brian didn't have time to clamp on the other side when the world dissolved into blinding white, and the archaeologist was back when he'd started.

June 2000

It was the start of a new season, not just for the site, but for Brian. Not only had Evans finally gotten out of the game, but the university had hired Brian to keep the program going. Now that more permanent structures had been established onsite for living and housing their finds, it was the perfect setting to bring undergrads. He wasn't all that keen on the teaching aspect; the most important thing was finding *more*. But Charlie had also stayed with the project in the intervening years, and he was happy to take on that part of the day-to-day workings as a co-director.

Brian had bounced between a few one-year lectureships after completing his dissertation. Tenure was still out of the question, but as an unmarried academic, he could afford to be flexible for a time. He'd operated on a few "hunches" over the past seasons that led to the excavation of the altar at the foot of the long-ago staircase, and he'd given Charlie the bath he'd always wanted, but there was still much work to do be done. The temple in the cave, however, he'd kept to himself as Saturnus had declared he would.

The dissertation and subsequent book had been cited a few times here and there, which was exciting for the young scholar–though as often as not, his work was criticized for making too many leaps without enough evidence. The walls were easy enough to find after a few more trips to visit the ancient city, but walls weren't nearly as sexy as the hoards of coins and other objects his competitors had been pulling out of the ground in other parts of the former empire. The earthquake that had destroyed the route up to the temple had also caused a huge amount of destruction, leaving very few intact pottery and statues to find. Even with his "uncanny" ability to figure out the best places to dig, excavating a complex the size he knew lay under their feet would take decades. And he didn't want to wait decades to get the recognition he deserved.

It was time to take a new approach.

Saturnus was happy to see him when Brian once again entered the cave. Or at least, he thought the statue was happy. It was difficult to tell when its face refused to stay still.

What have you brought me this time?

Brian rifled around in his backpack and produced a leg of lamb. He had smuggled it out of the kitchen's freezer, but it had already begun to thaw and drip pink blood by the time he presented it to the stone god. It would be a bitch to get the stains, not to mention the smell, out of his backpack, but that was a problem for the washer women. The staff on the project not only had expanded to include the undergrads, but also a cadre of locals to do much of the actual earth moving and upkeep for the professors and graduate students they'd brought along.

Luckily, the thawing meat juices had not penetrated the insta-fire log he brought along. Though Saturnus was happy to take Brian's blood as it was, the statue insisted on the meat of dead animals being cooked. Something about getting what it needed from the smoke. Brian didn't much care; as long as Saturnus was happy, he could continue his work.

He kicked away the ashes from what he had designated as the cooking spot a few summers ago, and lit the corners of the packaging. Under normal circumstances, he never would have dreamed of setting a fire inside of such an important archaeological space. The smoke damaged the interior of the temple, but Saturnus was always able to fix the smudges and dispel the haze within a moment using the scythe.

With the fire lit, Brian went to the crate where he stashed his gear. Since that first visit, he'd put together an ensemble that would keep him from drawing too much attention. He'd also gotten a hold of some coins here and there, which could always come in handy. The costume would have made any historical reenactor cringe; there was very little about the materials that were authentic. Thankfully, the average person never looked too hard at what he was wearing as long as it was roughly the right shape and color.

"Saturnus, I need your help with something."

Hmmm? The statue was standing over the offering, enjoying the smell and sight of the flesh burning to honor him. Like the sunlight Saturnus kept within the confines of the tunnel, the smoke never ventured out of the opening. *And what might that be?*

For Brian, the plume of smoke was getting hard to breathe around, and he waved as much of it away from his face as possible before making his request. "Could you tell me some places here in the valley that weren't destroyed by the earthquake?"

Saturnus became silent for a minute the way it always did when it was sorting through millennia of memories. Eventually it sighed.

Unfortunately, no. The whole city was levelled, then stripped and abandoned by the survivors.

"Shit. I was afraid you were going to say that." Brian rubbed at his stubble as he contemplated.

Why is it important?

"I need to find more, and I need to do it fast. My reputation is at stake." He explained the situation in more detail as the statue patiently listened. By the time he finished, his eyes were streaming from the smoke. "Do you have any ideas?"

Well, that seems simple enough to remedy. You could bury some things where you know you'd find them. You know better than anyone what you need to find. So make sure that you do. Simple.

Brian slapped his head against his forehead. "Of course! I can't believe I didn't think of it before." He began pacing as he considered. "The bath complex would be a good place to have found statues. Maybe I can pry up the cobbles behind it…"

I don't think that's a good idea.

"What, why? You're the one who suggested it!"

You already found the baths.

"So?"

Then you would have already found the statues.

Brian considered this for a few moments before nodding. "Yeah, okay. I see that logic, I suppose. I'd already know by now if I do it that way."

Exactly.

"Ok. Let's see. If we extend out to a new plot next to the current limit of the project, that would have us excavating…Yes! Perfect! That big villa. I wanted to do there next anyway."

Brian retrieved the scythe with a skip in his step. Since his regular tributes were feeding Saturnus, he'd been able to do away with the extra battery pack two summers ago. It still could not conjure the thunderbolt of its ancient counterpart, but the statue now had enough power to send him both backward and forward unaided. He held out the scythe and the statue infused it with the necessary energy.

Through trial and error, they'd figured out how much power was needed for him to travel but not knock him on his ass. He appeared in the temple in the past, and as usual, the fully manifested Saturnus was waiting for him. With his usual promise to leave the god something nice on the altar on his way back, Brian headed out into the city.

The villa belonged to a wealthy merchant. Excavation is a slow process, so it was not very far away from the baths. Brian could be away as long as he liked on these trips and still return to the same moment in his present, so he had plenty of time to observe the comings and goings of the merchant's family, business partners, and slaves. Using his small store of denarii, he bribed his way into the house when the family was away at their country estate and only a few slaves were left behind to manage things in their absence. He told them some story about being from a rival merchant's household and just needing an hour or two to look over some documents. They left a side door open for him in the dark of night, and he never saw a soul when he slipped into the house.

He let out a low whistle of appreciation as he stepped into the atrium. The ceiling opened to the sky over a shallow pool at the center. Columns were set at intervals around the rectangular room, and low couches were interspersed around the space. Without the family at home, the vases were bare and the pedestals for food and drink were empty, but as he inspected the rooms leading off the atrium, he found plenty of wonderful things he could later exhume. He was conscious on some level that he was probably condemning the helpful slaves by stealing from their master, but as they were already long dead from his perspective, it didn't bother him that much.

He chose a variety of items that were not only valuable to reinforce the "theories" from his book, but could also capture the imagination of the general public. A pair of finely painted goblets, a fish platter made of silver, a small ivory figurine of his patron god, and a few coins with Trajan's portrait stamped into the metal all went into a chest. Most ancient hoards were little more than a stash of coins that the unfortunate owner was unable to return to for some reason, so the chest alone would make this is a fascinating find for archaeologists. For the merchant to bury something in his own yard like this would be somewhat difficult to explain away, but he was sure he'd come up with something when the time came.

Brian dragged the chest out to the garden and chose his spot with care. The garden wall would be easy enough to find when it was excavated, and would hopefully protect his hoard from the worst of the inevitable earthquake damage. He considered lining the hole with stones or reinforcing it in some other way to ensure the quality in the future, but that would be far harder to explain when it came time to publish. Better to make it look as natural and consistent as possible. He settled for hiding the disturbed earth with a pile of gardening debris, then went back into the house.

As a last-second thought, he grabbed a votive figure from the family's shrine and slipped it into his money pouch. His white tunic was now a smudged mess. He'd have to get something new before he made another trip back. He crept through the streets, careful to avoid the taverns that were still open for business and any chance that anyone would spot him and ask him about his condition. After laying the figurine on Saturnus's altar, he made his way up the long staircase and back to the year 2000 as quietly as possible.

March 2009

Brian was famished, but he made a point of never eating in front of strangers, especially not mysterious strangers who had shown up to his office unannounced and said he had a "mutually beneficial matter to discuss."

During the few words they'd exchanged after the man offered to buy him a drink, Brian had recognized the tell-tale vowels and slight roll to the "r" that indicated a Slavic accent. So, he wasn't surprised when the man took a shifty look around the bar and addressed him in Bulgarian.

"You can understand me, Dr. Jeffries?"

"Yes," Brian replied in the same language. "I've picked it up over the years."

"Good," said the dark man, then he took another quick glance at their surroundings. There were a few college kids scattered around, but they were either talking with friends or paying attention to a textbook and never gave the men a second glance. "May I ask, how are things going with your project?"

Brian bristled. If this man knew who he was, and he must, then he already knew things were going terribly on that front. He'd enjoyed almost a decade of success, only for it all to be threatened by some stupid housing bubble and a stock market plummet he didn't care to understand. Budgets for higher education had been slashed, which included things like study-abroad opportunities for undergrads. Grants were already few and far between, but now the competition was fierce. Brian had received yet another "We regret to inform you" letter that morning.

To make matters worse, his tenure application was due, and without its protection, they could lay him off at any time. Who needs Roman history courses when the economy is in the toilet?

"I do not know if I will make it back this year. Or ever. Thank you for the reminder." He said the last sentence in English, then took a long pull of his IPA. The foamy torrent cascaded down his throat and came to a sloshing stop in his empty belly.

The Bulgarian slapped him on the shoulder and continued in his native tongue. "What if I told you there was a way to guarantee you could go back this year, and for as long as you wanted?"

"I would say you have my attention." Brian leaned back so he could get a better look at the other man's face. He had the familiar brown eyes and black hair of most of his countrymen, along with the paranoid streak brought about by living through the rise and fall of the Eastern Bloc. The thick, gold chain that tangled with his exposed chest hair hinted at his occupation. Members of the *mutri* and their enforcers often opted for shows of conspicuous consumption.

"I am very glad to hear it. My name is Gergo," he said, presenting his hand for Brian to shake. He squeezed the scholar in a hairy-knuckled grip for a few moments while gazing hungrily into his eyes. Brian was becoming less and less certain he was in fact interested in what Gergo had to say when he continued. "You have been finding some very wonderful things. Or so I am told. I do not know very much about antiquities. But my employer, he is quite the collector himself. He has been following your career with interest."

Brian studied the bottom of his beer glass. "And who is your employer?"

Gergo waved away the question and gave the other man a wide, white-toothed grin. "That is not important. What is important is that he would like to *expand* his collection." He moved his hands together and apart a few times to make sure Brian caught his meaning. Evidently, he was less impressed by Brian's knowledge of Bulgarian than Brian was. "He would like very much to see you succeed. And he's willing to pay for you to go back to work this year. But there is a condition."

"Condition?" Brian repeated, doing his best impression of a secret agent despite the butterflies doing the tango in his gut. "What kind of condition?"

"He wants…oh, what is American term?" Gergo stretched back, his elbows out by the sides of his head as he thought. Brian's façade cracked slightly when he was hit by the other man's musk, and he took another swig of his drink to drown out the smell. The thug finished his extension, then snapped his fingers in recognition. In English, he said, "First dibs. That is term!" He shifted back again to Bulgarian. "He will pay you handsomely, too."

Brian was lucky his beer didn't come out of his nose as he choked. Some of it sloshed over the side of the glass and puddled on the bar top. He had enough good sense at least to keep his volume down as he spluttered, "You want me sell antiquities?"

"You get to dig and he gets his trinkets." Gergo made a theatrical shrug. "Everyone wins."

"If they catch me, I'd be ruined. I'd never work again."

The thick man at his side gestured at the bartender to bring over a towel and take care of Brian's mess. "They? Who they?"

Brian waited for the bartender to finish mopping up the spill before he hissed, "The government. The police."

Unexpectedly, the other man responded by letting out a hearty laugh and slapping him again on the shoulder. "My dear Dr. Jeffries. My employer is as good the government, the police. He's the one who gets the roads built, who keeps the businesses going. Nothing will even be transported across the border. You don't need to worry about anyone finding out about this arrangement, trust me."

The mafia. Gergo was asking him to get in bed with the mob. And what was worse, Brian was considering it. He was the one burying the artifacts to find, after all. The site was only still being excavated because of his hard work. Hard work and the help of Saturnus, but he'd been the one to find the temple in the first place. The god would still be dormant if he hadn't woken him. Really, there wouldn't be any harm in putting a few extra things in the ground here and there for a generous patron. Not if he had the protection he needed to stay out of jail. Not if it meant he could continue his work and secure tenure.

In English, Brian muttered, "a mutually beneficial matter to discuss."

"Now we understand each other!" Gergo picked up his own glass and tapped it against Brian's. *"Nazdrave!"*

"Cheers."

June 2019

The climb was becoming more difficult every year. At forty-nine, Brian wasn't old, but he wasn't getting any younger either. Of course, he was only forty-nine to the outside world. Over the nearly two and a half decades since discovering the temple, he'd put in plenty of time in the past. He'd never bothered with the math, but he was certainly somewhere in his fifties by now.

Starting around 2010, Brian came out to the site a week or so earlier than the rest of the crew and students, and always stayed later. They had to rent construction equipment to help with moving around the fill dirt every season, so Brian "generously" offered to stick around and oversee the process of drop-off and pick-up. With the new road leading right up to the site, the delivery never took more than an hour. To explain the whole week of extra time on each side, it was easy enough to convince his co-director that he was processing the finds and making room in the dig house storage area before the new crop of students came.

Charlie, or "Dr. Charles Montgomery" as he liked to be called now that he'd traded his long, blond waves in for his own tenured position, had continued to be a vital part of the project. It didn't matter what he called himself, he was still the same, solid guy he'd always been. His guitar came along every year. He had a way with "the kids" as Brian called them, and Brian kept them viable both financially and by publishing their findings. It was a match made in heaven.

In reality, these early arrivals gave Brian a chance to make his trips to and from the past without needing to sneak around in the dead of night anymore. Gergo would come as soon as the season ended and take photos of the artifacts with his phone, and a voice on the other end of the connection told him what to take and how much to pay. Brian made plenty of money to keep the project going and then some. Charlie had no idea what he was up to, and he wanted to keep it that way. It wasn't only that he didn't want to share his cut of the lucrative business, but Charlie was a real boy scout and would probably make too many waves if he knew what was what.

Brian had signed off for the delivery of the construction equipment, then made the long plod up the far side of the hill. The disadvantage of making the descent during the daylight hours was the ever-growing patch of sweat dribbling down his back. If he wasn't careful, the day would come all too soon when he could no longer get down to the temple at all.

Hello Brian.

Saturnus's voice invaded his brain before he reached the entrance. This was new and more than a little unsettling. There was no denying that the trapped god had been getting stronger with each of his annual sacrifices, but if Brian started to hear the god all of the time, then it was going to make it much harder to accomplish his work. Or worse, harder to keep his secret.

He puffed his way down to the entrance before returning the greeting. "I brought you a special gift this time."

The statue stood over his shoulder as Brian rifled through his pack. As time went on, the speed of the shifting faces had slowed considerably, as if the god was gaining more control the longer he was awake. It made it much easier to look directly at him. When the archaeologist pulled out a small device, Saturnus's hungry expression changed to one of disappointment, but it quickly morphed into bemused interest.

What is it?

"You're always asking me about music. I thought you might enjoy catching up."

It wasn't the newest MP3 player (why waste the expense on someone who wouldn't know the difference?) but it did have a very long battery life. The tinge of melancholy remained on Saturnus's face, but Brian didn't bother asking what was wrong. He'd done plenty for the stone god over the years, he had no right to complain.

After exchanging a few more niceties and lighting up the customary fire to charbroil the haunch of meat, Brian made his trip back. He'd been careful not to steal too much from the same year or person, and had ventured a little ways backward and forward from where he started in order to keep himself from being discovered. At the site, they'd uncovered several city blocks worth of buildings. Some of the artifacts they found were even there naturally, which was always a pleasant surprise.

If he had wanted, Brian probably could have had a wonderful life back in the past. But as much as he enjoyed his sense of superiority over the residents of his study area, he also preferred the creature comforts of his current time. He stayed in the past for a few weeks, then he was off again.

When he arrived back to his present, the Saturnus statue was standing in its alcove as still as the day he first encountered it. The fire was still going strong and all logic would dictate that it should be enjoying the sacrifice instead of acting like the stone it was. Brian was about to ask it what it was up to when another voice at his back sent him wheeling around.

He was little more than a silhouette at the mouth of the cave, but his disapproval was clear in the slant of his shoulders. "How could you keep this from me?" Charlie asked.

In his shock, all Brian managed to do was blurt, "What are you doing here?"

"I decided to come out to the site early this year, too."

"You're spying on me?" Brian placed the scythe into the statue's waiting hands, but he saw no trace of the ever-shifting face under the stone hood. It was impossible. Saturnus said no one else ever found out about the temple. No, he realized as icy tendrils of dread spread down his spine. Saturnus said he never *told* anyone about it.

"*That's* all you have to say to me? Jesus Christ, Bri." Charlie sighed and crossed his arms in disapproval. "I sent you an email. I guess you didn't get it."

Brian approached his co-director with his hands stretched out before him. "I can explain."

"I mean, Jesus actual fricking Christ, mate. I knew you were keeping something from me, but I didn't think it was something like *this.*"

"You thought I was keeping a secret?" Brian asked coolly. He glanced at Saturnus again, but the statue betrayed no hint of movement.

"Yeah, I did. I was looking over the finances and—" The other archaeologist gestured at the burning meat. "Having a barbeque, are we? What the hell are you thinking? You're destroying everything in here." He picked up the hunk of meat by the bare bone and tossed it out of the cave. It had so far to fall, it didn't even make a sound when it hit ground far below.

A lump gathered in Brian's throat. If Charlie was looking at the finances, then he might suspect the black market sales. He was just short-sighted enough to turn Brian in, whether or not it would spell the end to the project. Of course, if the project continued, it would be with Charlie as the sole director from here on out. That's probably what he wanted.

Brian crept closer as Charlie glanced around him for a way to douse the flames, but settled for kicking that over the edge as well. The frayed hem of his polyester pants was all too happy to invite the fire to creep around his ankle. He took off his floppy hat and batted at the smoking pants to keep the flames from spreading. The idiot was standing right next to the cave mouth, on one foot no less.

It was just too easy to push him over the edge and out of Brian's hair.

Unlike the leg of lamb, Charlie did not fall silently. His scream ripped through the bucolic quiet of the pastureland until it was cut off by a stomach-churning thud and crack of shattering bone.

Brian wasn't sure how long he stood there with his heart pounding in his ears. It took the sound of Saturnus's voice rattling in his skull to break him from his reverie.

You've done well.

He fought the numbness enough to move his mouth. "How…how can you say that?"

The statue had moved impossibly fast and now stood at his side, peering out over the drop-off. When it turned its attention back to Brian, the face was holding steady in the shape of man in his sixties. He smiled and gave his acolyte a double thumbs-up.

Because you were right on target.

"I just killed a man!" he spluttered. "What the hell do you mean by target?"

Saturnus pointed at the ground, and despite his better judgment, Brian moved closer to the edge. The movies may have been wrong about archaeologists, but they were right about the way contorted, rumpled bodies looked after a fall. If he had harbored any hope that Charlie had survived, his twisted form fifty feet below and the spreading pool of blood tore that hope to shreds. At first, he had no idea what Saturnus was getting at with his talk of "targets," then Brian realized in horror that the altar lay directly below them. It had been covered by back fill for years, but the body was oozing blood onto it through the dirt and stone.

"This…this isn't right. This can't be right. This isn't me!"

Sure, it is.

Brian tore himself away from the view and put his back against the frescoed wall. Bile rose into his throat and he wretched into the corner.

When his stomach was empty and his body stopped shaking, he wiped at his sour mouth and cried, "This can't be happening. I'm not a murderer."

No, no. Not murder. Sacrifice. There is a difference. Trust me.

Saturnus was no doubt trying to be comforting, but he sounded more like a used car salesman than the avuncular figure he was going for with that face and those assurances.

Brian raked his fingers through his cropped hair, dislodging his glasses. His frenzied movements stilled as a new idea came to him. "I need to go back. I can fix this. Make it never happen!" Brian reached for the scythe only to find that Saturnus was not holding it. When he squinted at the far end of the tunnel, it was nowhere to be seen. "You have to help me," he begged. "I have to make this right."

Oh Brian. My dear Brian. The statue shook its head sadly, its painted skin taking on a more lifelike hue with every drop of Charlie's blood it absorbed through the altar below. *Haven't you learned anything? We already know that you don't because you did not. You would have stopped yourself just now if you went back to stop yourself. Right?*

It took Brian's muddled brain a few moments to take this in, but it was true. There was nowhere to go now but forward.

"What am I going to do?" he asked, his voice barely above a whisper. "No one can ever know."

Bury him, for starters. That's what happens to all sacrifices eventually. I'll even help.

With a wave of its hand, Brian and Saturnus stood at the base of the cliff. Brian balked and scrambled back a few steps when he saw how close Charlie's blood and gray matter was to touching his shoes. He would not have guessed he had more to give, but he wretched again.

Once he had his heaving under control, he turned back to the god. The hooded figure was kneeling beside the dead archaeologist's crushed body and humming contentedly.

"You're…you're outside."

You're very perceptive. Saturnus straightened and regarded Brian with a wry smile. *Come along now, it's time to bury him.*

When Brian tried to look at the corpse, his head swam. "I don't think I can do it."

I certainly don't know how to run that thing. You're going to need to drive.

The statue was pointing at one of the digging machines lying in wait for the season to begin. The shovel was tucked against the arm like the chin of a swan against its neck. A half-formed memory of him thinking these machines looked like dinosaurs floated into his mind. What a strange moment to think of it. What a strange moment, period. An unexpected bark of laughter leapt from his throat at his own strangeness, then he stepped over to the machine.

It took several tries to get it started and even longer to figure out the controls, but eventually he dug a whole next to the body and used the scoop to push it in. He never even needed to get his hands dirty. After he covered it up, he jumped down from the machine to admire his handiwork. After one good rain, the ground would look the same as everything else around it. That trench had already been filled back in for years. No one expected to open it this or any other year anyway. This might just work.

Saturnus had grown bored watching Brian's progress, and he found the hooded figure wandering around the edge of the excavation zone. Tender blades of young grass waved in the afternoon breeze just beyond the most recent trench. They'd be breaking ground on a new section again this season, and thanks to his last sojourn into the past, there would be some wonderful things waiting for them to unearth a few feet down.

The deep purple cloak draped over the god shifted in the wind, fabric now instead of stone. *You've done well. And you will be remembered for it.*

Brian blanched. "What do you mean 'remembered'? I thought you said that I needed to bury him, and then things would be fine."

Saturnus inclined his head over his shoulder in Brian's general direction, then returned to gazing over the field. *Did I? I don't remember saying that.*

"What happens to me, then?" His voice grew shrill with panic as he demanded, "You have to do something! You said it yourself, this was a sacrifice. For you."

And for you. Another in a long line. But no matter. The effect is the same. I am strong enough now. And it is all thanks to you. I will show you what will come to pass. The scythe flashed mirror-bright as Saturnus pulled it from the depths of his cloak.

"The future? You never talk about the future," Brian said warily. He stepped closer to the god all the same and rested his hand on the device.

This is a special occasion.

June 2095

The roar of the crowd bounced off of every flat surface, amplifying the people's rabid joy to a dizzying volume.

On reflex, Brian recoiled and covered his ears. He blinked around the plaza that had been a quiet meadow a moment before. At first, he thought that Saturnus had made a mistake. There were white buildings and wide streets surrounding them. This had to be the past. But as he surveyed the screaming people around him, their clothing told a very different story. Though the fabric appeared to be natural linens and cottons, the cut and fit of all the garments were foreign to him—neither the tunics of the past nor the blue jeans of his own time. To confuse matters, several people were holding up devices that resembled smart phones, but impossibly thin. Holographic representations of his own face stood upon several of them, and the people were looking between the image and him as if confirming his identity. More screens as tall as the buildings they were mounted on showed his movements in real time.

Something far above his head caught his attention, and he spied a series of blimps crisscrossing the clear, cerulean sky like manmade clouds. Their progress was silent, regal. He shielded his eyes to make out the writing on the nearest blimp, and nearly fell over in shock when he read the words "Welcome Back Brian!"

See. I told you that you would be remembered.

The living statue at his side had doubled in size. His velvety cloak had been replaced by a living carpet of plants and blossoms that flowed out behind him. Everywhere the garment touched, sprigs of new growth sprang to life. Vibrant butterflies alighted on the leaves and bees buzzed between the flowers. A series of concentric circles ringed his head in an oblique reference to his planetary association.

"I don't understand," Brian stuttered. "What is all this?"

They're here to honor you. They've been waiting for decades.

"But why? Why me?"

This is the 100th anniversary of my awakening. They are all here to express their gratitude. Saturnus lifted his massive hands, then lowered them, and the obedient crowd quieted enough to allow Brian to think. The air was thick with expectation, and hundreds of pairs of eyes were fixed on the man and the god. Saturnus's steps were so long, Brian had to jog to keep up with him as the crowd parted and they began to walk through the throng.

"All of these people worship you now?"

Even though his face remained shrouded, a hint of a smile seeped into the god's voice. *All of the people on the planet worship me now. The human race has entered a period of peace and tranquility not seen since Janus and I reigned in Latium. It is a new Golden Age.*

As they made their way down the middle of the street, musicians struck up a tune behind them. It was made up of layered, competing melodies that was not entirely pleasant. The crowd continued to part to let them pass, but the gap was immediately swallowed as people crushed in to be as close to them as possible. A few times, eager hands reached out and touched Brian, and one person even made a bold attempt to snatch his glasses for a souvenir.

Brian batted the man away, and he slunk off into the sea of faces. "So, what you're telling me is that once you could leave the cave, you what, snapped your fingers and made world peace?"

Saturnus let loose a full-belly laugh. *Do you really think it would be that easy? No, it has taken time and I have taken great pains to arrive at this moment. I had to gather more followers so I could demonstrate my power. There have been plagues and famines in the meantime, often of humankind's own making. I offered another path, one of clean air and growing things. Though, the transition of power was not without its detractors.* The giant directed Brian's attention to the corner of the next block. A huge bronze statue jutted into the roadway. The figures were larger than life size and, because of the festivities, wreathed in flowers. Only when they were abreast of the monument could Brian make out the scene of one set of soldiers viciously slaughtering another while a hooded figure looked down on it all.

There were many sacrifices along the way. If I had to guess, probably at least half of the humans perished in the struggle. And each and every death of a follower fed my power. Now, no one bothers to resist.

"Sacrifices…" Brian murmured. The scale of death the god talked about was so large, Brian's mind could barely hold the idea. Despite the chaos all around him, he fell silent and contemplative. "But, did you really just say half?"

Give or take. Saturnus shrugged, dislodging a bird that had taken up its roost in the tangle of vines on his massive shoulder. *But don't let that worry you too much. Nowadays, I've grown so powerful that I don't require nearly as many. Just on my festival days, the occasional blessing for a good harvest, marking important dates, that kind of thing. You know, you should really try to enjoy this more.* Saturnus sounded perturbed even in the confines of Brian's skull. *At least wave or something. Give the people what they want.*

"You're talking about 'sacrifice' like it's the most reasonable thing in the world. Like killing people is no more than flipping a switch."

You know all about sacrifices.

A vision of Charlie flashed before Brian's eyelids and he stumbled. A few friendly people in the crowd rushed forward to help him, and he returned an anemic smile of thanks. When he got himself steadied, he said, "That was an accident."

I don't mean that. The god flapped his massive hand dismissively, as if

Charlie's death were no more than one of his bees that got too close. *I am talking about all of the other times. You've been chipping away at your soul for decades in service of your goals.*

Their strange procession reached the foot of a monumental staircase, but the god never paused. The building at the top was a clear homage to the Roman temples that Brian studied, a triangular roof held aloft by an army of columns. The crowd here was even thicker. People were clinging to the roofs of surrounding buildings just to catch a glimpse. Children snaked in and out of the legs of adults to get a few feet closer. Flowers rained down from all sides just to be crushed beneath stomping feet.

"If everyone is so happy to see me, I suppose that means I was never tried for murder."

Correct.

"So, when I go back, do I become a priest for you or something? Help you spread the good word and find followers?"

Back? Why would go you back?

This brought Brian up short, and he paused a few steps from the top of the staircase. When Saturnus realized he no longer followed, he stopped and turned around. The scholar's mouth was suddenly painfully dry, but even over the murmur of the crowd, the giant heard him rasp, "I have to go back. My life is there. My work."

Saturnus shook his head slowly, then continued mounting the stair. *Your proper place and time are here and now. I told you. Today is very special.*

Brian reluctantly followed. When they reached the top of the stairs, Saturnus stood to the side of a dais. He motioned at Brian, and he understood he was supposed to climb on top of it. With far less grace than one would wish for, given the size of the audience, he got himself up. His head now reached the height of Saturnus's shoulder. The undulating multitude below stretched as far as the eye could see. The nearest giant screen showed a panned-out version of him atop the stone table, but the image shifted closer as he watched. It took only a moment to spot the drone that was making its dramatic swoop up the stairs to focus on him once more. He had the feeling that someone, somewhere must be doing a running commentary as if it was a sports game.

At the far end of the thoroughfare, Brian could just make out the cave that housed the original temple to Saturnus. The light of the sunset bathed the entire cliff in its amber glow. Which made the cool shadows gathering around him all the stranger.

The sky above was a swirl of bruise-colored clouds. The whirlpool grew thicker with every passing moment and the temperature dropped. Massive urns to either side of the dais whooshed to life with tongues of flame to compensate, but it did little to stop the shudder creeping up Brian's spine when everyone gathered grew silent. The drone buzzed closer to the altar, then started on a path that sent is slowly spiraling higher and higher around the dais.

Brian leaned a little closer to Saturnus and whispered, "Am I supposed to do something? They're all staring at me." He fidgeted with his dirty shirt, unsure what to do with his hands.

Of course, they're staring. I told you, they're all here to see you.

The giant tipped his head back and stretched his arms out beside him. For the first time in their long relationship, the god allowed the hood to slip away from his head, revealing a tumble of gray curls. In the screens, Brian could see the piercing emerald of his irises for a moment before Saturnus closed his eyes. Tendrils of lightning flashed across the gray expanse like the glowing white roots of an electrical tree digging into the earth. Saturnus took in a deep breath, and when Brian exhaled, it came out as a puff of steam.

"Yeah, okay." Brian followed the god's gaze to the rapidly darkening sky. "But see me do what?

The god exhaled as the first drop from the thunderhead hit the altar.

Sacrifice.

The Hornbill and the Lame Horse

By Ali Abbas

Amarna pinched a coil spring in her needle-nosed pliers and settled it on its pin. Holding her breath, she drew out the tongue of the spring and teased it through a maze of wheels. She gripped the edge of her desk with her left hand to steady herself, let go and clamped the spring in place. She let out her breath with a surge of relief.

From there the work was easy. She reassembled the control unit with brisk efficiency and limped over to the dented husking machine that loomed over everything in her workshop. The control unit slotted in place with a satisfying snap.

Her timing was perfect. Netta, the machine's owner, blocked the sunlight streaming in through the wide-open double doors. "Is it working, dear?" the hunched old lady asked.

"I'm about to test it, auntie," Amarna replied.

"Just as well I brought something for all your trouble." Netta held out a small hessian bag in one mottled fist. She kept her eyes on Amarna's face, politely not glancing at the younger woman's left leg as Amarna approached.

Amarna pasted on a smile. She gave a small bow of respect as she took the rice and poured it into the hopper. There was barely two cups worth. Once the husks were removed, she would struggle to scrape together enough for a meal.

She cranked up the machine and pulled the long-handled lever. Nothing happened. She reset the controls and tried again. The machine stayed stubbornly silent.

"Just a moment," Amarna said. In two ungainly steps, she was back at her bench. From her canvas tool roll, she picked out a heavy, flat object with a handle at one end. The tool had no discernible purpose, but there was a reassuring heft to it.

She limped back to the machine and rapped it smartly on the side. Something chimed inside. The machine came to life with a rattle and clank. Amarna hooked the now empty bag over the outfeed pipe and gave a genuine smile of satisfaction as pearly white rice poured into it.

"There you go, auntie. I'll have Jaun load it on the cart and take it for you tomorrow."

"Oh, no thank you, dear. I'll send my nephew to pick it up." Netta added a little stress to "nephew."

Amarna schooled her features again. "Of course, auntie."

It was late when Amarna's brother Jaun returned from his rounds. Amarna laid out dinner as he secured the cart and saw to the horse.

Jaun folded himself down onto his mat. "Here." He held out a bright yellow pear.

Amarna took it with a quizzical look.

"I gave Colek a lift home, he gave me this in return."

"An hour out of your way for a single pear. That sounds fair."

"Oh, and what did Netta pay you for the hours of your time, and the parts, and the years you spent learning your craft?"

Amarna dipped her head sheepishly and lifted the lid on the small basket of steaming rice. Jaun laughed, and after a moment of hesitation, Amarna joined him.

"Since we're celebrating getting paid, I brought something else for you." Jaun pulled a small metal canister from his pouch. Amarna froze. Machine oil. Not the runny stuff she made from used cooking oil. This was the heavy oil that stuck to metal parts to provide long-lasting protection and lubrication.

"For your leg," Jaun explained. "The joints are getting a bit creaky."

"We can't afford this," Amarna whispered as Jaun placed the canister in her left hand and closed her right over it with his own. He smiled as his ring chimed against the twin ring she wore.

"I had a busy day. The pear from Colek was a bonus."

Amarna hid her face behind her long, dark red hair. "You should eat before it gets cold," she said without looking up.

Jaun had left by the time Amarna woke the next day. He would be looking for work between the outlying farms and the village with their trusty old horse and mechanical cart. Amarna's work came directly to her. Their neighbours could not afford anything new, and she had inherited her father's knack for fixing things.

She allowed herself a few moments to enjoy the sounds of the morning. Birds chittered and trilled; the wind carried distant snatches of farmers chanting as they worked in the rice fields.

Amarna took a deep breath. The morning's work would not wait. She flipped back the light blanket and pushed up on her elbows, dragging herself into a sitting position. Despite years of practice, she hated this part of the day. Slowly, she drew up her sarong to reveal her legs. Their pale, washed almond tone darkened suddenly at her ankles, her feet lined with stripes from her sandals.

Her right leg was whole and healthy. The left fared well in comparison as far as the knee, although there was a band of calluses across her thigh. Below the knee was a different matter. Her calf withered and twisted to her ankle.

The metal callipers that allowed her to walk without visible aid had been made by her father. In the years since his death she had not found a way to improve on the design, copying the prototype until, at the age of eighteen, there was no need to make larger versions.

She carefully bound the leather straps, checked the minute gears and pistons, and rose to her feet. Her sarong slipped back down, the edge dragging on the floor. Other girls wore theirs a little higher, showing off their ankles, more if they could evade the sight of their elders.

A creak from her callipers reminded Amarna of the oil canister waiting beside her sleeping mat. Breakfast first, she decided.

Her tea was steeping when their meagre flock of chickens began to squawk, breaking the peace of the morning. She took the long-handled broom and went outside, expecting to chase off a feral dog.

Something rustled in the trees above the chicken coop. Leaves drifted down. The whole tree shook. Metal glinted between the branches.

Fear gripped Amarna. It must be a man with a sword. She took a couple of steps back, her left foot slipping out of its sandal. Her crossbow hung inside the front door of the house, and Jaun would not be back until evening. She could defend herself for a while, but an armed man would not be stopped for long by a broom.

"We don't have anything worth stealing," she called, wiping the sweat from one hand then the other and resetting her grip on the handle, trying to avoid the thought that he might not be here to steal.

The tree rustled in response. The branches parted, scattering leaves. A bird launched itself out of the foliage, extending its vast wings and diving directly at her. She stumbled back, momentarily blinded as sunlight reflected off its body.

The bird crashed into the hard-packed ground with a screech of tortured metal. Its beak dug into the surface, twisting its neck.

Amarna's scream died in her throat. It was a mechanical hornbill, larger than any real specimen. The wings flapped once, twice, then stopped. From the steel bell of its body came the unmistakable sound of a spring snapping. Eyes wide, she approached and dropped to the ground beside it.

Each feather was individually made, she could see that at once. Not cast but hammered then cut and etched into shape. Its wingspan was longer than Amarna was tall. In wonder, she ran her hands over the body. Across the broad sweep of its back she could see the outline of a hatch to access the mechanism inside, the shut lines so fine she could not slip in a fingernail. Afire with curiosity, she hunted for a latch, pressed and prodded to see if there were some means of opening it.

Nothing worked. There was no way she could drag something this massive into her workshop. She gave a frustrated yawp and thumped the ground. She wanted to know how it worked, to admire the skill and artistry, and she wanted some clues to its maker.

As if in response to her shout, there was a faint click from the hornbill. She reached out, gently lifting the feathers around the hatch. Where the enormous horned head and neck met the body a slot had opened. Amarna could have sworn it had not been there before.

It needed a key, of course it did. No one would make such a marvel and leave it free for anyone to poke around inside. Defeated at last, she pushed herself to her feet and stepped away. Her stomach growled. She would have breakfast and then figure out how to get past the lock.

Her tea had gone cold. She swigged it with a grimace. Too agitated to eat anything, she paced unevenly around her workshop. Her eye caught her tool roll. An idea formed. She flipped open the roll and pulled out the heavy, blunt instrument she had never found a proper use for.

It wasn't a rasp or a file, the sides and edges were perfectly smooth. It wasn't a chisel, there was no sharp edge. The unusual weight distribution and small handle made it an ineffective hammer. She took it outside. The rectangular profile fit into the slot precisely. She eased the tool into the body of the bird. There was no lateral movement, no twisting. Two-thirds of the way down the tool stopped. She felt a little give in its motion. She pressed. With a sharp click, the tool dropped fully into the hornbill's body, leaving only the handle exposed. She gave the handle an anti-clockwise twist. Two feather-covered doors sprang open on the bird's back.

Amarna tumbled away in surprise, her rigid left leg twisting and pivoting her body into the dirt. She did not move for several ragged breaths.

It was hours later than Jaun found her sitting at her desk in the dark. She watched as he lit a lantern and approached with silent steps in case she was asleep. Weighted by odds and ends, a paper lay unrolled before her. Her eyes must have caught the light, he put the lantern down with a heavy tap.

She didn't look up, and her voice made him jump.

"We have to leave, Jaun."

When he didn't answer Amarna looked up. There was a bloodless, sickly cast to his skin, as if a sick premonition had settled on him. He could not have missed the enormous metal bird in the yard. He might not understand the science that led to its creation, but he understood well enough that it was a harbinger of change.

"The flight engine of that bird is one of our father's designs. He never had the materials here to make it." Jaun would know by the set of her jaw and the crease at the edge of her eyes that her mind was set. To make sure she filled her tone with every ounce of certainty and determination she could muster. "Someone sent it for us. We're going to follow the hornbill's path back. I have to know who made it and what it is they want."

It took almost a month for them to make ready. Amarna barely left her workshop in that time. The hornbill represented a level of technology she could not hope to replicate, and without her father's plans and notebooks, she would have been lost in her attempts at repairs. Even so, the direction-finding controls defeated her. All she could do was reverse the hornbill's record of its journey and hope it would follow the route back.

Meanwhile, Jaun quietly sold what they would not be able to take with them. The home where the siblings grew up would be locked in the hope they would one day return to it and their father's grave under the shade of a palm tree.

At last, the day came when Amarna inserted the reversed metal ribbon of flight directions, and Jaun gave a final crank to the bank of springs, winched the hornbill to the roof of their home, and removed the heavy, flat key from the base of its neck. He then flicked a switch beneath its wing.

It took a moment for the bird to wake. The hornbill raised its head and rotated its neck as if stretching or orientating itself. It took off with a mighty sweep of its wings, circled the house once, and flew away.

"I still think we should have put a message in its claws," Amarna said as Jaun climbed down.

"We don't know what we are heading into. Let's just be cautious."

"I know, I know. Now hush, I'm working," Amarna replied. She added the bearing of the bird's flight to her notebook, scribbling furiously. With a bright smile, she lifted her head. "I knew it."

"What?"

"If the makers were anywhere south or west of us, I would have heard of them. To the north, there is open ocean that stretches beyond the reach of our ships, let alone the bird. But northeast we have mountains. It is flying straight at them. The hornbill does not fly high, and its navigation instructions were filled with twists and turns. We have a map to cross the mountains and find what lies beyond."

Jaun sighed and checked the lock on the door, then climbed up on the cart beside his sister.

"It's good weather for travelling, no point in hanging around here any longer."

"Wait. Look back at the house," Amarna instructed. "That way you know we'll return."

Jaun indulged her superstition, then flicked the reins.

The journey took them away from the village, away from the frequented paths to rutted roads along overgrown tracks. The land gave way from farms to pastures to forests. Through the lowlands, the bird's flight meant it could ignore the terrain, but for Amarna and Jaun the six rivers they crossed formed a formidable barrier, taking them miles off course as they sought bridges and fords. The easy pace of their aged horse was accompanied by the regular clicks of Amarna's measuring wheel as she charted their journey with her small, neat notation.

Their path led through the foothills and into the rugged terrain of the mountains.

"Look," Amarna said to Jaun as they paused to consider their route. She pointed between the steep rock walls on either side. The old water trail they followed now forked. "The hornbill could have flown above this. Making it fly at a lower altitude and follow the terrain was deliberate. I'm sure now, whoever sent it wanted us to follow it back."

She snapped her notebook closed and pointed to the right-hand fork.

Jaun leapt down from the cart and strode up to the horse.

"I'll lead," he said. "You'll have to loosen the suspension a bit and be ready to run the spring drive if it gets too steep."

"But I need to keep tally for my charts," Amarna complained, pointing at the paraphernalia of compasses and dividers that littered the writing desk across her knees.

Jaun cocked his head to one side and waited. An exasperated huff from his sister signalled her acquiescence.

It was only when they stopped for the night, a fire lit between them and Amarna settled on a mound of blankets, that he asked the question that had troubled Amarna since the hornbill landed in their yard.

"Do you really think this has something to do with our father?" When she did not answer he went on. "How did the sender know where to find us?"

Amarna stared into the fire, rolling a cup of tea between her palms. Their father had spent more time with her than Jaun, and he always deflected questions about his life before the village, and about their mother. Amarna had hoped he would open up on the matter as she grew older but his death, shortly before her fifteenth birthday, robbed her of the opportunity to find out.

In the five years since she had scoured his records and notebooks and found no hints to his history. It was as if he had carefully edited his life.

"Promise me you won't laugh?" she asked.

"When have I ever –"

"Please."

"Very well. I promise."

Amarna took off her destiny ring. In childhood, she had worn it on a chain around her neck until it fit, first on her thumb and now on the ring finger of her right hand. She held it up to the light of the fire.

"I know what it says, Amarna. 'A path home.'" Jaun offered gently.

"What if this is our path home?" She asked, her voice trembling. Across the fire she saw Jaun start to speak, his hand raised, then dropping it again. Whatever argument he was about to raise was left unsaid, and she was grateful he did not pursue his original question.

"Let's see."

She nodded and gifted him a wide smile.

"Stalwart," she said. "That's what your ring says and what you have always been for me."

His smile in return showed her he would follow the path with her.

After days of struggling against the terrain, the land fell away from them. Coming around a sharp bend the vista opened up. A dense forest covered the horizon. Between them and the forest was a vast river, wider than any they had crossed. There was no sign of civilisation.

Brother and sister shared a grim look. Had they come so far to be defeated at last? Amarna pulled out her spyglass and searched the horizon, then the banks of the river. Something caught her eye, fractionally unnatural.

"There." She pointed. "Something isn't quite right. We'll find a way across,

I'm sure of it."

It took most of the day to descend to the river. The dipping sun scattered sparkling jewels across the swift-flowing water. Lush, deep green grass spotted with moss-covered rocks carpeted the shore.

Amarna made a beeline for the bank. A squared edge of turf jutted out into the river. Amarna dropped to her knees accompanied by a squeal from her callipers. She felt through the dense sward, fingers crawling in search of an anomaly.

"The grass is a bit lighter where you are." Jaun's voice came from unusually high up. She twisted to see him standing on a boulder, hands on his hips. "I'd say the patch is about six feet wide and twelve feet long." He hopped down and pulled a couple of tent stakes from the cart. He drove a stake in just short of Amarna's foot with a mallet. It sank deep into the soil. He drove in another, a little closer to her, and she snatched her foot away with a yelp, noting his smirk for future retribution. The stake stalled after a couple of inches. A hollow, metallic sound reverberated under Amarna.

She scrambled to the water's edge, dragging her left foot, then peered into the darkness underneath the overhanging bank. After a moment there was a splash and Jaun's bare knees appeared before her.

Amarna knocked sharply against what her questing fingers had found. The same dull boom rose from the turf. Jaun ducked into the water, careless of his clothes. Amarna felt a rumble underneath her. She gasped as the gleaming prow of a boat emerged from under the bank. Jaun came up beside it, huffing and blowing.

"There's a boathouse hidden in the bank," he said. He pulled the boat out a little further, then went hand over hand along its rail, legs kicking. It seemed the riverbed dropped away steeply. He stopped on the other side of the boat. "There's some kind of rope here. It stretches across the river, but well under the waterline."

He pushed the boat back under the bank.

"What are you doing?" Amarna demanded. "We should cross now before it gets completely dark."

"No." Jaun hauled himself out of the water and peeled off his shirt before wringing it out. "We camp here tonight, behind that pile of boulders." He pointed a hundred yards back up the slope. "We can't take the cart with us, the boat is too small, so we have to plan what we leave behind. Also, someone has taken great pains to hide the way across. I'd rather have the river between us and the unknown overnight. Plus…" He flicked water from his shirt at Amarna. "I'm cold and wet and hungry."

"You definitely needed a bath, though," Amarna muttered as she limped back to the cart.

The next morning Amarna chafed, shoulders dipping and rising as she paced on the riverbank while Jaun took the cart back up the trail and hid it under a dusty tarp. Only after he had tested and retested the balance of the boat were they ready to leave.

Their horse stepped sedately on board, as if he had done this many times. Amarna was less assured, finding her callipers could not adjust to the rocking motion. She thumped down onto the backboard rather than risk tipping over the side.

The turn of a windlass pulled the boat along the cable. Before they were halfway across Jaun was drenched in sweat, and the boat had stretched the cable noticeably downstream, bowing away from the anchor points. As Jaun hauled on the windlass he was now having to pull against the current. An ominous creak ripped along the side of the boat.

The horse stamped and shuffled, its placid demeanour ruffled by the impending danger. Jaun chanced a look at Amarna, at the distant bank, and at the horse.

"Get on his back," he barked.

"What?"

"Get on his back. He can swim, you can't." Jaun went back to the windlass, his straining shoulders set against any argument.

Amarna struggled to her feet. As the boat pulled and tipped she threw both arms around the horse, holding on to its reassuring bulk. Jaun locked the windlass and boosted her up onto its bare back. She wrapped the reins in one fist and draped her arms around the horse's neck, crooning as much to soothe herself as to calm her mount.

Jaun unlocked the windlass and pushed. A loud crack boomed through the boat. He fell forward, the windlass spinning free. The cable had snapped behind them. The boat swung in an accelerating arc towards the far bank.

"Get ready to jump," Jaun called. Scrambling, he shovelled their gear to the sides, trying to clear a path along the flat bottom. As the bank closed in with alarming speed he scuttled back and slapped the horse's rump.

Amarna yelped as the horse bolted forward, taking two steps along the boat and hopping out just as the boat smashed into the bank. The horse scrabbled, slipping sideways as Amarna held on, left leg afire as she tried not to slide off its back. Jaun was thrown overboard the other way, a splintering shriek signalling the boat's demise.

Their gear was ruined. Amarna tore through packs. She dumped a dripping pile of papers onto the muddy bank. All her father's notes, his plans and blueprints were lost. Ink bled through the pages and over her fingers. She collapsed among the soaking debris of their lives and wept.

They trudged, weary and disheartened, through a dense forest. At first, Amarna tried to trade her place on horseback with Jaun, at least for short spells, but he would not hear of it, joking that he was better off walking than riding on the pile of blankets she used as a saddle.

It was in this state of despair that their world changed. Amarna rode in a daze; it took her a moment to register the horse had stopped. She dragged herself out of a deep well of introspection.

Jaun was off to the left, his blue shirt peeking through the underbrush. She was about to tease him over his sudden need to relieve himself when she noted the unnatural quiet of the forest. Jaun crouched, tense, ready to spring into a small clearing. Amarna nudged the horse forward. The trail veered left, and she might find a better vantage point.

A break in the trees opened up her line of sight. A woman lay in a clearing, pulling desperately at her leg which was caught under a tree root. She kept glancing up, as if danger approached. The low bushes shivered behind her.

Blue flickered at the edge of Amarna's vision. Jaun rose from his crouch just as a brown bear surged into the clearing. Jaun launched a rock at it, sailing over the woman and hitting the bear squarely on the forehead. The bear roared and turned away. Jaun leapt up and raced to the woman, yanking up the root so she could pull her foot free.

She tried to stand and fell into his arms. The bear roared again, only a few feet from them. Time slowing to a crawl as the bear lashed out. Jaun snatched the woman out of its reach, swung her over his shoulder in one smooth motion, and took off. He jumped, catching a low-hanging branch and boosting himself and the woman into a tree with a kick against its trunk.

The bear was upon them. It took another swipe then stood upright trying to reach them, shaking loose leaves with every motion. The horse whinnied in fear, twisting to flee. Amarna tugged its head back to hold it steady.

The bear turned and Amarna's insides melted. She was now its prey. It dropped down to all fours and took a step her way. Jaun dropped out of the tree onto its back, one arm wrapping around its neck. The bear reared up. Jaun pulled out his knife and stabbed it into the bear's neck. Once, twice. Blood sprayed the clearing. The bear shook and bucked. If Jaun were thrown off he would surely be crushed. He stabbed once more. The bear gave a last gurgling croak and slumped to the ground.

Thunder erupted from all sides. The clearing and trail filled with riders, their mounts lathered, stamping and snorting. Amarna slid from her own horse and lurched to her brother. Before she could reach him a young man ran up and extended a hand to help him off the ground, relief and wonder etched into his face.

The newcomer turned as Amarna approached. His eyes went wide, the colour draining from his face. She stopped. The young man gathered himself, shake his head slightly, and drop into a deep bow.

"Madam, it seems I owe your…" he paused.

"Brother," Amarna supplied.

"I owe your brother an enormous debt, for he has saved my sister," the young man said. He slapped Jaun on the back and dropped to one knee to retrieve and clean the knife. Two female riders in soft brown leggings helped the stricken woman out of the tree, she hobbled forward in obvious discomfort.

Amarna had both Jaun and the woman in her sight, so she saw the moment it happened. Their eyes met and locked. Colour rose in their faces. They looked away as the woman's brother got back to his feet.

"I am Cuman; this is my sister Cara. If you'll permit me, I would like to take you to our home and introduce you to our mother."

Amarna nodded for them both, sure that she knew what Jaun's desire would be. She turned and limped towards her horse, which was nibbling on a tuft of grass, acting unphased by the tumult and new arrivals.

"You're hurt," Cuman said with a gasp.

"Not hurt. It's no matter," Amarna replied. Suddenly self-conscious among all these strangers, her next step was a stumble. Jaun was at her side in an instant, his distraction with Cara dispelled by Amarna's need. Cuman's hand was outstretched, slower to react than her brother.

"Please, take my horse. We'll let yours have a rest."

At Cuman's insistence Amarna allowed herself to be handed up onto his horse, several hands taller than her own, its mane brushed and braided, its sweaty flanks unblemished. Cuman's thumb brushed against her destiny ring. She marked him noticing it and that he did not comment. He wore one too.

Cuman had not put himself out unduly, one of his party gave up a mount for him, and another gave way for Jaun. It seemed the brother and sister were people of influence.

The party picked its way through the forest until they reached a path which opened out into fields that swayed with heavy heads of golden grain. Cuman slowed a fraction to allow Amarna to catch up. Amarna guessed he was a little younger than her, despite his obvious authority. Jaun and Cara rode knee to knee, deep in conversation.

There was a directness and curiosity in Cuman's gaze that unnerved Amarna. She remembered Jaun's warnings that they did not know what they were heading into, or why their father left it behind. She hoped Jaun would remember that too.

"Forgive me for saying it," Cuman said, "but you seem a little unprepared for a trip through the forest. May I ask whence you came?"

"My brother and I were seeking out a new life," Amarna replied. "Our village was poor, and there were few opportunities for us." She took a breath, marshalling her thoughts. The evidence of their route would be easy enough to retrace. "Our boat sank as we crossed the river; what we did not lose to the water was ruined." Her voice choked at that, the memory of her father's life's work still raw.

"The river!" Cuman's eyes widened. "I've not heard of anyone successfully crossing it for years. The current is too strong and the banks rarely passable."

Amarna pursed her lips. "I'd hardly call our crossing a success."

"Indeed. Pardon me a moment." Cuman tugged on his reins and dropped back through the riders. Though Amarna resisted the urge to look back, she listened carefully, and after a moment heard rapid hoofbeats disappearing away behind her. Cuman had sent someone to check her story.

Jaun trotted up beside her, his face flushed and a smile tugging at his lips. It faded as he saw her clouded expression.

"Be on your guard," she said quietly. This time she did glance back at Cara. "There's a gulf in our stations, Jaun. I fear she'll break your heart." A clatter from the rear announced Cuman's imminent return. "And best not mention the bird for now." Her heart sank at his stricken look. "Quickly, what did you say?"

"Nothing about you fixing it, or that it landed in our home. Only that we took our direction from a huge silver hornbill, hoping it was a sign."

She let out a breath. "Good, that works. I told Cuman we're seeking a new life and we crossed the river. It seems that is an unusual feat."

Cara nudged up beside them. Amarna pointed at a tall building on a nearby rise that caught her attention.

"Is that a windmill?"

"Indeed it is. Are they common where you are from?" Cara tilted her head as she asked her question, the sunlight catching in her rich mahogany-coloured hair. Brother and sister were much alike.

"Not really. Our climate was placid, so we used them to wind up our clockwork machines and fill reservoirs for water pumps rather than as a reliable way to get work done."

"You speak like an artificer," Cara observed with a raised eyebrow.

Amarna fixed on a smile, realising she might have given away more than she intended.

Jaun stepped in to rescue her. "It's a fact of rural life. Everyone needs to know a little of how things work."

"What an interesting thought. Machines are rare for us, and the skill to make or mend them almost non-existent." She twisted in her saddle. Cuman still hung back a little way. She leaned forward and pitched her voice low. "Most of our windmills are not in good working order. The artificer who built them is no longer with us, and our country is hard to reach. Few visitors come with new ways of doing things. It is something my brother hopes to change."

"Your brother?" Amarna asked. "Is he…"

Cara's laugh was like a cascade of bells. Amarna felt a surge of warmth towards her even as her jaw dropped.

"My brother will be king one day. We are twins, but he pushed his way past me to come out first." Cara's eyes twinkled with mirth.

"Your highness, I'm sorry I spoke so…" Jaun's face had gone stark white, and he could not finish his sentence. Cara rocked in the saddle as she laughed. It wasn't a cruel or teasing sound, but one of genuine joy. The look she gave Jaun was at once frank and warm.

"I would not have had you talk to me any other way. I owe you my life." Her own voice faltered, and a blush rose up her neck to suffuse her face.

Amarna cleared her throat, uncomfortably aware that she rode between them.

"Do we have much further to go?" she asked.

Cara's bright smile returned. "Just over this next rise." She called out to Cuman. "We are nearly home, Brother. What reward do you propose for the man who saved my life?" Her eyes danced with mischief.

Cuman was not to be outdone. "Our new friends have but one horse, Sister. A faithful steed it might be, but I think they could do with another. I shall offer Master Jaun a horse."

"A horse! The life of your sister is worth but a horse?" Cara halted and turned to face her brother.

"Peace, Sister. Not just any horse, they shall have their pick from our stables, any horse they choose." Cuman bowed deeply in his saddle.

Cara lifted her chin and nudged her horse on. "Very well, that is a suitable place to start."

Within the city walls, Amarna saw evidence of Cara's words. The basic mechanisation she expected at the wells and among the tradesmen was absent. The city seemed less advanced than the poor village she had left behind.

The palace was beautifully maintained. A long, gravel drive through shading trees and blooming gardens led to a broad courtyard of creamy flagstones. Stewards in immaculate livery appeared to take the horses. Amarna and Jaun were whisked away to prepare for an audience with the queen.

By the time Amarna emerged from a restorative bath, a selection of clothes was laid out for her. She chose a long-tailed shirt and the trousers the local women seemed to favour. The wide legs would serve to hide her callipers.

Her scruffy satchel stood out against the clean, richly embroidered clothes. After casting around for a solution she emptied it out. Her tool roll, writing, and navigation equipment littered a velvet divan. None of it was appropriate to take to an audience with royalty. She unrolled her tools, finding a moment of contentment in their familiar shapes and weights. Her fingers lingered on the strange, flat tool that had unlocked the hornbill. She had taken to thinking of it as a key. Unsure why, she took it out of its slot and, rolling up the leg of her trousers, strapped it to her callipers. She felt better leaving the rest behind knowing the key was on her person.

She met Jaun in the corridor, pleased to see he had chosen similar colours to her, and that his usually unruly hair had been flattened into an approximation of tidiness.

Another liveried servant approached with a curtsey. "The queen is engaged presently. Prince Cuman has asked for you in the stables."

The servant adjusted her pace to Amarna's slow gait. They were led through a series of hallways until a pair of large doors opened out into the stable yard. Cuman, washed and dressed in more formal clothes, was waiting for them.

"I promised you the pick of the stables, although I would count it a favour if you did not choose my mother's favourite horse."

Amarna could not resist returning his charming smile. Then hers died as she saw him notice her awkward steps. She felt Jaun stiffen beside her, always alert on her behalf.

"It is no trouble to have the stable hands bring them out one by one," Cuman offered, his face a mask of polite neutrality.

"Thank you, but no. I'm just a little less elegant than some other ladies."

"Elegance has many measures," Cuman replied with a little tilt of his head. Amarna sensed the tension drain out of Jaun as her smile returned.

There were many beautiful horses; all tall and broad-chested. Their own placid, unremarkable mare seemed to be a different species. Despite the attraction, none of them would do. Could this city really be their destination? Nothing there pointed to the level of sophistication required to make the hornbill. They would have to journey on, and for that, they needed a stout and sturdy creature.

The far end of the stable was deeply shadowed, pierced by the odd shaft of sunlight from an open shutter or gap in the wall. Amarna wandered into the gloom as Jaun and Cuman chatted about the merits of one horse over another.

The stables were many times larger than her home, and yet she found something familiar about them. They were well-engineered, with a vaulted roof. The spacing and dimensions of each stall stirred her memory. Although the last few stalls were unoccupied, a sense of knowing pulled Amarna forward. The last stall, she was sure, would be larger than the others.

It also had an occupant.

Amarna's gasp brought Jaun running.

"Oh," he said when he saw what she had discovered.

"When you said any horse in the stable, did you mean it?" Amarna asked Cuman as he hurried up to join them.

The horse was made from a burnished, silvery metal, its skin a myriad of tiny links that flowed over lifelike musculature. Jewelled eyes shone in the gloom. Amarna paced around it, admiring the artistry of its construction. The metal mane flowed like hair, each filament smooth and tapered. Her fingers found the small imperfection that hid the crank cover on its hindquarters, exactly where she expected it to be. She continued around the horse, out of sight of Cuman, under the mane there was a slot. Amarana could not measure it, but she knew, without a shadow of doubt, that it was the same dimensions as the key slot in the hornbill. Her father had made this horse.

"This is not something I think I can give," Cuman stammered, his urbane demeanour lost.

"You offered them a horse, Brother. Any horse in the stable. You should make your promises with greater care." Unnoticed, Cara had joined them, a crutch under one arm, her injured foot off the floor. Close enough to Jaun that their sleeves touched.

Cuman looked stricken but nodded helplessly.

Amarna could not sleep. The bed was too soft. She missed her floor mat and the familiar sounds from her home. She clambered out of bed and strapped on her callipers. She had to see the horse again. She considered waking Jaun, she even peeked into his adjoining room but his deep, settled breathing from a lump on the floor stopped her. She would let him rest, he deserved it.

An oil lamp burned at the entrance to the stable. Amarna took it and stepped inside quietly, taking extra care to lift and place her left foot, rather than let it scuff or drag. There would be stable hands nearby, and alarming the horses might rouse them.

The metal horse had not moved. She ran her hands over a flank, marvelling at the fine links. They may have lost the trail of the hornbill, but this was undoubtedly where they were meant to be. What she could not make sense of was the disparity. Here was a mechanical marvel, even if it never moved, the artistry alone rendered it priceless. Yet somehow the nation that could conceive and construct this could not maintain its own infrastructure or create basic water lifts and wind pumps.

She sighed. Cara had mentioned an artificer who had brought new learning and left again. Amarna was sure that was her father. What had brought him here, and what made him leave? She knew first-hand that he was as gifted a teacher as he was an engineer. Why abandon these people to their fate?

A horse nickered near the stable doors. Footsteps pattered. Amarna froze as she heard a girlish giggle.

"Someone will find us," a female voice said.

"No one comes here at night," a male voice replied.

Another giggle. Amarna sank back into the wall. They were coming towards her, and as long as the tryst lasted she was trapped. She squeezed her eyes shut and jabbed the wall with her elbow in frustration. Something clicked and the wall give way behind her. She overbalanced, falling into a dark room as the hidden door pivoted behind her. The lovers were immediately silent.

The lamp was left behind on the stall floor. The secret room was pitch black. Her fingers found walls on both sides and brushed what she hoped was the catch for the hidden door.

She dared not return, not yet. She had no way of knowing if the lovers had made their escape or come to investigate. Her questing right foot found a stair leading down. Gingerly she rose to her feet, hand above her head in case the ceiling was low.

It took several minutes to traverse the dozen or so stairs. Amarna's final step echoed, suggesting a large space ahead of her. Feeling her way along the wall, she bumped into a table, its edge jarring her thighs. She sucked in her gasp.

Tentative passes of her hands discovered a bowl of matches. She lit one and found oil lamps on the table. With a sigh of relief, she lit several.

She turned and screamed. A stern face stared; implacable eyes bore into her. Amarna fell back into the wall, scrabbling towards the stairs, slipping. She screamed again, there were more.

None of them moved. They were statues, soldiers lined up ready to march, but all immobile. She approached, fear overwhelmed by her curiosity. Not statues, automata, alternately armed with swords and pikes. She picked up a lamp and raised it above her head. The soldiers stretched away into the distance, rank upon rank, an entire army.

Dust lay thick on their shoulders. A spider's web ran from a pauldron to the cast metal ear of the one nearest her. She hadn't seen a design for anything like this in her father's papers. She shook her head. On closer examination, it was not her father's work at all. The castings were crude, with small gaps between the plates and defects in the finish that he would never have tolerated.

She undid the clasps on the nearest one. The chest cavity opened with a squeal. Belt drives looped up from the legs and spread out to the arms. The motor was missing. The space would accommodate something the size and shape of the hornbill's impressively powerful and efficient unit.

Amarna opened another, it too was missing a motor.

She paced along the row, looking for some clue to what she had found here. Something deeper in the room caught her eye, a break in the dizzying ranks of soldiers. She zigzagged her way through towards what seemed to be the centre of the room. The hornbill perched on a plinth, beak tucked into its chest.

"Does he live?"

Amarna almost dropped the lantern, startled by a woman's voice. A figure carrying a shuttered light emerged from behind a soldier. A twist opened the shutters, bathing the woman in a golden glow. She was tall, almost as tall as Jaun. Grey shot through dark hair that fell down below her shoulders. From her looks and her bearing, Amarna had no doubt this was Cara's mother. She bowed to the queen.

"Your father, Kudus, does he live?" There was a fragility to the question, as if the queen's voice was about to break.

"How…" Amarna stopped, realising she was answering back to royalty. "A short illness took him, Your Majesty. The red cough."

"He used to say 'I wish I could fix people…'"

"The way I can fix machines," Amarna finished the quote. "He built this hornbill and the horse, didn't he?"

"He did. The hornbill was to celebrate your brother's birth, the horse was for yours. Before and between he waged a single-handed war to bring my people the fruits of modernity." The queen came up and stroked the hornbill, as if it were a pet and not a machine.

Curiosity burned through Amarna, a chance at last to fill in the holes in her father's life story. "Why did he leave?"

"I don't think anything could have kept him here after your mother's death. When he and I differed over a matter of policy, he took it as his moment to depart."

"The soldiers," Amarna whispered to herself, forgetting how close the Queen was.

"You are perceptive."

"You wanted his motor to power your army, but he refused." Amarna blurted with a flash of accusation. "He couldn't have made those soldiers, they're too shoddy."

The queen laughed, a full-throated, head-back laugh. "You are just like him. Truth bubbles out of you, and you can't control it." She reached out and touched Amarna's cheek. "So like him. And you are right again. When he learned of their existence he would have nothing to do with them."

"Did you think he would have changed his mind when you sent the hornbill?"

"At last an incorrect deduction. I counselled against sending it, but Cuman has been raised on the legend of the artificer. He will be king after me, so I gave in. He was sure the artificer would return and mend all that has fallen into disrepair."

"How did it find us?"

"That secret your father took to his grave. We had no idea where the bird would fly, if it would even return, or who it might bring. Cuman judged it to be worth the chance. We could not follow when it went over the river. I thought the horse would be all I had left to remind me of Kudus." The queen threaded an arm through Amarna's and paced around the plinth. "Your father was a deep one. He planned everything meticulously, even his departure. It has been almost twenty years since he left, and only today did we find the remains of the cable he used to make the river crossing."

"What was he to you?" Amarna asked, not knowing if she would get another chance to pose the question that burned in her.

"A friend once." The fragility in the queen's voice returned. "I comforted him when your mother died, but it wasn't enough to overcome our differences." Her eyes locked with Amarna's. "It may comfort you to know he valued you both over his creations. I had the hornbill and the horse guarded, but not his children. It seems I made a habit of misjudging him." She stroked Amarna's cheek again and turned away. "The horse is yours; it was always yours. It will not do you much good. It was the only time I knew Kudus to be cruel. At least, I like to believe he did not know I was pregnant." With that, she left.

Amarna stood rooted to the spot, only as the lantern began to gutter, and her tears had run dry did she return to the stairs and drag her weary body back to her room. The sky had begun to lighten as she collapsed on the bed and sank into an exhausted, dreamless sleep.

The audience with the queen in a spacious, vaulted, and mirrored chamber was brief. Amarna and Jaun were thanked and invited to stay as long as they wished. The queen remained cool and aloof, giving no hint of her late-night encounter with Amarna.

Throughout, Amarna could not bear to face her brother. All her life he had been her support, cheerfully, without complaint. The blossoming romance with Cara, already doomed by the difference in their stations, could not even give him a moment of joy. Amarna dreaded the moment she would have to tell him of her discovery.

As they departed the audience chamber, Amarna glanced at the mirrored wall. Cara hobbled ahead, injured ankle unsettling her steps. In that moment, as both women measured their steps with care, it was obvious to any onlooker that they were closely related.

Amarna's eyes met Cuman's in the mirror. He'd noticed too. She watched the colour drain from his face, his fists clench, nostrils flare. He hurried out of the audience chamber, almost at a run by the time he reached the tall, ornately decorated doors.

When at last she was back in her room, Amarna closed the door and leaned heavily against it. Her lips quivered, and tears blurred the light from the windows. She had to be the one to tell Jaun. But her strength failed, and she slid down the door and clasped her knees.

She blinked away the tears. Something was not right in her room. The rug had moved, and the angle of her satchel had changed. She clambered back to her feet and lurched over. Her things were still in the satchel, almost, but not quite, in the precise order she liked to keep them. Someone had searched her belongings.

A knock on the door made her drop the satchel. Jaun strode in without waiting for an answer.

"I think someone has searched my things," both said at once. In two steps Jaun was at her side. He tilted her head up.

"You've been crying."

Amarna tried to hold onto his gaze but failed. She wrapped her arms around him in a tight hug, she needed his strength to break his heart.

Hours later, brother and sister sat at opposite ends of the room, each lost in their own thoughts. The afternoon sun cast golden squares on the dark wooden floor. Their reveries were broken by a quiet tap on the door.

"Yes," Amarna said, her voice hoarse.

The door opened a fraction, and Cara slipped in. Her normally dancing eyes were lined with red; a hollow, haggard look replaced her customary smile. She glanced at where Jaun sat, his head hanging down, hands loose between his knees. He looked up, and they both looked away.

"You have to leave," Cara said without preamble. She limped over to Amarna and took her hands. "The notebooks have been found. Mother knows they are ruined and useless. She's determined to learn the secret of your..." she took a deep breath, "our father's motors. She dare not tear down the hornbill nor the horse for fear of destroying them, but she has no such reservations with you." Her eyes were drawn back to Jaun. "Either of you. In fact, you are a complication she could do without."

"Will she let us go?"

Cara pulled Amarna to the window. Guards now patrolled the small garden.

"How can we leave then?" Amarna asked, desperation edging her voice.

A smile pulled its way through the sadness in her half-sister's features. Cara reached up and unclipped her hair, allowing it to fall freely as Amarna's did. "Cuman made the connection already. I didn't. Or didn't want to. Mother confided in him today, and he came to tell me. He and I will ride out in your clothes and draw the guards to the river where they expect you to go. You head for the hills. I don't know where you can go from there, but you'll be out of immediate danger."

"I understand why you are helping us," Amarna said, looking over Cara's shoulder to Jaun, then back. "Why is Cuman in on it?"

"You don't know?" Cara took half a pace back. "Your mother was my aunt, my mother's elder sister. Jaun's claim to the throne precedes everyone." She tripped over his name and the set of her head showed she was resisting the urge to turn to him.

"Can Cuman be sure we won't raise a rebellion or cause trouble?" Jaun asked.

Cara turned to Jaun at last. "No, he can't. But I can. I won't even ask for your word." She looked back at Amarna, a fierce challenge in her eyes. "Tell me I'm wrong."

Amarna shook her head.

"Very well, in a short while Cuman and I will cause a commotion and ride out dressed as you. Wait in the stables until sunset. You'll have our clothes, the guards will not be looking too closely. If anyone asks, tell them you are going to the city to see a play."

"Thank you." Amarna took Cara's shoulders in her hands. "Jaun has been my rock but I always envied those girls who had a sister." Her words faltered, and the two women clasped each other then broke away. Cara left without a backward glance.

Amarna tried to block out the sound of Jaun's pacing. They waited in an empty stall at the back of the stables. An hour earlier, the shouts and clatter of guards running had announced the beginning of the ruse.

She fidgeted with her destiny ring. *A path home.* A certainty grew within her. This was not her home. Returning here was not her destiny. Whichever way they fled, she and Jaun had to cross the river and make their way back to the village. Their work and their people were all there.

While the hornbill remained, they could be found.

"Come on," she said to Jaun. She dragged him past the metal horse and through the secret panel into the chamber below, leaning on his arm to hurry down the steps. The hornbill stood in the centre of the room as she remembered. Amarna rolled up her trouser leg and unstrapped the key. In moments she had the case open and the route instructions reversed. She slipped the key under the cuff of her shirt.

There was a glass dome directly overhead. Amarna looked around and saw what she was looking for, a lever by the base of the plinth.

Jaun cranked the hornbill as the sky overhead darkened. Judging the time to be right, he pulled the lever. The glass dome above parted, the hornbill pushed off and rose out into the night.

They hurried back to the stable. Jaun was turning out of the stall when Amarna called him back. "We have to take this," she said.

"We don't even know if it works, or how it works," Jaun objected.

"Trust me. Trust our father. He prepared for everything, I'm sure he prepared for this as well." Amarna paced around the horse, feeling its flanks while Jaun brought the loaded travel bags Cara had prepared and saddled the horse for them both to ride.

"I hope you know what you're doing. They'll never believe we're Cuman and Cara on this thing."

"I know. Let's go."

Jaun lifted her up onto the horse and mounted behind her. Amarna took the soft, braided silver reins and nudged the horse forward with gentle pressure from her knees. The horse took an awkward step forward.

She guided it out of the stable. Its limping progress raised a sick feeling in her stomach. Something was wrong. The queen's words echoed through her growing horror. *It was the only time I knew Kudus to be cruel.* Was the horse a mockery of her own disability? Had her leg driven her father to make this horse as a parody?

Overwhelmed by a surge of grief, she didn't see the ring of torches waiting for them outside the stable.

"You won't get far on that," the queen's voice rang out. Cuman was on his horse beside her. "Your father made it lame like you." Disdain dripped from her tone.

Amarna's horse, lame like her, made by a man she thought she knew and understood, who had sought solace in the arms of his sister-in-law.

Jaun's arms tightened around her. "You know that's not true."

Stalwart. Her courage surged. Jaun was right, she did know that. Her father was a man of peace, who believed in helping people. The leg was what others saw, not what she was. That was the lesson her father had taught her. She would not misjudge him the same way the queen did.

This was her horse, of course it would not run for anyone else. She slipped the key out of her sleeve and dropped it into its slot. She pressed and turned it clockwise. She felt gears shifting, cogs falling into place.

Amarna touched her heels to its flanks, the horse took a half step backwards, its steel muscles bunched, power burst forth in a torrent. Dimly, Amarna heard shrieks and shouts. In a moment they were gone, lost as the horse accelerated out of the palace.

The darkening landscape blurred, hoofbeats hammered. It seemed they had barely taken a breath before they were at the edge of the forest. The horse did not slow down, it dodged and weaved through the trees. The siblings clung on, Jaun's arms around Amarna, hands gripping the saddle's edge; Amarna pressed into the horse's neck, knuckles white on the reins.

They burst out of the treeline onto the swathe of sward at the river's edge. The horse found another burst of speed, took one step into the water, and leapt. Amarna would never forget that moment. Moonlight glittered on the horse's silver flanks. Beneath her, its reflection was pacing them.

They landed on the opposing bank, and only there did the horse trot to a halt and drop to its knees.

Jaun rolled off first with a groan. Amarna managed to step off herself. She caught her breath when she saw what lay behind them.

Cara watched from the opposite bank, her horse's drooping head a testament to its exhaustion. She raised one hand in greeting. Jaun raised his in return. With slow, deliberate steps Cara waded into the river.

Jaun jumped in. The breadth of a meadow separated them, there was no way he could reach her. Cara kept coming. The water reached her waist. She lost her footing. The current caught her. She raised her hand as she was swept downstream by the torrent.

Amarna screamed. She lurched to the water, pushing past the still, solid form of her brother to stretch impossibly for her sister. She felt the current tug, her left leg collapsed under her. A strong arm gripped her around her waist and pulled her back to the shore.

Muddy and wet, they sat in silence, keeping vigil through the night.

"Why?" Amarna asked as the sky blushed with the new day.

"Her destiny. Her ring said 'love once.'" Jaun replied in a flat tone. He stood and held out a hand to help Amarna rise. "And your destiny is to take us home."